FEARSCAPE

THE DEVOURING BOOK 3

FEARSCAPE

THE DEVOURING BOOK 3

BY SIMON HOLT

LITTLE, BROWN AND COMPANY

NEW YORK   BOSTON

Also in  series:

The Devouring (Book 1)

Soulstice (Book 2)

Text copyright © 2010 by Spex Studios, LLC

Smoke images by Yamada Taro/Riser/Getty Images, and Don Farrall/ Photographer's Choice/Getty Images.

Little, Brown and Company

Hachette Book Group
237 Park Avenue, New York, NY 10017
Visit our website at www.lb-teens.com

Little, Brown and Company is a division of Hachette Book Group, Inc.
The Little, Brown name and logo are trademarks of Hachette Book Group, Inc.

First Edition: October 2010

Library of Congress Cataloging-in-Publication Data
Holt, Simon.
  Fearscape / by Simon Holt.—1st ed.
    p. cm.—(The devouring ; bk. 3)
  Summary: Pursued by the Vours, supernatural creatures who feast on fear and attack on the eve of the winter solstice, Reggie tries to hold on to her humanity as she finds herself gradually morphing into a Vour.
  ISBN 978-0-316-03570-5
  [1. Fear—Fiction. 2. Supernatural—Fiction. 3. Horror stories.] I. Title
  PZ7.H7416Fe 2010
  [Fic]—dc22

                                                                                          2010006364

10 9 8 7 6 5 4 3 2 1

Book design by Alison Impey

RRD-C

Printed in the United States of America

TO MOM AND DAD

# PROLOGUE

Dear Eben,

I know that it has been many years, and that we did not end things on the best of terms, but I am writing you now because I have little time left and nowhere else to turn. I made a choice a long time ago, and it was the wrong choice. You were right to get out when you did. Those I trusted have proven untrustworthy, and I fear that my latest assignment will be my last. Even now the enemy is closing in; I can only hope I am choosing correctly now by putting my faith in you.

I must speak generally, in case this falls into the wrong hands. I infiltrated the establishment as ordered, but what I discovered there was entirely unexpected, and unprecedented. There is a woman who possesses a special skill that could end this war forever. She is beyond my reach now, but I managed to obtain her journal. I wish I could be more explicit, but it is too dangerous—read it and let it guide you. What you do with what you discover, I leave up to you.

Even now my mind plays tricks. The moments of lucidity grow fewer daily. Soon I will be dead or lost to the void. The nightmare is always the same—I wake in the mausoleum, laid out on a cold stone slab. The skin has rotted from my bones, and the rats gnaw on my organs. I am a blackened skeleton, not dead, not alive. I hear the whispers of the other corpses. They narrate my life, and they detail every life I took or tormented. I relive it all—I feel the slit of the knife in my gut, the tweezers plucking the fingernails from my hands, the spoon gouging out my eye, the water rushing into my lungs. Death matters not; my hell has already begun. Has yours, I wonder?

Be wary, my old friend. Our sins live with us for eternity, and that is perhaps the most frightening thing of all.

—Sims

The bell rang, and Aaron looked up, surprised. History class had passed quickly, probably because he had been so much more absorbed in the letter than in the lecture on the Louisiana Purchase.

So Macie Canfield's journal—the detailed account of the monsters called Vours—had been sent to Eben Bloch on purpose by someone named Sims. Perhaps it wasn't significant, but Aaron wasn't certain. Maybe there was more in that journal that could help him now. He would have to think about it.

 **1**

"What fresh hell today, Dr. Evil?"

Reggie Halloway lay stretched out on an operating table, the restraints on her wrists and ankles tied so tightly that they lacerated her skin. There was no reason to secure them so, other than the Vours' malice. After months of captive torture, she was frail and weak. Her own body looked foreign to her—knobby legs, rail-thin arms, protruding ribs, and pale skin pocked with unnatural black marks beneath the surface. They routinely denied her food and water, and her tongue felt swollen in her parched throat.

Next to her was another operating table with a comatose, middle-aged woman lying on it. Her chest rose and fell in a steady rhythm, and to most she would have looked like a normal, suburban soccer mom taking a nap. But not to Reggie.

This woman wasn't human. Not anymore. Her body had been possessed and her soul banished to a faraway hell, and in just a few minutes Reggie would be following her into it. For some reason it was the Vours' will to send her into these fearscapes, one after another, to defeat them.

Reggie had first learned of the existence of the monsters nearly a year ago, when she had read about them in an old diary and one had taken over the body of her younger brother, Henry. Vours were the essence of fear, and their methods were straightforward, if the stuff of horror movies: On Sorry Night, the night of the winter solstice, they could enter a human's mind and inhabit his or her body, sending their victim's consciousness to a place called a fearscape. Like snowflakes—if snowflakes were twisted and demonic—all fearscapes were unique, landscapes crafted from a victim's deepest, darkest fears. Here the victim would live in torment, while the Vour lived a human life in the human world, with no one the wiser.

But Vours were devils, hateful and soulless, and they brought certain devilish powers into the human realm. They could sense fears and implant hallucinations in a person's mind, incapacitating them or, worse, driving them crazy. They also inherited all of their victims' memories, which made it easier for them to assimilate into life. And while their human bodies were not invincible, they did become tougher and stronger when a Vour moved in.

But Reggie and her best friend, Aaron Cole, had discovered some of the Vours' weaknesses and how to spot them. They couldn't cry, and they couldn't handle extreme cold—their blood even turned black when exposed to freezing temperatures. And the Vours weren't the only ones with powers, now: Reggie had developed the ability to travel through people's fearscapes and help them defeat their fears, thereby destroying the realms and the Vours that had taken them hostage. She had saved Henry and others this way, but it had come at a price.

There had been the death of her friend and protector, Eben Bloch, a man more like a father to her than her own dad. And now she herself was a captive and a guinea pig. The Vours' human lackey, Dr. Unger, had kidnapped Reggie from her own home months earlier, at the end of June, and had whisked her off to some new psychiatric hospital that apparently didn't mind having psychopaths run their wards. Ever since, he had been pushing her into fearscapes, forcing her to complete them. For Reggie, it was an impossible situation: She didn't want to be part of his endgame, whatever that was, but the victims in these fearscapes needed saving. And she was the only one who could do that. By traveling through the fearscapes and helping the entrapped conquer their fears, Reggie assisted in killing Vours and bringing these lost souls back to the real world. What she didn't understand was why Unger seemed to prefer it when she did defeat the fearscapes.

"This is Dominique," Dr. Unger replied from his perch by the door. He never did any of the dirty work himself, of course. He only gave orders, or asked questions, or jotted things down in his little notebooks. His voice made her cringe. She wanted to rip free of her restraints, wrap her hands around his neck, and squeeze until the life left his body. It was the only fantasy that gave her sustenance in this place.

But if she was going to be forced to traverse these fearscapes, Reggie was glad to know the names of the victims; it helped, when she found them trapped inside. Fearscapes robbed humans of their identities, and the simple practice of calling them by name helped bring them back.

One of the Vour orderlies bound the woman's hand to Reggie's; Reggie could feel the pulse, faint beneath her icy skin. The black closed in around her, and she tumbled down the rabbit hole.

———————

Reggie awoke—the surrealistic projection into another human being's fears was best described as a gruesome kind of *awakening*—in near perfect darkness. Though she could see almost nothing, her other senses screamed. The air was frigid and stale, and the scent of decay hung around her like a noose. With every breath, she tasted the rot of this place slathering her throat. She struggled not to gag as her eyes adjusted to the room around her.

She was lying next to a fireplace filled with logs, and the wood felt dry enough to burn. Reggie found a flint on the crumbling mantel and struck it against the cold stone floor until it sparked. After a couple of attempts, a weak flame crackled beneath the wood and set the logs on fire. Reggie crouched in front of the small blaze and rubbed her hands together, but no matter how close she pressed her hands to the flames, she could take no comfort from them. The fire burned, but it didn't warm her.

From her many monstrous journeys into dozens of fearscapes, Reggie had grown accustomed to this kind of quiet cruelty. No matter how innocuous an element appeared inside these forsaken places, nothing ever provided true peace or rest. Whether overtly grotesque or achingly subtle, all aspects of each fearscape had been designed to achieve the same result: despair. Forced to move deeper and deeper into their own fears, human beings pushed ever inward with a fever of desperation. This fire was no different. It offered nothing.

Reggie rose and explored her surroundings, the light of the blaze showcasing the room enough for her to make out more details. The putrid smell grew stronger, and Reggie covered her mouth with her hand. As she did so, something crawled down her cheek.

She swiped at it, and it flew off, buzzing. A fly. It had left a gooey trail along her skin.

Orange light flickered about the room, and Reggie saw the outline of a long table. Perhaps a dining room? The firelight glimmered off something metal at the edge of the table, and Reggie realized it was an antique candelabra. She reached for it; it was tarnished but heavy—real silver, she thought. The candles were burned low, small humps of wax melted into their stems, but each had a bit of wick left. Reggie wrenched the largest candle from its stick and placed it into the fire's embers, then used it to light the rest of the tapers.

She approached the table again. With every step, the odor grew worse, and Reggie kept the lit candles as close to her nose as she could to fight off the smell.

She realized the source of the stench soon enough: a platter of food so rotten it had almost liquefied. The lump on the platter writhed with the presence of hundreds of flies. Reggie walked slowly along the side of the table, the meager light from the fireplace dying behind her. She held the candelabra out farther, using its glow to fold open the stale darkness.

Something lurked beyond her sight, something just past the weak ring of candlelight in front of her. She could hear something moving: a slow squishing sound. The stench only grew worse. The deformed outline of a head rose from the center of the table, and Reggie shuddered. No matter how many times she explored the inner workings of the human psyche, she never grew immune to the base fear of the unknown. She fought against herself and cautiously leaned in, bringing the candles close.

"This little piggy went to market...."

The voice was garbled and thick with mucus.

Reggie realized she was staring at the decapitated head of a roasted pig.

"This little piggy stayed home...."

The head scrabbled slowly off of the plate toward Reggie, leaving a sluglike trail of copper-colored blood. Its charred mouth curled up into a demented smile, and the short tusks on either end grew long and sharp. The pig opened its mouth, and the entire head convulsed. It appeared to be choking on something.

The beast squealed, and a rotten apple spewed forth, flying at Reggie. It struck her right shoulder and burst open, the acidic juice burning into her flesh. She frantically wiped at it, feeling it sizzle into the veined flesh on the back of her hand.

"This little piggy had roast beef...."

Another apple flew out, aimed right at her face. Reggie ducked, and the apple careened past her with a searing buzz.

The pig's snorting laughter echoed throughout the room.

A cockroach skittered through the beast's eye socket as

another apple fired at her, knocking the candelabra from her hand and sending it flying. It hit the stone floor, and the candles scattered. A few of them winked out, but two rolled to the wall, their flames still lit. There was a crackle, and the fierce flame arced upward, devouring the dry, peeling wallpaper. Within seconds the wall was ablaze.

From the fire's light, Reggie could see the entire room. It was, indeed, a dining room, and the table was loaded with plates and platters and tureens all filled with moldering food, covered with flies, maggots, and other insects.

At the opposite end of the table sat five diners, their bodies as rotted as the food on the plates in front of them. Their skin had wasted away, leaving just a thin layer of flesh over their skeletons. Strawlike hair hung in patches off their heads, and their Victorian-era clothes were threadbare.

Reggie gaped in horror at the sight. It wasn't just the mummified corpses—she'd seen plenty of those in fearscapes by this point—no, it was the way they sat, upright in their chairs, facing each other. One even had a hand on the table, gripping a blackened fork. But they were so thin, so wasted away, it looked like they had died of starvation in the middle of a dinner party.

A coughing fit from the increasing smoke brought Reggie back to the problem at hand: She needed to find a way out of this room. The only door was beyond the pig and the bodies. She ran for it, but as she passed the corpses, a hand shot out and grabbed her by the wrist. Reggie cried out as the bony fingers dug into her skin, but the hand would not let go. The mummy turned in its seat. A disintegrating lace blouse suggested that it had once been a woman. She looked at Reggie with empty eye sockets, but her jaw clacked open and she spoke.

"Hungry," she croaked at Reggie.

A huge apple slammed into the side of the woman's skull, knocking it from her shoulders.

"This little piggy had none! None! NONE!"

The pig's head had grown to an immense size, and it slithered across the floor toward Reggie, its tusks now like curled spikes.

Reggie pulled away from the headless woman, but the mummy sitting to the left—at one time a man, judging from a moldy ascot wrapped around his neck—caught hold of her other arm.

"Food. Please." His voice was like the snapping of twigs.

The two groped at her, tearing her skin with their sharp bones. The other mummies began to shudder and reached for her as well; all of them moaned and wheezed.

"So hungry…"

"Starving…"

"Feed us…."

The pig head, slobbering and spitting chunks of apple and burnt flesh, crunched down on one of the mummies, crushing its bones between its teeth. It skewered a second mummy with one of its tusks as it turned for Reggie.

"NONE!"

The fire had spread to the ceiling, and Reggie's eyes and lungs burned from the smoke and heat. The pig was nearly upon her now, chomping on the brittle bones of the corpses and spewing them out from between its tongue and jagged teeth.

"NONE!"

Reggie pushed toward the door, stumbling through the desperate grips of the dismembered mummies littering the floor.

"Feed us…."

She reached the door, but it was sealed completely shut. She rammed her shoulder into it, praying for the wood to splinter, but it felt as sturdy as concrete. Some mechanism was at play here, and sheer force would not give passage through this layer of the fearscape. But she could not think clearly. Her vision was blurring; she was losing consciousness from the lack of air. The pig yielded for a moment, reluctant to pass through the growing flames to attack Reggie.

One of the burning corpses moaned again on the ground. "Food…"

A huge feast, but they are all starving, Reggie thought. *Why?*

She instinctively picked up a handful of rotting meat from the ground and held it out to the broken corpse that writhed on the floor in front of her. It opened its mouth to take it, but then it turned away.

"Mustn't eat…get fat…"

"This little piggy had NONE!"

The boar roared and spit at Reggie, now making its way through the flames. It howled in pain but continued to come for her.

The bodies refused to eat. These corpses hadn't starved at the hands of this pig or anything or anyone else. They had starved *themselves.* The twisted scene playing out before her had been born from some fear of eating, Dominique's irrational phobia of losing control and getting fat. Of becoming a pig in the eyes of others.

The realization bathed Reggie in both anger and pity.

She lifted the clump of fetid food to her face and stared at the monster boar. It growled furiously and pushed through the fire, its flesh searing and melting from the bone.

Reggie stuffed the clump into her mouth, ignoring the stench and the grotesque texture and taste. Oils and slime oozed from between her teeth, but she forced herself to swallow.

"*NONE!*" squealed the pig, its skin folding down and dropping to the floor in charred, smoldering chunks. "*NONE!*"

The entire head disintegrated into a pile of ash before Reggie's eyes.

Instantly, the corpses were again upon her. Grabbing at her ankles, begging her to feed as the entire roof became engulfed in angry, voracious flames.

Reggie turned the knob on the door, and it opened effortlessly.

"Feed us…"

"Starving…"

Reggie kicked the skeletal hands from her ankles and lunged through the door into blessedly cold, fresh air, then collapsed on a cobblestone patio.

She lay there a few minutes, hacking the smoke from her lungs. When her breath started to come more easily, she sat up. A mummy's hand still clung to her wrist like a gruesome bracelet. Disgusted, Reggie pried the fingers open and tossed the hand away. It shattered upon hitting the stony ground and left a puff of smoke in its wake.

When the smoke cleared, Reggie saw a dusty golden ring

lying on the stone. She picked it up and pocketed it—many times she found tokens like these that victims had dropped as they were pushed deeper into the fearscape. These objects helped guide Reggie through, and, in turn, helped the victims remember who they were when she found them.

She had solved the first layer of Dominique's fearscape.

Now it was on to the next circle of hell.

2

There had been only five or six actual witnesses the day two orderlies had dragged a struggling Reggie Halloway from her house and strapped her into the back of a Thornwood Psychiatric Hospital van. Her father had been one of them, as well as a passing jogger, some homeless guy, and a few neighbors who had wondered what all the fuss was, marring such a lovely June evening. Still, not more than twelve pairs of eyes had actually seen the disturbing event: Reggie screaming for help as she flailed in vain against the strong-armed orderlies, half her hair shaved off her head and her face and arms covered in cuts and burns. But by opening business hours the following morning, the entirety of Cutter's Wedge knew about it.

"Did you hear about the Halloway girl?" seemed to be the most commonly asked question of the morning. Most people had. And most of them remembered how "the Halloway girl's" mother had skipped town almost two years ago, and how her father always seemed ready to slit his wrists any minute, and, worst of all, how her little brother had flipped out at school mere weeks before and nearly stabbed another boy in the neck with scissors.

Some said, "That poor family" and shook their heads. Others thanked the heavens that Reggie had been taken away before she put someone else's child in danger like her brother had. All in all, it had been the biggest news to hit sleepy Cutter's Wedge since high school quarterback Quinn Waters had disappeared last December. That is, until midday, when the story broke that Quinn had been found.

At first no one believed it—there had been false reports before. But bit by bit the truth spread: Quinn had shown up at a homeless shelter in Boston, out of it and with some minor injuries, but alive. His frantic parents were on their way to collect him. The local news carried the story on their afternoon broadcast, with a chirpy correspondent standing outside the shelter and announcing that the Waterses were inside and had just been reunited with their son. An hour later cameras caught the family leaving, Mrs. Waters sobbing and gripping Quinn around the waist like she thought if she let go he would simply vanish, Mr. Waters on Quinn's other side with a hand on his shoulder, trying to shoo away the swarming cameramen. And Quinn. He looked emaciated, and his face was crisscrossed with scars. His green eyes, known for their twinkle, were vacant, and he stumbled forward, relying on his parents for support. His right hand was bulkily bandaged where two of his fingers had been cut off above the knuckles. It was hard to believe this was the same kid who had, not even a year ago, been an all-state athlete with college recruiters at every game.

Still, wounds could heal. He was alive. He was found. He was coming home. And Reggie Halloway was forgotten.

Aaron Cole had not forgotten her, however. He was Reggie's best friend, and he had been with her the night Henry had been possessed. Together they had stumbled upon the existence of Vours and learned how to defeat them. He had been by her side through everything, except, it turned out, when she had needed him most. In a wicked twist of irony, he had been driving back from Boston when she was taken, having just dropped Quinn Waters off at the homeless shelter.

It wasn't Quinn's fault, not in the strictest sense, but that didn't stop Aaron from blaming him. It had been one of the biggest shocks to discover the previous winter that Quinn Waters, town golden boy, was actually a Vour—and it was one of the first lessons that anyone could be one. He had nearly killed them both before drowning in Cutter Lake; or, at least, that's what Reggie and Aaron had thought. Against all odds, Quinn had managed to survive, and he resurfaced that summer, weakened and deformed, seeking Reggie's help. He claimed that the Vours had turned against him and that he could help Reggie destroy them, but of course it had all been a lie.

Aaron still rued Reggie's decision not to tell him straight away about Quinn's return. How things could have been different! If only he had known, he could have convinced her of how stupid it was to team up with Quinn. But Reggie had, inexplicably, kept him in the dark, and trusted the Vour over him.

Well, not entirely inexplicably. Reggie had always had a thing for Quinn, and apparently finding out he was a homicidal monster hadn't completely obliterated the attraction. That part Aaron really couldn't understand.

In the end, though, Reggie had saved the real Quinn and brought him back from his fearscape, destroying the Vour in the process. It was what she did, the credo she lived by: Save the soul, kill the monster.

But it hadn't been as simple as just taking Quinn back home to Cutter's Wedge and throwing a ticker tape parade. He had been missing for months, and at one point Aaron had even been under investigation for his murder (another notch against Quinn, in Aaron's book). No, Quinn's reappearance couldn't be tied to Reggie and Aaron, so Aaron had staged the homeless shelter affair. But if it hadn't been for Quinn, if he hadn't had to go through so much trouble for a guy he didn't even like, maybe he would have been there when the Vours showed up. But he hadn't been. He had failed Reggie.

Aaron had devoted the rest of the summer and that fall to trying to track down where Dr. Unger and the Vours had taken his best friend. Their old headquarters, Thornwood Psychiatric Hospital, had been exposed—and half of it blown up—after the events of the summer solstice. The story fed to the authorities was that a gas leak had caused the fire, but rather than rebuild, Unger had relocated his patients. Reggie's father, who thought his daughter was mentally disturbed and blamed Aaron for it, refused to give up her location, so Aaron spent his days trolling the Internet, newspapers, library, and any other reference source that could point him in the direction of the Vours. He had also collected as many files as he could from the house of his old mentor, Eben Bloch.

Aaron also couldn't help but think that things might have

turned out differently if Eben had revealed his secrets earlier. Aaron and Reggie hadn't learned of his very personal connection to the Vours until June, when he admitted that he had once been a member of the Tracers, a league of assassins bent on destroying the monsters. Eben had known as much or more about the Vours than anyone, but he had specifically kept this information from Reggie to protect her. Aaron had to wonder, though, if his silence hadn't had the opposite effect. Reggie had been determined to involve herself in the fight against the Vours despite Eben's warnings, and maybe his knowledge could have kept her safer.

It was moot now. Eben had finally succumbed to the injuries wreaked on him from decades of killing Vours, but he had left behind stores of information on the monsters. Unfortunately, none of it had been particularly useful yet, and it was already nearing November.

What Aaron really hadn't expected were the frequent phone calls he'd begun to get from Quinn at the end of the summer. The guy claimed just to want to talk, but Aaron didn't have time for chitchat or hand-holding. Besides, the golden boy had about eight hundred friends he could turn to.

Aaron's fellow classmates had always categorized him as the weirdo genius type, but he had returned to school that fall a different kid. He sat in the backs of the classrooms these days, rarely participating in class discussions unless specifically asked by the teacher, and the notes he scribbled in his notebooks had nothing to do with the subject matter he was supposed to be studying.

Now, deep into October, he stared at an ever-evolving list with the header *Possible Vour Hideouts/Fronts*. Some of the entries were circled or starred, but most had been crossed out and replaced with new ones. His search was not yielding much fruit.

When the bell rang and he returned to his locker, Aaron didn't bother to load up his backpack with books—he had other plans for the evening besides homework. He just grabbed his bike helmet and headed to the southeast exit of the school. He was already running late, so he was none too pleased to see Quinn Waters leaning against the bike stand, blocking his way. In a previous life this would have been a threatening scenario for Aaron—the nerd versus the jock—but Aaron knew there were much worse things to fear than meatheads now, and he had vowed to stop fearing Quinn a long time ago.

It was hard for Aaron to look at Quinn. There it was before him, the same face as the Vour, the same features handsomely assembled, the mask that had deceived so many. Vours liked to insert themselves into powerful places in society, and the attractive, athletic, charming Quinn had been a powerful Vour indeed, known and idolized throughout the community. But Aaron had come to see that face as abject evil—the face of the monster that was responsible for Reggie's predicament now.

And yet, it was a different face, too. It wasn't just that the scars had mostly healed, though there was still a faint mark along his cheek—there was just something that was off. Like Quinn was a shattered mirror that had been put back together, but not all the shards had been glued in the right places. If he were being charitable, Aaron could have pitied Quinn—the kid had, after all, spent a decade in a fearscape, where he'd been skinned alive by a gym teacher, chased by a demonic scarecrow, and forced to relive his best friend's tragic death over and over again. Of course he'd be a little off now. Still, Aaron could never bring himself to be charitable when it came to Quinn.

"Don't you have a dead pig to toss around right about now?" Aaron asked.

"Not anymore," said Quinn. "I quit the team."

Aaron's eyebrow rose involuntarily. He hadn't expected that. Even with missing fingers, Quinn had been welcomed back on the team—it wasn't his throwing arm, after all. Quinn's parents, his coaches, his teachers, practically the whole town had placed him right back up on that Big Man on Campus pedestal the moment he'd resurfaced, and part of that role included quarterbacking the team to at least a division title.

"What do you want?" asked Aaron.

"I want you to tell me what happened to me," Quinn answered.

"What makes you think I know?"

Quinn took a step forward.

"Because I remember you being there."

Aaron contemplated Quinn. Part of him had known that this moment would come, that Quinn would start to remember things. It's why he'd been avoiding him and ignoring his calls.

"Then your memory is playing tricks on you."

"I don't think so. I know you were both there—you and Reggie." Aaron winced when Quinn said her name, but Quinn didn't notice and continued, his words coming faster now. "Bits and pieces—they just appear in my head, horrible nightmares, but they're—they're memories, and you and Reggie are in them."

Quinn's eyes burned intently. Aaron had become accustomed

to certain of Quinn's more dominant expressions over the years: the arrogance of a star athlete and, later, the cold hatred and sadism of a Vour, a desire to inflict pain and an enjoyment in witnessing endless misery. But Aaron had never seen this—desperation, maybe even fear.

Quinn reached out and grabbed Aaron's arm. His grip was fierce.

"I need to know what I am," he said urgently.

Anger shot through Aaron as he was reminded of the bully of old, and he shoved Quinn backward against the bike rack. The metal clanged, and Quinn reached out to stop his fall, nicking his hand on Aaron's bike chain. Blood spurted up from his skin.

"You don't have the right to ask me for anything," Aaron spat at him. "You're human, that's what you are. A living, breathing human being, though you have no right to be."

The two boys glared at each other, but Aaron thought he could see Quinn's intensity give way to confusion, then worry. But no, he was not going to feel sorry for this prick. He and Reggie had sacrificed enough for him.

A sporty VW pulled up next to them. Nina Snow was at the wheel, and she leaned across the seat, giving both Quinn and Aaron an impressive view of her cleavage.

"Quinn, there you are," she purred. Her eyes fell disdainfully on Aaron for a moment, then snapped back to Quinn. "What are you doing here, baby? I've been looking all over for you."

Quinn didn't answer her, but continued to stare at Aaron. He seemed to be looking through him, though, as if his thoughts were someplace else. He absentmindedly sucked the blood from the cut on his hand.

"I guess your ride's here," Aaron said.

Finally Quinn glanced at Nina, who was now impatiently clicking her nails against the steering wheel.

"Yeah, can we go already?" she huffed.

Quinn sighed, and with the utmost reluctance he turned and got into the car. Again Aaron was a bit surprised—not many adolescent boys would look so put out at the thought of joyriding with Nina and her low-cut tops.

"Seriously, Quinn, what is going on with you?" Nina asked as Quinn slammed the car door shut. "First you quit the football team and now you're hanging out with that loser?" Nina didn't bother to keep her voice down, but Aaron missed the rest of the conversation as the car peeled away. He rolled his eyes as he unlocked his bike, then took off in the opposite direction.

3

A few hours later, Aaron flipped the microfiche machine off and rubbed his eyes. Even with them closed he could still see the black-and-white text imprinted on the backs of his eyelids. He'd been staring at newspaper clippings for too long.

The *Cutter's Wedge Progress*—Aaron couldn't help but appreciate the irony of the newspaper's name—had not yet digitally archived their old editions dating back before 1990; hence the archaic method of search. He hated not being able to type in a few keywords and have all the information he needed appear at his fingertips. Microfiche was so slow and inefficient: Aaron had to use a special machine to scan through filmstrips that were photographs of articles and painstakingly read each one to see if it contained anything useful. It was such dark-ages technology that the library had moved all the files and equipment to a dingy corner in the basement. Obviously the advent of personal computing had changed the world, but Aaron really did wonder how people had accomplished anything before the Internet.

It hadn't been a wasted day, though. He'd found a few promising stories of murder, assault, and suicide that could be

Vour related. He was trying to establish a pattern of Vour activity over the past century that could suggest what they were up to now, and what they might want with Reggie. He packed up his notes and headed back upstairs to the land of the twenty-first century.

As he was returning the film to the librarian at the research desk, he happened to glance at the kids' section a few aisles over. Henry Halloway was standing on his tiptoes, straining to reach a book on a shelf just above his fingertips. It was remarkable, really, how well he seemed after the literal hell he'd been through. Sure, he had had a couple violent outbursts the previous spring when memories of being in the fearscape had returned, but those had mostly passed. And now, with his sister missing and likely in some kind of unspeakable hell herself—well, it was a lot for a nine-year-old kid to handle.

Aaron hadn't seen Henry for many weeks—over the summer he had tried to stop by to see how he was doing, but Mr. Halloway had made it clear that Aaron was no longer welcome in their house. Henry had been trying to persuade his father that the Vours were real, and Mr. Halloway blamed Aaron for the influence. Before he had left for the last time, Aaron had whispered to Henry to stop talking about the Vours, to pretend like he didn't think they existed. He'd been afraid Mr. Halloway would ship his son off to Dr. Unger if he thought Henry was headed down the same path as Reggie.

Now Aaron turned away, but not quickly enough. Henry had spotted him, and a smile lit up his face. He waved. Aaron waved back and walked over to him, peering surreptitiously about for signs of Thom Halloway.

"Don't worry," said Henry. "Dad's at the hardware store. I just came over to get some books."

Aaron eyed the shelf Henry had been reaching for.

"Hardy Boys, huh? Good stuff."

"I like that they always solve the mysteries," Henry said. Aaron nodded, not quite knowing how to respond.

"We're working on it, Henry," he said finally. "We're going to get your sister back."

"How?"

The question wasn't ill-tempered or challenging, but Aaron still felt a stab of guilt. He didn't know how. There weren't always tidy solutions to real life's mysteries, not that he had to explain that to Henry. Aaron's hesitation gave the boy all the answers he needed.

"You don't know yet, do you?"

Aaron shook his head.

"Not yet."

"I've been trying to figure out where she is," Henry continued. "Dad is so secretive about it. I've been asking him if we can go see her, but he always says no. Dr. Unger says visitors will be bad for Reggie's 'recovery.' Aaron, what do you think they're doing to her? Do you think she's…" He hesitated, and Aaron guessed he was going to say "dead." Fortunately, he didn't have to answer the question.

"Henry!"

The word was curt and perhaps too loudly spoken for a library. Aaron knew the voice. He turned around to see Thom Halloway standing behind him, his arms folded across his chest. He glowered at Aaron.

"I thought I made it clear that I didn't want you talking to my son."

"I was just saying hi," said Henry. "Aaron didn't do anything."

"Then you can say goodbye now," Mr. Halloway replied.

Aaron reached toward the bookshelf and pulled out *The Secret of Wildcat Swamp*, then handed it to Henry.

"This was one of my favorites," he said.

"Thanks, I haven't read it yet."

"Henry, why don't you go check that out?" his father said. "I'll meet you at the car."

"I'm serious, Dad. Aaron was only helping me pick out a book."

"And that was very thoughtful of him." Mr. Halloway's tone and gaze left no room for argument. Henry offered Aaron a weak smile and headed off toward the front desk.

"See you, Hen," said Aaron.

"No, you won't," said Mr. Halloway. "I don't want you anywhere near him."

Aaron's eyes narrowed and he returned the older man's hateful look.

"How's Reggie doing?"

"She's doing much better now that she doesn't have you filling her head with lies and conspiracy theories."

"So you've seen her, then? Your daughter will be coming home soon?" Aaron's voice dripped with disdain.

"Dr. Unger is happy with her progress."

"But you haven't actually spoken to her, have you? You haven't seen this 'progress' for yourself—you're just taking Unger's word for it."

Mr. Halloway took a step forward. Aaron had grown quite a

bit in the last year and was now pushing six feet, but Mr. Halloway still loomed over him, and he was twice Aaron's girth.

"I trust a professional, celebrated psychiatrist who is considered an expert in the field more than a deranged kid who preyed on an impressionable girl."

Aaron felt the wrath building inside him.

"If you think Reggie's impressionable, you're even more blind than I thought." He shook his head, disgusted. "Just try to see her. Go visit her—see if Unger lets you. I bet you all your good intentions he'll give you the runaround, some excuse why you can't be in the same room as her, why you can't even look at her. He's keeping your daughter away from you, Mr. Halloway, but once you figure that out, it'll be too late."

"You're insane," Mr. Halloway seethed. Both of their voices had risen, and other library patrons were starting to give them looks. "You stay away from Henry, you hear me? You stay out of my family's business. You're never going to see Reggie again."

"At this rate, neither are you," Aaron shot back.

Mr. Halloway's hands balled into fists, but at that moment a librarian appeared behind him.

"Excuse me," she said firmly. "I'm going to need to ask both of you to leave. Now."

"Just about to," said Aaron. As he pushed past Mr. Halloway, he added quietly, "Try it. See what happens. Then give me a call."

That Saturday, despite the freezing rain, Aaron pedaled his bike out to the neighboring town of Wennemack. He pulled up to an apartment complex in the shadier part of town and dragged his bike down the steps to the garden unit. He knocked on the door, and it was answered by a short, attractive African-American woman.

"Hi, honey, come on in," she said.

"Hey, Crystal. I didn't know you'd be dropping by today."

"Just delivering a little goody bag."

Aaron followed her back inside and wiped his wet shoes on the doormat. He left his soaked coat by the door and entered the small but cozy ground-floor apartment.

A man with cropped brown hair and a full beard sat at a kitchen table cataloging some pretty serious–looking weaponry, including guns, grenades, and other specialty items. With his new facial hair, hair color, and wardrobe, he didn't look much like the man who had taught Reggie and Aaron Shakespeare the previous year, but he was.

Arthur Machen had shown up in Cutter's Wedge with the specific purpose of keeping an eye on, and then killing, Regina Halloway. Posing as a high school English teacher, he had actually been a member of the Tracers, the same league of assassins to which Eben had belonged. The Tracers would break any moral or ethical code if it meant protecting the greater society from the Vours, and this included murdering humans who got in their way or posed a risk. Reggie had done both. She disagreed with their lethal methods, and they saw her powers as a threat to the balance between worlds. Machen had been sent to eliminate her, but in the end he had defied his orders and gone into hiding. Reggie was unaware of his transfer of allegiance, but he was now Aaron's only ally in his quest to rescue her.

"Wow. That is quite the arsenal," Aaron said, approaching the table.

"Specially modified by yours truly," said Crystal. "The ultimate in anti-Vour technology."

"You're the best, Crystal. This is perfect." Machen rose from the table and walked her to the door. "You're sure you're not sticking your neck out too much, getting this stuff for us?"

"It's worth it, baby. We all play our part."

Machen smiled at her and surreptitiously handed over a wad of bills.

"Plus the cash doesn't hurt," Crystal added. "Let me know how things go, and when you need another shipment. And be careful."

"You too."

"Any new deserters?" Aaron asked as Machen closed the door behind Crystal. After news of Reggie's power had spread among the Tracers, some of them, like Machen and Crystal, had balked at the group's unbending way of battling Vours, now that there was another option that didn't require killing the human victim trapped in the fearscape. The league had lost many members, but Aaron's question was purely rhetorical. Machen never shared the names of Tracers, current or former. The only reason Aaron knew Crystal was because she had walked up and introduced herself to him.

"You bring your gloves?" Machen asked. Aaron grinned at him.

"Oh, yeah."

The other thing Aaron had done over the summer was start a

training regimen with the ex-Tracer. Weight lifting, boxing, even some martial arts work. In only a handful of months, his beanpole frame had developed muscles he hadn't even known existed, and he could now actually run a few miles without getting winded. His entire life, Aaron had been the hacker guy, more known for his computer skills and nerdy exploits than an ability to bench-press something more than just the weight bar. But Aaron never wanted to be the weak, gawky kid again.

After a sparring match, which Machen won handily, Aaron pulled out the new information he'd gotten at the library, as well as the letter he had found among Eben's personal files.

"Do you think it's significant?" Aaron asked Machen after he had read it. Machen scratched his beard.

"You're sure this refers to Macie's journal?"

"It must. I don't think Eben received any other diaries by mail. Plus it talks about a special ability, and Macie had that Vour confined behind the wall in her basement. Sims must have been an old Tracer buddy of Eben's, but they had a falling out when Eben quit the group."

"That's a logical deduction. But I don't see how it can help us now. The house burned down, didn't it?"

With Reggie almost trapped inside, Aaron thought.

"Yeah, and from this it sounds like the Vours did get their hands on the old bat after all. Poor crazy Macie."

They moved on to the newspaper stories, which they cross-referenced with the files Machen's contacts had recovered from the Tracers. After deciding which seemed like probable Vour cases, Machen added pins to a wall map where the crimes took place; a heavy concentration of the pins were already stuck in the area surrounding Cutter's Wedge.

"It's like ground zero," Aaron said, standing back and examining the map. "Why do you think that is?"

"I wish I knew," Machen replied. "I spent years following orders, killing whom I needed to kill, never asking the bigger questions. There didn't even seem to be bigger questions, because Vours never seemed organized—they could only act one by one. Now I feel like a real idiot."

"So the Tracers really never knew about Unger or the experiments or anything like that?"

"It's possible that they did and I wasn't privy. We operated like sleeper cells, to keep our identities as secret from the Vours as possible. I could be sitting next to another Tracer on a bus, in a bar, wherever, and neither of us would know what the other was. At any rate, we all worked on a need-to-know basis, and if the Tracers were aware of Unger and his activities, I didn't need to know about it."

"And we're left with nothing." Aaron sighed. The frustration was almost unbearable.

"Based on these pins, we can make the educated guess that wherever Unger has Reggie, it's relatively close, probably within a two- to three-hour drive. Whatever it is about this area, he most likely won't want to be far from it."

"So she's probably not in Tacoma. Wonderful. We still need a way to narrow it down."

"And we will."

"How?" Aaron found himself asking the same question Henry

had. "We've been at it for months now, and gotten exactly nowhere!"

"Not nowhere." Machen crossed to his desk and pulled a manila envelope out of a drawer. He tossed it down in front of Aaron. Aaron flipped it open and examined its contents.

"Where did you get this?"

"Crystal. She's good at tracking things down."

"And you think it's for real?"

"It's the best lead we've had so far. But we should get visual confirmation."

"Can you give me a ride to the station? Looks like I'm headed to New York."

Reggie wobbled on one bare foot atop a pedestal that was no larger than ten square inches. Her toes had curled around the edge of one side and gripped the dais so hard that her entire foot had turned purple. Gray clouds surrounded her, their dampness soaking her skin and making the bottom of her foot dangerously slippery. As Reggie teetered on the pedestal, the inside of her calf aching with a hot, stabbing pain, the clouds parted.

She stood atop an impossibly tall and thin makeshift tower comprised of desks, chairs, rickety ladders, and other nondescript furniture and junk. The ground was so far down that cars on the streets looked like ants crawling in single file. She was too high up to make out any people.

Unger had shunted her into the fearscape of Trevor, a man

who was about thirty, and whose body, in the real world, was covered in bedsores from months of inactivity. This early layer revealed his fear of heights.

The pace of Unger's wicked experiments upon Reggie had only accelerated during her captivity, and at times she could feel that her mind had started to unravel. Her ability to distinguish between wakefulness and dream, between reality and fearscape, was disintegrating. For all she knew, Unger was trying to break her, to crack open her mind and drive her insane.

If this was his objective, he was close to accomplishing his goal.

The atmosphere up this high was almost too thin to breathe, and Reggie was getting light-headed. Fright seized her heart as she wobbled on the tiny platform. Falling likely meant failing—she'd be kicked out of the fearscape, and Trevor would be left in hell.

"Trevor!" she called out into the atmosphere. If he could hear her, maybe he could send her a sign. She needed to know how to get to him, where he had gone in this nightmare. "Trevor!"

Frigid winds lashed across her body, swallowing up her voice and making her sway precariously in the wet, gray sky. Lightning crackled in the distance, and thunder rippled low and raw like the growl of a waking demon. The Vour knew she was here.

It wasn't just facing fear after fear that was getting to her; it was also the exhaustion of having to put the puzzle pieces together and find the way through. She had to be brave, but also smart, wary, and, most difficult of all, optimistic. It was such a burden, and a joke, trying to muster optimism in the face of so much horror. The toll this pressure was taking on her mind was far greater than that on her body.

"Trevor!"

A bolt of lightning streaked down and hit the platform, just missing Reggie. But an electric shock surged through her body, frying her skin, and she lost her balance. She toppled over the side of the platform, just managing to catch the edge with her fingertips before she could plummet to the ground miles below.

There she dangled, her fingers gripping the ledge with the last of their strength. But they were wet with dew and sweat, and they were slipping....

Would it really be so bad to fall? To fail? Reggie wondered. Maybe she couldn't beat this one. Maybe this was one she just couldn't save.

"Trevor!" she called again, less sure now.

The ground had disappeared, replaced with swirling gray mist. The emptiness tugged at her.

Reggie strained to hear something, *anything* that might give her hope that the person she sought felt her presence. But aside from the whistling wind and the boom of closing thunder, the only voice she heard seemed to reverberate from within her.

Give in....

She was so tired. Everything ached, her muscles and her mind.

It's okay. Give in....

She hadn't asked for this. Why shouldn't she give in, just this once?

Leave....

Reggie exhaled sharply. She didn't know if the voice was the Vour's or her own. If it was the latter, then she had nothing left, and that was far scarier than anything the fearscape could show her. She would not give in. Not yet.

"TREVOR!"

A spot of red appeared in the gray, far below. Slowly it grew, rising up on the air currents to meet her, and soon Reggie saw that it was a balloon, with a matching red ribbon trailing along behind it. A bread crumb. He had heard her.

Just before she thought her arm would pop out of its socket, the balloon floated up past her head. With her other hand Reggie grabbed the ribbon, and she began to slowly and gently descend through the storm, the helium-filled balloon keeping her from falling too fast.

But as she drifted lower, the air around her grew darker and darker, until she was surrounded by blackness as complete as a starless night sky. She could see nothing, not even the tips of her fingers. She couldn't tell if she was still floating or not: Her body felt weightless, but now she thought maybe she was lying on her back. She tried to get up, but her legs didn't move. It occurred to her that she felt weightless because she couldn't *feel* any of her limbs. She couldn't move her legs, or wiggle her toes, or raise her arms. There was no feeling anywhere in her body. Her eyes were closed, and she had no power or control to open them. She had battled against the pull of a gray oblivion, so why could she no longer move?

She was stuck in some kind of paralytic limbo, and panic gripped her like morning frost. She could feel her heart pound harder and faster, verifying that her body was in some way still *here*. Did Trevor fear paralysis? No sights, no sounds, no feeling. In her growing catalog of ghoulish experiences, never had Reggie found herself completely without the ability to *move*.

But then, as if from very far away, she heard something. It was hard to discern over her racing heartbeat, but slowly it grew louder.

The arthritic sound of thin metal, stretching and grinding.

Voices, muffled at first, grew in clarity. Someone approached her.

Then there was a bang like a door being thrown open, and new, strange voices mumbled unintelligibly all around. She strained to understand, but the voices sounded submerged beneath a rolling tide. Her surroundings bustled now, but she still could not see or feel. She wanted to call out, but she could only listen. The voices finally molded into words she understood.

"Tumor," said a gruff voice. "Routine."

"Patient anesthetized. Begin when ready."

Oh, God, thought Reggie. *No! No, I'm not all the way under!* But neither the doctor nor the nurse could hear the screaming in her head.

Metal clinked and Reggie imagined surgical implements on a tray.

Scalpels, clamps, staplers. Sharp, cold, and harsh.

"Sharpen."

Sounds of a blade filing down. *Zhip, zhing, zhip, zhing, zhip, zhing.*

"Staples."

Snap, chink, snap, chink.

"Staples ready."

Help me! Reggie shrieked in her mind. *Trevor! Can you hear me? Are you out there —*

Without warning the knife sliced into Reggie's abdomen. It moved from one side of her stomach to the other, and she felt her guts moving around as the doctor dug around her insides.

"Prepare for incision."

The blade cut into her again, this time a little higher, sawing across her body.

Again, lower this time. The scalpel dragged across her hip bones.

Searing, stabbing agony, and all Reggie could do was scream in her thoughts.

"Scissors."

She heard the sickening *snip snip snip* of the blades as her abdominal muscles ripped like tissue. A monitor in the dark beeped rapidly. A red-hot coal burned inside her chest.

"Cardiac arrest."

The pain was too intense, and she had no idea how to get out of it. How could she move to the next level of a fearscape if she couldn't *move*?

Endure. Endure this.

That was the challenge here; that was the only chance at victory. Endure. Wait it out, and pass to the next level.

Reggie concentrated on deep, even breaths. She thought of Aaron in one of his stupid hats, and she felt her bottom lip

twitch. The pain washed over her. Her heart slowed. The burning in her chest ebbed.

Ftwop went the staple gun. *Ftwop ftwop.*

Her stomach riddled with holes, Reggie endured.

Breathe. Just breathe.

4

Machen stopped the car in front of the train station. The windshield wipers squeaked back and forth, the blades dull.

"Are you sure you want to do this on your own?" he asked Aaron.

"There's no reason both of us should waste a day if it turns out to be a false lead. I'll confirm and return."

Machen nodded.

"All right. Good luck."

Aaron pulled his hood over his head and got out of the car. The cold rain pattered against his jacket as he ran up the station steps to the ticket counter. He bought a round-trip ticket to Boston, where he'd transfer to the express to New York, stashed it safely in an inner pocket, then headed out onto the platform. Machen had dropped him off early; the train wouldn't arrive for another fifteen minutes.

It was one of those chilly, wet October days that signaled the approach of winter. Aaron stayed pressed against the cold brick of the station walls under the roof's overhang. Everything looked gray under the overcast sky—the platform asphalt, glistening and slick from the rain; the dark overcoats of the few other waiting travelers; even the leaves that hadn't yet fallen from their trees, still fire-colored but tinged with the browning creep of decay. Only one person seemed unaffected by the depressing weather. A little girl dressed in a pink wool coat, with matching hat, scarf, and mittens, skittered back and forth on the platform, singing to herself, completely oblivious to the world outside.

Aaron watched her, amused. It was refreshing to see some childhood innocence. She stood out on the slate background like a stem of pink cotton candy, wispy and sweet. It was unclear to whom she belonged; there were only a few other men and women on the platform, and no one seemed to be paying her any attention. Aaron's thoughts turned to what possibly lay at the other end of this trip. If perhaps, this time, they could catch a break...

The clanging of bells signaled the approach of the train. As one, the passengers cowering under the overhang, Aaron included, leaned out and gazed down the track at the blinking lights in the distance. The little girl was jumping in puddles on the platform now, making up her own version of hopscotch and singing softly to herself. She was close enough to Aaron now, though, that he could hear what she sang. It seemed to be some kind of nursery rhyme:

"Little Polly Flinders sat among the cinders,
Warming up her pretty little toes.
Mother came and caught her and whipped her pretty daughter
For spoiling her nice new clothes."

Aaron almost laughed. It was such a nasty nursery rhyme for a cute little girl to sing, but then, "Ring Around the Rosie" was about dying from the plague.

Hop. *Splash.* Hop. *Splash.* She landed alternately on one foot, then two, water droplets spraying up from beneath her shiny black patent-leather shoes. Her once-white tights were soaked now and streaked with dirt. Aaron couldn't believe one of her parents wasn't stopping her. *Splash.* She landed on one foot and wobbled. Her shoe skidded a few inches on the wet pavement.

"Careful!" Aaron called out. "It's slippery!"

The girl cocked her head at him for a moment, then went back to her game. The bells on the train were loud now; it was just about to reach the station. Then Aaron heard a scream.

All heads whipped toward the girl. She had jumped too close to the edge of the platform and tumbled off onto the tracks. Aaron rushed forward; she was lying sprawled across the train tracks, her foot lodged between two slats. A gash in her head was bleeding profusely, staining her pretty pink coat. She was wailing.

"Help!" Aaron cried. He waved his arms like a madman. "Stop the train! Stop the train!"

But he knew the train couldn't stop in time—it was moving slowly, but it was too close. No one else on the platform moved; everyone seemed frozen in shock. The girl's screams were nearly drowned out by the pealing train bell.

"Help me!" she shrieked. "I don't want to die!"

Aaron glanced frantically around, but there was no rope, nothing to toss her. Not that that would have helped—her foot was still stuck.

"Help me! Please!"

The girl's terrified eyes bore into Aaron's, pleading with him. Aaron felt his heart racing. He could hear the clacking, the banging, the whooshing of the train bearing down, but maybe there was enough time. The conductor would have pulled the emergency brake, slowing the train even further. He wouldn't even need to try to hop back up onto the platform—if he could get down there, get her loose, he could carry her over to the opposite tracks. One more glance at the train confirmed it; it was slowing down. It was far enough away. He could make it. He couldn't just watch this little girl die.

Aaron took a deep breath and ran the last few steps to the platform's edge. But as he was about to leap down onto the tracks, something grabbed his coat and yanked him back. Aaron felt wind on his cheek as the train rushed past, missing his head by centimeters. How could that be? He'd just seen it yards away still. He stumbled backward, slipping and falling hard on the asphalt.

"No!" he shouted. "No, the girl!"

He jumped up again and ran frantically along the platform as the train rolled to a stop.

"The girl! The girl!" he kept repeating, but people seemed just to stare at him. The train doors opened, and a handful of people disembarked, apparently unaware of the terrible accident that had just occurred. Aaron scanned the crowd for a conductor.

"We've got to help the girl!" he cried, running up to one.

"What girl?" the conductor asked.

Aaron wanted to tear out his hair.

"The girl who just got hit by the train!" he practically screamed in the conductor's face. The man took a step back, his expression dark and suspicious.

"What are you talking about?"

"This train just ran over a little girl," Aaron insisted. "Didn't anyone see? She fell off the platform—she's under there right now!" He pointed to the tracks.

"Son, that's really not funny. I think you better get on or move along." The conductor turned his back on Aaron and climbed aboard.

Aaron cupped his hands over his head, confused and exasperated. And then he heard a voice that made his blood turn to ice.

"Little Polly Flinders sat among the cinders…"

He turned slowly to see a little girl in a pink coat hopping in puddles, not ten feet away.

"Aaron!"

Aaron whirled around to see Quinn.

"What the hell was that? Do you have a death wish?" he demanded.

"What?"

"You were about to jump in front of that train!"

Realization dawned on Aaron.

"You were the one who pulled me back."

"Of course I did. You're welcome, by the way."

"I thought…I thought I saw…" Aaron began. He looked down the platform again. The girl was still there, still oblivious.

Hop. *Splash*. Hop. *Splash*.

"Aaron, are you okay? What's going on?"

"She fell. She fell on the tracks. I saw her fall."

"Who, that kid? Obviously not." Quinn shivered. "God, it's freezing out here."

Aaron looked at him sharply.

"You're feeling chills?"

"Uh, yeah, it's October in New England."

Aaron grabbed Quinn's shoulder.

"Are you sure it's just that? Or is it like you're losing heat? Like it's being sucked out of you?"

Quinn raised an eyebrow.

"Yeah, the second one, I guess. I was fine when I left my house this morning, but now I just can't get warm."

"Shit," Aaron muttered.

"What's the matter?"

"We've got to get out of here now."

Aaron ran toward the train just as the doors were closing, Quinn on his heels. The whistle sounded and the train lurched forward.

"*Shit,*" Aaron said again. He stepped back as the train picked up speed and rumbled past them, out of the station. His brain was on full alert now. He'd just seen something that wasn't real, and now Quinn had the shivers. The Vours were here.

He looked up and down the platform. It was empty but for him, Quinn, and the hopscotching girl. The girl with no apparent parents.

"*Mother came and caught her and whipped her pretty daughter,*" she sang.

"Let's go," Aaron whispered to Quinn.

But men had begun to appear, one by one, in the doorways leading back into the station. They all stood nonchalantly, checking their wristwatches or reading the paper, but there was no way to get out without pushing past them. One of them tightened his scarf around his throat.

Another bell rang out in the distance; a train heading the other direction was approaching. Quinn rubbed his arms vigorously.

"God, I am so cold. Maybe I'm getting sick."

"You're not sick," Aaron said, glancing at each man in turn, then the little girl, who continued to play and sing. All the exits were covered now. They were trapped.

"We're in danger, Quinn." He kept his voice low but tried to appear as if he were having a normal conversation. "Right now. I don't have time to explain, but those men are here for us. You were right, about Reggie and me being involved with what happened to you, and this is part of it. I'll tell you everything, but now we just need to get out of here."

"Okay, but how?" Quinn's eyes were wide. Aaron was just thankful he was accepting their predicament without question.

"Do you have a car here?"

Quinn nodded.

"Where's it parked?"

Quinn started to raise his hand in the direction of the parking lot on the opposite side of the station, but Aaron grabbed it.

"Don't point. It's over there? Which one?"

"The black Toyota by the B sign." Quinn inclined his head, pretending to scratch his ear.

Aaron casually scanned the station once more. There were a handful of people on the opposite platform now, as well, though he couldn't be sure which, if any of them, were Vours. The north-bound train was nearly there, its lights flashing through the rain.

"On the count of three, we're going to jump and run. Can you make it?"

Quinn glanced at the track as if making a mental calculation. "Yes. Can you?"

"Let's hope. One…"

The men standing in the doorways began to saunter toward them.

"Two…"

The little girl stopped hopping and looked straight at Aaron. Her hair and coat were soaking from the rain, and her face glistened with a deathly pallor. Aaron thought he could see black lines spreading down from her eyes across her cheeks. She'd been out in the cold too long. Still, a smile played on her ghostly lips, and she raised a finger, pointing at Aaron and Quinn.

"GET THEM!" she screeched in an earsplittingly high-pitched voice. The men rushed forward. The first car of the train passed the edge of the station.

"Three!"

Aaron and Quinn ran and leaped down onto the tracks. Quinn came down solidly and raced ahead, hoisting himself up onto the opposite platform. But Aaron stumbled on the landing, and his boot caught on an uneven slat. He rolled forward into the flashing lights of the oncoming train. People on the far platform screamed, and the train's whistle blew again and again.

"Aaron, come on!" Quinn shouted. "Move your ass!"

Aaron jumped up and staggered forward, his ankle throbbing with pain at every step. Quinn crouched on the platform, his hand extended. Aaron reached for it, and Quinn started to pull him up.

"Hurry! They're coming!"

And then, again, something caught Aaron's jacket. One of the Vours had him. He heard a hiss in his ear.

"Sorry, kiddo. You'll never be the action-hero type."

The Vour yanked Aaron back and they both fell to the ground. The train was bearing down on them. The Vour began to drag him back across the tracks where the others waited. The little girl was there, clapping her hands and shrieking with delight. Aaron struggled, but the monster was too strong. And then, in a flash, Aaron unzipped his coat and slacked his arms, letting the jacket slide off. The Vour fell backward, surprised by the sudden give. Ignoring the pain in his leg, Aaron bounded toward the opposite platform and leaped, catching Quinn's hand. In one motion Quinn pulled him up just as the train passed, plowing into the Vour, still prostrate on the tracks. Smoke billowed up from where the body lay under the train and rushed away into the rainy sky, but only Aaron seemed to notice that in the ensuing chaos.

He lay on the platform, his breath coming too fast to control, his brain a blank mass of adrenaline. He barely heard the screams all around him, the running feet, the incessant howl of the whistle, or felt the arms pulling him to his feet.

"You are one psycho son of a bitch," Quinn said, panting equally heavily. "Come on, we've got to get out of here."

Aaron nodded and, using Quinn for support, limped down the stairs heading to the parking lot. He knew the Vours would be circling around from the other side, and police would be descending upon the station to investigate the accident. They had to get to the car first.

"Faster, man, come on," Quinn urged. They emerged from the stairs onto the pavement, and Quinn began to run, practically dragging Aaron along behind. He pulled a keychain from his pocket and unclicked the door locks on his car. He threw Aaron into the front seat, then raced around to the driver's side, and within minutes they were peeling out of the station parking lot to the music of approaching emergency vehicle sirens.

 5

"So where are we going?" Quinn asked once they had put some distance between them and the train station.

"Are we being followed?" Aaron asked curtly.

"I—I don't know," Quinn answered. "I don't think so. But it's not like that's a skill I learned in driver's ed."

"Okay." Aaron sat forward and rolled up his pant leg. He massaged his leg and ankle—he wasn't an expert, but it didn't seem to be broken. Probably just a bad sprain.

"Where do you want me to take you?" Quinn asked again.

"I was going to go to New York—"

"Great. That'll give you four hours to explain just exactly what the hell is going on."

"You're going to drive me to New York?"

"Would you rather wait around for the next train?"

"Not really." Aaron leaned back in his seat, and finally his body began to relax, warmed by the air spraying from the heaters. "Why were you even there, at the station?"

"I followed you," Quinn said, a bit guiltily. "I was going to try to get you to talk to me again. Luckily I saved your life—twice—so you owe me."

"Actually, that makes us even."

"Okay," said Quinn, drawing out the word. "I guess we'll get to that. But first, why were you going to jump in front of that train? The first time, I mean, when I pulled you back."

"It was like I said, I saw that little girl—who, it turns out, is not just any little girl—fall onto the tracks. I was going to try to save her."

"Hero complex, huh?"

"Something like that. But what I saw, I think it was just a vision that she sent me."

"*Sent* you?"

Aaron sighed. There was no avoiding the conversation now.

"Look, it's better if I start from the beginning. You're not going to like what I'm about to tell you, but you're just going to have to deal for the moment, okay?"

"Sure."

"I'm serious, Quinn. You can't freak out, you can't steer the car into a tree, or start screaming, 'It's not true, it can't be true!' It's all true, but *you* are out of the worst of it now."

Quinn seemed to notice that he emphasized the word *you*. He glanced sideways at Aaron.

"I woke up in a homeless shelter with no memory and two missing fingers. I've been pretty certain for a while now that whatever happened to me was bad."

Aaron nodded, then started talking. He filled Quinn in on the whole truth of the Vours and how Reggie had brought him back from the fearscape. Aaron didn't sugarcoat any of Quinn the Vour's diabolical actions; in fact, he took some small pleasure in relaying them: how Quinn had tried to drown them last December, and then, when he returned, how he'd betrayed Reggie and nearly gotten her killed again. Quinn's fingers seemed to tighten on the steering wheel during those parts of the story, but he kept calm and didn't interrupt. Sometimes he even nodded slightly, as if Aaron was giving him missing pieces of a puzzle, and he was finally able to put it together. Still, by the time Aaron finished, Quinn had gone very pale.

"So there are such things as monsters, and I was one of them."

"Yep. A pretty nasty one."

Quinn swallowed.

"I feel sick."

Aaron refrained from pointing out that how Quinn was feeling was below his radar of caring.

"Good. That's a pretty human reaction—I'd be worried if you didn't."

"You don't understand. I've had…thoughts…about murder…and torture.…They've been trapped in my head, and I didn't know where they were coming from. I really thought I had gone crazy! Like I had a split personality and one of them was a psychopath."

Aaron grunted noncommittally.

"But then, on the other side, there are these memories of the most horrible things. Fear and pain and death and dread…I just…I didn't know if they were real or all bad dreams or what. And it turns out that everything was real—all of it—they're just memories from my two different…lives."

"Look, I can't give you a handbook on how to deal with this," said Aaron. "Henry, Reggie's little brother, has experienced some of what you're talking about, remembering things from both worlds. I think it's just a part of you now."

"So I'll always have a little bit of psychopath in my head?"

"Maybe. It's up to you not to act on it."

Quinn sighed. He looked stricken.

"Thanks, Aaron, for being straight with me. I get it, why you brushed me off for so long. I'm really sorry about Reggie."

"Thanks" was all Aaron said.

"So you didn't know that girl was a Vour when you were waiting for the train?" Quinn asked.

"No, I didn't. Maybe I should've." Aaron thought back to the platform, to the girl jumping in puddles. "There are signs, but they're subtle. She was playing in the cold rain and didn't seem to be bothered by it. And the vision she sent me, it wasn't like the others I've had. Most of the time they're nightmarish, like unbelievable things happen but they feel real. But this time, there was no fantasy involved. A girl's playing on wet asphalt, she slips, she falls on the tracks. It's a freak accident, but believable." Aaron paused. "I've come to know when I'm seeing a Vour vision, even if I can't fight against it. I know that it's happening to me. But this—this *was* real."

"Why do you think this one was different?" Quinn asked.

"I can't be sure," Aaron said. "But when Vours send visions, it's usually either to incapacitate you, or just to mess with you, drive you crazy. I think that girl wanted me to jump on the tracks and get hit by the train. She was trying to kill me."

"And everyone would think it was suicide, or an accident."

"Welcome to the wonderful world of the Vours."

"But the reason I started feeling especially cold is because I can detect them," Quinn went on. "That's what we think. This is further proof. But with Henry at least—it's not an exact science. You can tell that a Vour is close, but it doesn't pinpoint them."

"So it's handier if I'm in a room with one other person than in a crowd."

"Exactly."

"Still, it's something."

"Yes, it's something."

"So what's in New York? Is that where you think Reggie is?"

Aaron hesitated. This was not necessarily part of the tale he was anxious to bring Quinn in on. Quinn sensed this.

"Come on, I'm in it now. Whatever you're up to, I want to help."

Aaron exhaled.

"Not Reggie. Her mother." Saying it out loud somehow made it more real. After all this time, could they really have found her?

"What's she doing there?"

"She…left…a while ago. Disappeared, changed her name, the works. But when we find and rescue Reggie, she's going to need to disappear as well. I'm hoping that her mother will take her in."

"You're going to rescue Reggie?"

"Of course."

"How?"

"We're still working out the details."

"You and this Machen guy?"

"At any rate, it's imperative that we have a plan for Reggie after she's out. She can't go back to Cutter's Wedge. It's too dangerous."

"It might be too dangerous for you, too, you know."

"I'll do anything to make sure she's safe," Aaron murmured to the car window.

They didn't talk much for the rest of the trip, and Aaron's thoughts turned to Mrs. Halloway. He wasn't going to engage her on this trip, if it really was her out there in Brooklyn. He just needed to confirm her identity. They'd have to wait until after they'd found Reggie to approach her—no point in doing it before then and risking the rescue operation. On the one hand, he hoped that as her mother, Mrs. Halloway would drop everything to ensure her daughter's safety; on the other, it's not like she deserved any awards for motherly instincts as of late.

Aaron had always liked Mrs. Halloway, too. Sure, she had been a bit frazzled at times, but that made her fun. She would do the unexpected, like wake Reggie and Aaron up on sleepover nights to go for midnight ice cream runs, just because she was having a craving. Or secretly give the two of them driving lessons on backcountry roads when they were only thirteen. Aaron loved his parents deeply, but theirs was a somewhat regimented household. Once upon a time, the Halloways' had been an escape for him, a carnival where new rides were always opening.

But then everything had changed. It had happened slowly and subtly; Aaron couldn't even put his finger on the moment when he had realized that Mrs. Halloway was somehow different. She just grew more distant, and cared less about what Reggie and Henry were doing. She'd disappear for hours at a time, leaving Reggie alone to babysit Henry without any explanation as to her whereabouts. Mr. Halloway had always worked long hours, and the fights between him and his wife had begun in earnest when he would routinely arrive home to find Reggie preparing microwave meals for the family and no sign of her mother. Reggie didn't openly complain, trying to shield Henry from most of the strife, but she had grown more reserved, withdrawing from almost all of her friends except for Aaron.

He had mentioned Mrs. Halloway's behavior to his own mom at one point; being a psychiatrist, she had told Aaron to look for signs of alcohol or drug abuse, since they were often involved in cases of such drastic personality shifts. But Aaron had never found any evidence to suggest that Reggie's mother was drinking or popping pills, not that that proved anything. Addicts became experts at hiding their vices. And then Mrs. Halloway had simply disappeared.

But now she had been found. Hopefully.

When they stopped for gas, Aaron offered to drive. Two hours later they were rolling into Brooklyn, and half an hour after that, Aaron parked on a quiet neighborhood street in front of a redbrick building. He peered out the windshield. The sky was getting dark, and a light flipped on in a second-story window.

"She's home," Aaron said.

"So what now?" asked Quinn.

"I guess we have to wait until she leaves," said Aaron. "I have to make sure it's really her."

"But she could be in for the night."

Aaron shrugged.

"You're the one who wanted to come along."

Quinn frowned and slumped in his seat. When they'd been waiting for twenty minutes, a pizza delivery guy pulled up and headed to the building's front door.

"Hang on, I've got a better idea."

He jumped out of the car before Aaron could stop him and waved down the pizza guy. They chatted for a few seconds, Quinn handed over a few bills, and the guy gave him the pizza. Then Quinn began to climb the front stoop.

"What the hell?" Aaron hopped out of the car and ran after Quinn. "Quinn!" he hissed. "What do you think you're doing?"

"Delivering pizza," said Quinn, looking at the names on the buzzer.

"I'm serious."

"I'm just going to get into the building, then go knock on her door and say I thought the pizza was for her. She doesn't know me. Then I'll pretend to get a phone call and snap a picture of her with the phone cam. Genius, right?"

Aaron grudgingly agreed.

"Yes, that's pretty good."

"Then let me get to it."

Aaron retreated down the steps and back to the car. He heard the buzzer go and the door slam as Quinn entered the building. This time he sat in the passenger seat, and he noticed his stomach rumbling. The pizza had smelled awfully good.

His cell phone buzzed, and he pulled it out of his pocket.

Expecting his mother's or father's name on the caller ID, or perhaps Machen's, he was shocked to see "Reggie" flashing on the screen. He touched the answer button and slowly put the phone to his ear.

"Hello?"

"Aaron, is that you?" It was Henry—this was Reggie's home line, not her cell. Aaron felt foolish.

"It's me, Henry. What is it? Is everything okay?"

Henry spoke softly and quickly.

"I don't have a lot of time. I just wanted to tell you that Dad is going to see Reggie next week."

"He's what?"

"Whatever you said to him at the library, he's been acting weird ever since. And then today he told me that he set up an appointment for us to go see her."

"When? Where?" Aaron felt his hairs standing on end.

"He didn't say where. But next Saturday."

"Henry, this is fantastic. Listen, I'll talk to Machen, but we're going to need your help. You're going to need to spy for us."

"I've got to go. He's coming."

There was a click and Aaron's cell lost the call. He bit his thumbnail, lost in thought. So his words had struck home. Mr. Halloway wanted proof that Reggie was on the mend. Now it was just a game of surveillance, certainly something Machen knew how to organize. As long as Henry could pull it off, they would finally learn where she was. It was the break they'd been waiting for.

The door opened and Quinn got into the car. He had a funny look on his face as he slid into the driver's seat.

"So?" Aaron asked. "Did it work? Did you get the picture?"

"Ye-es," said Quinn hesitantly.

He handed over his phone, which showed a picture of a pretty woman with dark hair. She was slimmer, but it was definitely Sheila Halloway.

"That's her," Aaron said excitedly. "It's her—it's Reggie's mom."

"Aaron, there's something you should know."

"I did it. I found her!"

"Aaron!"

"What?"

Quinn took a deep breath.

"When she opened the door, I felt it. The cold. Like all the heat in my body was gone."

Aaron gaped at him.

"You're saying—"

"Yeah. She's one of them. She's a Vour."

———

The dirt crumbled all around her, blinded her, suffocated her, but still Reggie crawled on through the tunnel. She dug forward with her hands, shoving the earth out of the way, ignoring the pain in her fingertips where her nails were cracked and bleeding.

And then finally she felt air. She pushed forward and her arms were free of the tunnel. They were sore beyond measure, but she pulled herself out and sucked in the oxygen.

It wasn't the cleanest breath: She appeared to be in some kind of cavern now, lit dimly by moonlight, and the air was dank and close. But it beat the hell out of breathing dirt.

A gray abyss surrounded the cave entrance; she had been seeing this emptiness throughout the entire fearscape, the decay of memories that signified the human victim, Jacob, had been trapped here for years, maybe decades. Indeed, it was the most eroded fearscape she'd ever been to, as if it could crumble away into nothingness at any moment, and there was still no sign of Jacob. There was no sign of anything—no people, no monsters, no tangible objects. These outer layers had not been occupied for a long time, and whatever horrors once populated this realm had since melted together and hardened into emotionless, lifeless chunks of psychic rubble. Wherever Jacob was now, it was deep, deep down.

Reggie suspected he had long since been propelled to the core of the fearscape, where his existence would be one of only isolation and immobility in a fathomless dread. She knelt and sifted through the ash-colored dirt, seeking out anything that might offer a clue as to where Jacob now dwelled. No magic door would open, no chute would suddenly appear beneath her feet here. She needed to find a symbol of Jacob, some lingering bread crumb that tied him to this place. Through all her journeys, Reggie knew that while the Vours could strip away the identities of their victims, it was something else to destroy them completely. Jacob's identity was hidden, but it was not gone. At least, she hoped it wasn't.

Her fingers struck a small box caked in sand. She rubbed the dirt away, revealing the soft purple velvet exterior. She tried to pry it open, but it was locked tight. She shook it, but nothing sounded from inside.

"What are you telling me, Jacob?" Reggie asked herself. "What's in the box?"

A constant *drip drip drip* echoed in the cave. She hadn't noticed it before, but now the noise seemed to drum on the inside of her skull.

She walked toward the dripping sound but never drew nearer or farther away; it remained constantly beyond her ear, beyond her grasp. Paths and caves twisted and turned on one another, creating a sealed maze with no physical exit. Reggie knew she could sit down in the dust and wait forever. This place brought on the weighty feel of an infinite solitude. The immediate peril was nonexistent; the loneliness was eternal.

Reggie walked on, clutching the box and rubbing the velvet between her fingers.

"What's in the box?"

And then she took a step, and the ground fell away beneath her. She tried to pull back, to grasp anything that would stop her fall, but her hands found nothing. There was nothing behind her, nothing in front of her—she was tumbling into the abyss. She had walked off the edge of the fearscape.

Reggie thrust out her arms, grappling at the air, willing herself to find something to hang on to, but there was only the emptiness of the gray matter. She fell and fell and fell. *This is it*, she thought. There was no way out, nowhere else to go. She would be lost forever in the oblivion. Her comatose body would remain in Unger's prison as her psyche unraveled and at last dissipated into this void of forgotten memory.

Then, suddenly, she stopped. She did not hit ground—she simply stopped.

Around her there was nothing. Her mind struggled to comprehend, but it could not. It was not black or gray, viscous or dusty, dense or light. It was nothingness.

Reggie had no concept of time or space here. Emotions drained away, including fear itself. The only sensation she had was that of her existence slipping away. The feeling was not painful or sad. It was nothing. It was this place. It had always been this place, and she had always been one with it. She no longer mattered. Nothing mattered.

Nothing.

A small entity fluttered by her ear. Reggie called out from the nothingness that was both her and not her. The thing tickled her ear, only for a moment.

What are you?

"I am nothing," Reggie answered. "This is nothing."

I have dwelled in nothing forever. You are more than nothing. What are you?

"I…" Reggie struggled to trace a thought. "I am here…"

Why?

"…to save you…"

Tiny wings fanned her face.

Please…find my soul.

Jacob. It was Jacob.

And she…

"My name is Reggie," she said, pulling her mind back from the peaceful emptiness. "And you...your name..."

I have a name?

"Yes. Your name is Jacob."

Why am I here?

"You were taken. Stolen."

I remember...fear...neverending...

"It is ending."

What has kept me here?

"Nothing, Jacob. Nothing at all."

Reggie felt velvet, soft and warm in her fingers. She lifted her hand and held the box aloft in her palm.

"This is yours."

The flutter of wings.

"Open the box, Jacob."

She could see it now. A faintly lit mothlike creature flying around her hand. It circled over the box, the wings buzzing closer with each revolution.

"Open it."

The box glowed white. The hinges creaked back and the box opened. From inside came the most unexpected of sounds.

A man's baritone voice sang out loud and clear into the void. It was one of the most beautiful things Reggie had ever heard, strong and rich and deep and sad. It took her breath away, and for a few moments she actually forgot where she was, and her heart soared.

And then, a few moments after that, as the man continued to sing, thousands of tiny lights began to pierce the darkness, and they grew steadily, white light blasting away the black. As Reggie's eyes began to adjust, she saw the most incredible thing. A tiny moth, fluttering here and there, began to grow and shift and stretch, until it had two legs, and two arms, and a torso, and a head, and the most lovely of voices. It was Jacob as a young man, tall and lean and proud.

He continued to sing until all the darkness had faded away, and they were standing in the blank space of the obliterated fearscape. Only then did Jacob end his song.

"You found me," he said to Reggie. "I was so lost."

"So was I," she said.

A revolving door appeared. Jacob squinted and pointed upward, and looked the slightest bit afraid once again.

"What's that?" he asked.

Reggie was not surprised. Victims often witnessed something inside the defeated fearscape—something she could never see herself.

"I don't know." She gestured to the revolving door. "But this is the way home."

Jacob took her hand.

"Let's go, then."

6

Aaron tapped incessantly on the center console of Machen's car. He was lying stretched out in the backseat, mostly covered with a blanket so that he was hidden from the sight of people passing by.

"Not built for stakeouts, were you?" asked Machen, hunched down in the front seat.

"I'm sorry, I don't have the Zen master thing down yet."

It was Saturday afternoon, and they were parked on a side street not far from the school, around the corner from the house of one of Henry's friends. The plan was for Henry to tell his father that he was spending the night there, but when he got dropped off, meet Aaron and Machen instead. But they'd been waiting there for almost three hours, and there had been no sign of Thom Halloway's pickup truck. Every time a car drove by, Aaron's head would pop up, inciting disapproval from Machen.

"The point is for people not to see us sitting here, loitering suspiciously in the car," he said.

But Aaron could barely contain his worry. So many things could have happened—what if the Vours had found the hidden camera Henry was carrying? What if they'd taken the Halloways hostage or, worse, killed them? How could he and Machen have been so idiotic as to let that kid risk so much on his own? A small part of Aaron's brain replied to this, and he wasn't sure he liked the answer: Like he had told Quinn, he would do anything to save Reggie, even if it meant putting her little brother in danger.

The front passenger door opened and Aaron jumped. Henry hopped in the car and buckled his seat belt.

"Henry, thank God, you made it!" he exclaimed. "Are you okay? Did you see Reggie?"

"Not yet," Machen said. He started the car and pulled away slowly, glancing periodically in the rearview mirror. Only when they were on the road back to his house and he was satisfied that no one was following them did he address Henry.

"Henry, are you all right? Hurt in any way?"

Henry shook his head. "No, I'm fine."

"And you did go to visit Reggie today?"

"Yes, but they wouldn't let us—"

"Wait," Machen interrupted. "I need you to start at the beginning, so we don't miss anything. Do you think you can do that?"

Henry nodded.

"Okay, first, where are they keeping Reggie?"

"It's a hospital called the Home Institute of Psychiatry," Henry answered quickly. "And I remember we drove on Route eighty-four for a long time, and it was close to a town called St. Mary's."

"That's excellent, Henry. We'll definitely be able to find it again, then."

"The Home Institute?" Aaron scoffed. "Unger's holed up in a place called Home?"

"Can you describe the place?" Machen went on, ignoring the irony.

Henry thought for a minute.

"It wasn't like Thornwood. It was big and white, like a normal hospital. And very cold."

"Cold like *Vour* cold?" asked Aaron.

"Yeah. I had the chills everywhere there." Henry shivered, as if his body remembered the sensation. "There are Vours all over the place there, and they have Reggie."

"But we know where she is now. We can get her out." Aaron put his hand on Henry's shoulder.

"What happened next?" Machen pressed. "When you went inside?"

"They tried to stop us at first. We were in the lobby, and a doctor—not Dr. Unger—came out and told us we shouldn't be there. He said we couldn't see Reggie, and we had to leave. Dad started yelling and pushing. I've never seen him like that. It was awful."

Aaron had suspected it would go down something like that. There was no way the Vours would let them in to see Reggie. But he knew it must have been hard for Henry to witness.

"Dad got through the first security doors," Henry went on. "There was a long, white hallway with doors all the way along it, and elevators at the end. But that was all I could see. A bunch of security guards grabbed Dad and they called the police. That's why we were so late—they took us to the station. Dad was try-ing to tell the police that they had kidnapped Reggie, that they wouldn't let us see her, but the cops didn't care. They just threat-ened to keep him there if he didn't calm down. Once we got home I thought Dad might make me stay in tonight, but he seemed relieved not to have to deal with me."

"What's your dad going to do?" Aaron asked.

"I don't know. I don't think he knows what to do. He said he was going to talk to a lawyer."

"But of course he wouldn't think to ask me about it, even though I warned him this would happen," Aaron grumbled.

"I don't get why," said Henry. "After today, I really thought he'd believe us."

"Your father is a man of extreme rationality, Henry," said Machen. "He will always assume there is a sensible answer, even to the most inane questions. He won't believe in Vours until he gets some kind of visual proof, and even then, maybe not."

They had reached his house, and he parked the car and turned the engine off.

"You were very brave today, Henry. I know it can't have been easy to go through that. But now we're getting somewhere. The camera worked?"

"I think so," said Henry. "I did like Aaron showed me."

They went inside, and Machen set up the equipment for watching the video Henry had filmed. Throughout the week he and Aaron had met stealthily between the playground and the high school, and Henry had turned over one of his coats to Aaron. Machen had stitched a lipstick camera and mic—more goodies pilfered from the Tracers—into the lapel of the coat, creating a fake buttonhole for the lens. Aaron had explained how to use it, but they hadn't had the opportunity for a live run. Now they hoped for the best.

Machen cut the camera out of Henry's coat, careful not to damage the jacket too badly, and hooked it up to a monitor. The image flashed on the screen, and the three settled in to watch.

Henry had done a good job getting an exterior view of the Home Institute, as Aaron had instructed him to. Like he said, it was very unlike Thornwood. That hospital had been a rehabbed farm, the interior cozy and inviting. This place was a compound: large, generic, anonymous. Machen made notes about the perimeter and security as Henry and his father headed inside.

The interior was as sterile as the outside: white walls and floors, glass barriers keeping visitors out and patients in. They were staring at Mr. Halloway's back as he strode ahead to the reception desk.

The following minutes were hard to watch. As Henry had said, his father had quickly grown belligerent with the nurse on duty, demanding to see his daughter and threatening to call the police. A doctor in a white lab coat appeared and tried to calm him down, but Mr. Halloway was not having it.

"I want to see my daughter!" he shouted over and over again. "Regina Halloway! She's a patient here under Dr. Unger. I want to see her now!"

"Dr. Unger isn't here right now," the other doctor said. "I can't allow any visitors without his authorization. I suggest you contact his office directly—"

"I don't care about authorization! You can't keep me from my daughter!"

Aaron bit his lip. It was a terrible sight: Mr. Halloway, so big and capable, and yet so powerless. The desperation and confusion rang through his voice, and his entire body trembled. It was unnerving. He balled his hands into fists, as Aaron had seen him do that day at the library.

And then, as an orderly was passing through the security door leading to the patients' wing, he sprang, pushing the man aside and charging through the door. The view started to shake as Henry ran after, and shouting voices sounded around the camera. Mr. Halloway made it halfway down the hallway before security guards seemed to descend from all sides, barring his way. Aaron thought he could hear Henry's voice crying out meekly for his father, but it was drowned out by the jangling of an alarm. Mr. Halloway tried to push through the guards; it took four of them to subdue him.

All the while, Machen had been scribbling in his notebook. He wasn't paying attention to the theatrics on-screen; he was recording the locations of security cameras, the time it took the guards to respond, and all the other data that would be pertinent to staging a breakout. Aaron had to admire his focus, and he tried to follow Machen's lead.

The guards had cuffed Mr. Halloway and were leading him back to the lobby, where a sheriff's deputy waited. As they passed Henry, his father looked at him. "It's going to be okay, Henry. Son, it's going to be all right. Don't be afraid."

Machen jumped up and switched off the camera. The television went black.

"I think we got everything we need," he said.

Henry sat quietly on the couch, looking at his lap. Aaron scooched next to him and put an arm around his shoulder.

"I'm sorry you had to go through that today. But we have what we need now. We know where Reggie is, and we're going to figure out how to get her out. All because of you, Henry. We couldn't have done it without you."

Aaron wondered if Henry was trying to hide tears, but when the boy turned to him, his eyes were dry and resolved.

"I know. I'd do it again in a heartbeat."

Aaron began researching the Home Institute of Psychiatry immediately. Over the next weeks, he and Machen gathered as much information as they could on the place. It was located in Connecticut, just off Route 84; it wasn't a particularly renowned hospital, but on paper it appeared legit enough. They found schematics for the building in a local library's archives, and Machen made a few more trips out to St. Mary's to scout the area and get a better feeling for the property.

The real break came two weeks later when Aaron was able to hack into Home's network. Suddenly at his fingertips were the names of all the patients, their room numbers, the meds they were taking, the food they ate. And there she was: Regina Halloway, room 304. He pulled up the hospital blueprints and examined the floor plan. Third floor, west side, far from the elevators. It was the size of a prison cell.

Aaron looked at the information on the screen in front of him. It would be so easy to change her information, to delete her altogether—maybe to order a transfer? But it wasn't the smart move. Unger would be keeping a close eye on Reggie, especially after the incident with her father, and any computer glitch would be another red flag. The rescue needed to be a complete surprise attack. And that was Machen's purview.

"It's doable," he told Aaron over his cell one Tuesday morning in late November as Aaron was on his way into school. "I've figured out how to do it."

Aaron's heart soared. There was still a long way to go, but it felt like a weight had been lifted off his shoulders. Finally they had a plan.

"That's the best news I've heard all year," he said. "We should do it Saturday—I don't want her in there a day more than necessary."

"I agree, but there's a catch," Machen said. "We're going to need a third. We'll have to have two go in, and another in the car. I asked Crystal but she won't do it. None of my contacts want to risk exposing themselves like that, even for Reggie."

"Okay, we'll figure it out." Aaron clicked the phone off and pocketed it. His eyes fell on a black Toyota SUV pulling into the student parking lot. He gritted his teeth and racked his brain for another option, but none came to mind. Saturday was five days away, and he was running short on allies. He walked toward the car.

As Quinn hopped out and grabbed his backpack, Aaron was relieved to see that he was alone—no Nina or other hangers-on were in the vicinity.

Quinn cocked his head as he saw Aaron striding toward him.

"I need to know if you're still interested in helping Reggie," Aaron said once he got close.

"Of course. What do you need me to do?"

Aaron glanced at the car.

"Drive."

7

Reggie dove through the mirror and landed hard on cold stone. She whipped around to see the glass still intact—she had passed through it without it breaking—and the hag with the scissors slammed into it on the other side. She brandished her razor-sharp teeth and struck the mirror with her scissors again and again, their bloody tips leaving reddish black smears on the glass, but the boundary held.

She had passed into a deeper realm of yet another fearscape, and the witch could not follow her here. Eventually she backed away, scowling, and the room on the other side faded to black. Reggie was outside, looking at her own reflection in the window of a cottage. She winced. Her hair looked like it had been cut with a vacuum cleaner.

"Only a teen girl would be afraid of an evil hairstylist," Reggie muttered to herself, thinking of Missy, the petite brunette she was strapped to out in the real world. She had looked about sixteen, Reggie's age, and the relative solidity of the fearscape indicated she hadn't been a Vour that long, perhaps a year or two.

Reggie turned her attention to her arms. In addition to

mauling Reggie's split ends, the psychotic beautician had gotten in several good stabs with her shears, and the wounds were oozing a black, viscous fluid. Had she not been so exhausted, so strung out from fight after fight in Unger's endless parade of fearscape challenges, Reggie could have avoided this type of injury. Her skills for combating the wicked manifestations inside these forsaken places had grown immensely, but those skills would matter little if her mind was forced to battle without rest. Sooner or later, she would break for good. But until then, there was nowhere to go but onward.

Trees grew right up to the house, and their leafless branches scraped the cottage walls like spindly skeleton fingers. The front door stood open, but inside was only blackness. A few feet away, a dirt path led into the forest.

Reggie shivered, and her teeth began to chatter. Cold. Always so damn cold.

She had two choices—go inside or follow the path. Though she was loath to enter the uninviting cottage, she would freeze if she was out in this weather much longer without more clothing. But just then a gust of wind blew the front door shut, revealing a long, red cloak hanging from a peg on the wall. Reggie eyed it suspiciously.

Most objects that Reggie found signaled that she was on the right track, but they were often small tokens. She didn't know how an old-fashioned cloak would correspond to a teenage girl like Missy. Reggie tried the knob, but the door was stuck. The fearscape seemed to be telling her that the right direction was through the woods, but to go that way, she needed some kind of covering.

She gingerly removed the cloak, holding it out wide so that it fluttered open. She checked both sides and inside the hood but found no insects, rats, or other surprises waiting to jump out at her. Reggie took a deep breath and swung the fabric around her shoulders, fastening it at her throat.

She waited, but no magic spell took hold of her. It appeared to be a garden-variety cloak, and a warm one at that. Reggie snuggled into the thick wool and pulled the hood up over her head, so she was wrapped in a cherry-colored cocoon. She was about to head off when she noticed a basket sitting on the ground, covered with a handkerchief. Pinned to this was a note that said only, *For Grandma*. Kneeling, she removed the napkin, again expecting some horrifying surprise the fearscape had concocted, but the basket was filled with muffins. Blueberry, from the looks of it.

She sat back on her heels, frowning. A red cloak, a basket full of muffins, a path through the woods, and a note sending her off to Grandma's house.

Little Red Riding Hood.

"So be on the lookout for big bad wolves," she said to herself as she rose, taking the basket with her. She wished she had something more threatening than muffins to bring along.

She set off along the windy dirt path into the woods. Though it was winter and most of the trees were clear of leaves, they grew so closely together that it was difficult to see more than a few feet beyond the edge of the trail. The path itself was narrow and overgrown; she had to dodge branches and step over roots, making her an easy target for anyone tracking her, especially with her bright cloak against the colorless winter forest. Still, there was nothing for it but to plunge on.

As she walked, she tried to put the fearscape pieces together. There had been the outer layers that had been the surface fears — rats, the dark, a bad haircut. But she felt that now she was getting to the deeper terrors. She couldn't see how Red Riding Hood played into it, though.

The afternoon faded to evening, and she was quickly losing light. She tripped frequently, not seeing the vagaries of the trail in the deepening shadows. And then she heard it: a low snarl.

It was almost imperceptible at first, blending in with the wind blowing through the branches. But it came again from one side of her, and then the other. She heard twigs cracking, and the growl grew louder. It was behind her now.

Slowly she turned. The moon had risen, and in its spotlight she saw the flash of two yellow eyes. The beast was massive, its fur coarse and jagged, like wire. It trundled forward, black gums curled up around its snout, revealing spiked teeth dripping with saliva.

It growled again.

Reggie backed away. If she ran, it would be on her in a second. How did the fairy tale go? Red Riding Hood was on her way to Grandma's house, and the wolf distracted her so that he could get there first, devour the old woman, and lie in wait for the girl.

This wolf seemed uninterested in forgoing Reggie as an appetizer, though. Its fangs glinted in the moonlight.

"My, what big teeth you have," she murmured.

She glanced about for any kind of weapon, but the branches were too high above her head, and she couldn't spot any rock on the ground. All she had were the muffins.

She drew one out of the basket. It seemed like just a regular breakfast treat, soft and sweet-smelling. But as she lifted it, the wolf sniffed the air. When it snarled this time, it was higher pitched, more like a whine.

It took a step back.

Wary, Reggie held the muffin out, and the wolf retreated even farther. Then the creature threw up its head and howled, an ear-piercing screech that echoed through the forest. Its call was answered with other yowls, and soon the woods were a deafening cacophony of wailing wolves.

Reggie aimed for the wolf's open maw and hurled the muffin at it. It landed in the beast's throat; startled, it choked the muffin down and immediately let out a whimpering cry. It staggered back, and then, to Reggie's utter surprise and horror, it started tearing at its own stomach with its teeth. Black blood spurted out of the wounds, and its intestines spilled from its abdomen.

Reggie didn't wait to see what would happen next. She heard movement in the woods, and the howls around her grew louder: The rest of the pack was on its way. She dashed down the path, clutching the precious muffins to her chest. She couldn't risk spilling any.

Ahead she could see light, and at last the dense trees opened up to reveal a glen, and another cottage, warmly lit from inside with smoke wafting out of the chimney.

Grandma's house.

She staggered to the door and tried the knob, but it was locked. She banged on it.

"Let me in!"

The howls drew nearer. The wolves poured forth from the trees.

Someone moaned inside the house, and a meek voice called out, "Are you the Woodsman?"

"My name is Reggie! I've come to help you!"

"Only the Woodsman can help me."

Reggie saw flashes of yellow shining in the dark. The wolves surrounded the cottage, slinking closer on noiseless paws.

"I have the muffins you made. The muffins for Grandma. Don't you want them?"

The door swung open on squeaky hinges. Reggie raced inside, slamming and bolting the door behind her. She stood in a one-room cabin with a fireplace, potbellied stove, kitchen table, and washbasin. A bed was in the corner, steeped in shadow.

A red cloak hung from a hook by the door. It was warm in the room, so Reggie removed her own cloak and hung it there as well.

Haggard breaths labored from the bed, and she walked forward slowly.

An old woman was lying half under the covers, dressed in a threadbare nightgown and nightcap. Her face was lined with wrinkles, her hands knobby and liver-spotted. She gazed at Reggie with glazed eyes that looked almost dead.

"You brought me my muffins?" the hag croaked. When she spoke, Reggie could see that her teeth were rotted black. Reggie held up the basket.

"You can have your muffins when you tell me where Missy is."

"Who's Missy?"

"The girl. She's about my age."

The hag shook her head and looked away.

"No more girl. No more Missy."

"I heard another voice when I was at the door. A girl's voice. Where is she?"

The woman squinted at Reggie.

"Have to have the daughter before you have the grand-daughter."

Reggie frowned.

"Who are you?"

"I'm…I'm…" She trailed off. "I'm not sure. I lost me."

Reggie thought she was beginning to understand, and she crossed to the head of the bed. On a hunch, she held a muffin to the woman's lips. The hag inhaled the sweet scent and took a nibble.

Suddenly her wrinkles began to smooth away, as if someone were holding a steamer to her skin. Her straggly gray hair fell out in clumps, and within seconds thick, dark hair sprouted from the bald scalp and flowed down to the woman's shoulders. The bags under her eyes tightened, her lips plumped, and the age spots faded away. She winced in pain as her toothless gray gums turned pink, and white teeth pushed up through them. The transformation was equal parts grotesque and wondrous.

"Hello, Missy," Reggie said.

The girl looked at the muffin with awe.

"I used to make these with Gran," she said. "Before she died."

The haunted howls echoed outside again. The wolves were surrounding them. There was a thump and the scraping of claws at the walls.

Scritch scritch scritch.

"Missy, why are you here?" Reggie asked. "What are you afraid of?"

Missy looked petrified. She hugged her chest and rocked back and forth in the bed.

Scritch scritch scritch.

Lone wolves, Reggie thought. *Isolation?*

"You said your grandmother died. Was she alone? Did she leave you all on your own? Loneliness can be scary, but we can fight it together."

"I'm never alone," Missy whimpered.

"What do you mean you're never alone?"

"Only the Woodsman can help me."

The baying outside drowned out Missy's voice, and Reggie had to lean close to hear her.

"Why? What can the Woodsman do?" she urged.

The screeching halted, and all was silent. Three strong knocks at the door followed.

"It's him," sighed Missy, sounding both relieved and terrified. "Come in."

"I bolted the door, Missy. Nobody can—"

The door was already opened, and a hulking man stood on the threshold. He strode forward into the room, carrying an ax stained with black blood and fur. He looked every bit the fairy-tale hunter, with his leather breeches and boots, cotton tunic, and wool coat. His large jowls were covered with a furry beard, his cheeks rosy from the cold.

Was Missy stronger than she had realized—had she brought the Woodsman here to kill the wolves, to free her? But if so, the fearscape should be collapsing.

No, there was something yet to happen.

The man came up to the bed, and Missy held her hand out. He took it and squeezed it.

"I'm here," he said in a deep voice. "Everything will be all right now. Are you ready?"

Missy nodded.

"Ready for what?" Reggie demanded. "You killed the wolves. Missy can leave, right?"

The Woodsman turned to Reggie. For the first time she noticed how hairy he was—whiskers grew all down his neck, and the hair on his head was thick and shaggy, like a pelt. But worst of all, his eyes glinted yellow at her.

"You're a wolf!" she cried. She dove toward Missy, trying to shield her, but the Woodsman caught her with one hand and tossed her away. Reggie hit the floor hard, and a bone in her wrist cracked. "Missy! Get out of the bed! Run!"

"She can't," growled the Woodsman. "Not with that thing growing inside her."

Reggie felt a chill go through her.

"What thing?"

The Woodsman ripped the covers off Missy's body, and to

her horror, Reggie saw the outline of a rounded belly beneath the girl's nightgown. She was pregnant.

"Cut it out of me! Cut it out!" Missy shrieked.

In an instant the puzzle pieces clicked together in Reggie's mind like the tumblers in a lock. Pregnancy. Being a single, teenage mother. This was what Missy feared. And her mind had perverted a children's story so that the Woodsman wasn't the hero because he rescued Red Riding Hood from the wolf; he *was* the wolf, and he saved her by slaying her.

The Woodsman raised his ax high above his head. The black blood smoked and dripped from the cold steel, singeing holes in the sheets where it landed. Missy closed her eyes and waited.

"Missy, listen to me!" Reggie said. "This isn't the answer. He won't just kill your baby—he'll kill you as well. You don't need to be afraid of this—we'll find a way out!"

"No way out," Missy whispered.

Cradling her arm, Reggie staggered up. She saw a muffin lying a few feet away; the basket had toppled to the floor when the Woodsman had upset the bedclothes. She grabbed it and tossed it at Missy.

"These were made with love, remember? With your gran? She wouldn't want you to do this to yourself—she'd want you to be strong, to fight back!"

Missy picked up the muffin and looked at it. The Woodsman hesitated, his ax hanging in the air as if suspended by a string.

"That's right," said Reggie. She held out her hand toward Missy. "Come with me. The woods are clear. We'll get through this together—I'll help you."

Missy's eyes shifted from the muffin to Reggie. Tears brimmed in them, and her jaw hardened.

"You'll just leave me like he did!" she screamed.

With that, the Woodsman dropped his ax, but not on Missy. He whirled about, swinging the weapon through the air and slamming it into Reggie's stomach.

She let out a startled gasp as the blade sliced through her organs, all the way to her spine. She tasted the rusty blood as it rose up her throat and into her mouth, bubbling on her lips. He held her like that, skewered on his ax, then pulled it out, and Reggie collapsed on the ground. Black bile and inky smoke gushed from her abdomen, and there was nothing she could do to stop it.

As her final breaths sputtered from her body, and the fog closed in around her, the last thing she saw was the Woodsman taking another swing with his ax, this time splitting Missy's body in half. There was a scream, a fountain of dark blood spewed up from the bed like an erupting volcano, and then all went black.

8

Minutes or hours later, she didn't know, Reggie's vision began to clear, and she was staring at white now instead of black. White tiles, to be more precise, and they were moving. No, they weren't. *She* was moving. She was on her back and tried to sit up, but something was holding her down. Reason and familiarity began to creep back on the edges of her brain: She was on a gurney, her arms pinned to her sides with restraints. Two Vour orderlies wheeled her down the hospital corridor. She couldn't be sure where she was going. Sometimes after a fearscape they would take her back to her room; sometimes they would take her for more tests — painful ones that involved lots of needles and electrodes and injections. And, on occasion, Dr. Unger would see her, and ask her irritating questions about her fearscape experiences, as if he really were her doctor, really trying to help her get better. What a sick joke.

"Where to today, boys?" Reggie mumbled to the orderlies. They didn't answer, and she didn't expect them to. She had nicknamed them Click and Clack in her own mind because of the sounds their shoes made on the linoleum tiles. Click was white with sandy hair, and Clack was Hispanic with dark hair. That was the extent of her knowledge of them. Like always, they stared straight ahead and paid no attention to her, unless she struggled. Then one of them would inject her with something that knocked her out and left her with an excruciating headache when she woke up again. She had learned a while ago not to struggle. Not that it mattered much; when she came out of a fearscape, she was always terribly weak anyway.

Lately there have been other feelings, though, Reggie thought to herself. Not just the weakness and the lethargy. Sometimes it was like she could feel something foreign coursing through her veins, like some kind of drug. It could be a drug—she could never be sure what the Vours were pumping into her bloodstream—but somehow, Reggie didn't think that was it. It was more like adrenaline, like a naturally released chemical or endorphin. It was the strangest of sensations: Reggie wasn't sure if she had the strength to stand on her own, but at the same time, her body felt very alive, her senses heightened. But the feeling could pass as quickly as it had come, leaving her deflated and exhausted.

The tiles above her head swept by with maddening regularity; the gurney's wheels squeaked beneath her; the shoes went *click-clack, click-clack* on the floor. Reggie's stomach lurched and her pupils dilated.

Scritch scritch scritch.

She heard the wolves pawing at the walls.

Suddenly she was back in the cabin, lying crippled on the floor in a pool of her own blood. She couldn't move her legs; the ax blow had paralyzed her, and now she was a mangled heap of limbs and flesh. She felt something pressing on her stomach, and she looked down to see her intestines slipping out of a gaping hole in her abdomen. The pain was too intense to believe, and her breath came in choking gasps of air mixed with blood. She forced herself to look away.

Missy's corpse lay splayed on the bed, cut in two like two pomegranate halves with their gutty seeds spilling out. Facing her was the Woodsman with his yellow eyes. But now he had a third eye, bloodred, that stared out from the middle of his fore-head. He held up his ax and laughed at her, a deep, mirthless laugh that seemed to bounce around Reggie's skull. The ax came down again, this time on her neck.

She expected to lose consciousness, or to die; at this point, she wanted the blessed blackness to close in, the pain to go away. But instead, she felt the blade hit her, slice through her skin, sever her tendons, and split her vertebrae. For a moment the world spun around her, and when it righted itself again, she wanted to scream, but her vocal cords were no longer connected to her lips, and her tongue fell back down her throat. Her head had rolled across the floor, and she was staring back at her decapitated body.

And then the images around her began to shift. They were in the light-filled cabin—but no, they were in a light-filled office. The Woodsman's features melted off his face, and his whiskers retracted into his skin, revealing the countenance of an old man with burn scars, wearing not a hunter's jacket but a lab coat. The ax shrank until Reggie realized it was actually a pencil. She raised her head as her vision continued to clear. She was lying propped on a couch. Wires were attached to her fingertips, her arm, and her neck, and flowed out to a machine in the corner that recorded her brain waves. Dr. Unger sat behind his desk smiling at her, his thin lips making a twisted V.

"Welcome back, Regina," he said.

Reggie's extremities began to tingle as she regained feeling in her fingers and toes, her arms and legs. It had happened again—another flashback. This was another unwelcome new development from the constant immersion in the fearscapes. She'd begun reliving old fearscape experiences in the real world, the fantasy mixing with reality. It seemed that anything could trigger an episode.

"Good to see you, too, Doc." Reggie tried to sit a little taller, to show a strength that she didn't feel. The clock on the wall said quarter to three. At least eight hours had passed since they'd first tossed her into the fearscape that morning, not that Reggie could have told the difference. It could have been ten hours or ten minutes for all she knew. Time was becoming a less and less quantifiable entity in this hellish existence.

Dr. Unger contemplated her for a few minutes more. Though it was small comfort, Reggie did take some pleasure in his marred visage. When she had first met him, he'd looked like Santa Claus, with a jolly, cherubic demeanor. But now one half of his face was mottled with burn scars, with a particularly nasty one situated in the middle of his forehead. The nerves in one eye had been damaged, leaving his eyelid droopy, and his eyebrows had been singed off and had not grown back. To people like Dad, he had attributed his change of appearance to getting trapped in the Thornwood fire while trying to rescue patients. Really, he had sustained all of these injuries the night of the summer solstice, when he had tried, unsuccessfully, to use Reggie to open the gateway between the Vour world and the real one. Aaron and Eben had rescued her and blown up Dr. Unger's lab in the process, leaving him looking like the monster that he was.

"What just happened there, Regina?" Dr. Unger asked finally. He poised his pencil over a pad of paper, ready to record all pertinent data. But Reggie wasn't going to give him the satisfaction.

"Oh, I think I just fainted. My corset was probably too tight. You know us females — get us too excited and the vapors take us. Whew!" Reggie fanned her face melodramatically. She tried to keep her manner airy, but her breath came in rasps, and it took all her concentration to stay focused on the doctor, not to slip back into some terrible vision.

A shock ripped through her body, and Reggie involuntarily jerked forward, nearly falling off the couch. Panting, she glared up at Dr. Unger. He continued to smile back at her, but his eyes were like ice. He gestured to the brain-wave machine.

"Cute. But you know I have little time for cuteness. Shall we continue?"

Reggie thought the hate would overpower her, but she kept herself in control and nodded grimly at him. The machine didn't just monitor her brain; it shocked her when she lied. Unger was a lot of things, but stupid was not one of them. Their sessions often went like this: Reggie would resist at first, but eventually the pain, and Dr. Unger, would triumph. And Reggie seemed to have less and less will to withstand him these days.

"Excellent," Dr. Unger continued. "So, what just happened there?"

"I have no idea." Another shock. "Look, I don't! I had a flash-back, or a vision, or a living nightmare! What do you want me to say? You're the goddamned doctor!"

"No need to get angry, my dear," said Dr. Unger. "Simply tell me what you saw in this 'living nightmare.' I am thoroughly intrigued."

"I bet you are," Reggie muttered, but she did as he asked, try-ing to keep things as vague as possible. But every few minutes the electricity would jolt through her body and she would begrudgingly share more.

Dr. Unger kept at her for the next several hours, asking her all kinds of questions, some about the fearscape she'd just been in, some about how she was sleeping, what her appetite was like, if she was noticing any other physical changes. Every time Reggie would ask for food or water, he would put her off, telling her she'd receive anything she wanted when they were through. *I want to kill you*, was all Reggie could think when he said this.

At least the constant shocks kept her alert. Reggie could feel the endorphins—or whatever it was—creeping back into her veins. Her mind became sharper, and though she was weary and in pain, the feeling of being *alive,* of having some kind of power or strength she didn't quite understand yet, was getting stronger. Still, she had no trouble feigning exhaustion—physically her body felt like it had been hit by a truck and then steamrolled for good measure.

At last, long after the orange streaks of sunset had disappeared and the office was lit only by a few lamps and weak moonlight,

Dr. Unger put down his pencil. He had used up almost the entire legal pad.

"I think this has been a very constructive session, Regina," he said pleasantly. He poured some water from a pitcher on his desk into a glass and walked over to her. "You've done a lot of talking—you must be very parched."

Reggie took the glass and drank thirstily. When she was finished, Dr. Unger took it from her and refilled it.

"You see? When you cooperate, you're rewarded," he said.

"With basic human needs? You are too generous," Reggie seethed.

"One needs to start somewhere. Perhaps in time you shall eat cake."

Wrath welled in Reggie. Hate boiled up inside her like a churning sea, all of it directed at the monster before her. The irony was that he wasn't even a Vour—no, he was a full-blooded human, though Reggie doubted if he had a heart. He simply worked with the Vours, ran their experiments for them, carried out their work, and he did it all because of a morbid curiosity to see what new discoveries he could make, without regard to the people he hurt or killed in the process. As far as Reggie was concerned, there was no more despicable creature on the planet, including the Vours.

Reggie sipped the water more slowly this time, and as its icy coolness flowed down her esophagus, she felt that strange energy surging throughout her body, tingling, like the feeling the air has before an electrical storm. She breathed slowly in and out, in and out, desperately hoping she wasn't giving anything away.

But Dr. Unger seemed to notice a change.

"Are you all right?" he asked.

Reggie continued sipping her water and nodded at him.

"You should try sending ten thousand volts through your own body sometime. It's exhilarating."

Unger regarded her but still did not seem satisfied. He approached her again and put two fingers against her throat, checking her pulse.

When he touched her, a wave of nausea swept over Reggie, and she reached out instinctively to steady herself, grabbing the doctor's arm. Her hand wrapped around his wrist, and she felt the *ba-bump, ba-bump* of his own pulse as clearly as if he were drumming it on her fingertips. Her vision narrowed, and for a moment she feared that she was starting to have another fearscape flashback. The office around her faded into gray smoke until it was like she was looking down a tunnel, but she couldn't see what was at the end. And then her mind began to stretch like putty, as if it were trying to leave her body and travel down the tunnel. At first she resisted, but it was as though a magnet was pulling her, and the desire to know what was there, on the other side, was so great. Strangely, she was not afraid. She let herself go and felt a *whoosh* as her consciousness rushed outward. When she emerged from the tunnel, she was shocked at what she saw.

Dr. Unger lay screaming and writhing on a slab, not unlike the one he had strapped Reggie to in his underground lab. Wraithlike people swarmed around him—some of them had shaved heads, some were missing limbs, and they all had gray, rotting skin marbled with bruises and burn marks. They looked like walking corpses, but all of them wore twisted expressions of malicious glee.

Reggie chanced a few steps closer, but no one was paying her any attention. It was as if she were invisible. With a start she realized that she recognized one of the women standing by Unger. She was one of the patients the doctor had experimented on — Reggie had seen her imprisoned in one of the cages by the lab. Unger had driven her insane by injecting her with liquefied Vour essence, and she'd nearly beaten herself to death on the bars of her prison right in front of Reggie. But now, it seemed, she was exacting her revenge. She danced around the doctor's body, happily injecting him with IVs filled with thick, black sludge. The vile stuff flowed into Unger and turned his veins black beneath his white skin, and they pulsed menacingly. Reggie saw black ooze flow over the whites of Unger's eyes, and she cringed. Another man stood by his head with a scalpel in hand and was performing a lobotomy without anesthesia. Unger's screams were piercing.

Somehow, this was different from the previous flashbacks she'd had. It wasn't even a flashback — she'd never seen this event before. Moreover, she didn't feel the fear in the same way; it wasn't all around her, encompassing her, blurring the lines between fantasy and reality. Unger was feeling the pain, the fright, not her. It was as if she were just an innocent bystander, a fly on the wall, witnessing his torment. And, stranger still, in the background she could make out the outlines of shapes in Dr. Unger's office — the desk, the lamp, the brain-wave machine — but they were dim, as if behind a black screen.

And then it hit her. *She was in Unger's head*—deep in his psyche, accessing his terror. It wasn't his fearscape, but his subconscious. She was seeing what Vours saw when they read people's minds and retrieved their fears. And this was what Unger was afraid of—that the atrocities he'd committed would somehow come back upon him. Reggie had to admire the symmetry.

But did she have the Vours' other ability to then project those fears into the conscious mind? Could she make Unger see and feel these terrible things happen to him? Again Reggie felt the hatred and anger toward her captor rise within her, and she wanted to try.

Reggie focused on the image before her. Slowly, deliberately, she began to push it with her thoughts back down the tunnel. It moved like molasses, but gradually her own brain felt less stretched, and she knew she was getting close. Before she realized it, she was back in her own body, staring out of her own eyes at the doctor and the office around him. But her thoughts still held the image of his torture like a lasso, and as she glared into his startled eyes, she felt a connection, a pathway of sorts, open between them. With all her effort she pushed the image back at him, straight through his eyes into his visual cortex, where it gripped his neurons. The doctor's pupils dilated, and the color drained from his face. He began to twitch violently.

"No...no, no, no, no," he moaned. "No, it isn't possible...."

"Oh, it's possible, you son of a bitch. And it's happening. Enjoy your little trip." Reggie applied more mental pressure to Unger's terrors, searing them into his waking mind. She felt incredibly powerful, and electricity seemed to surge through her body—not painfully, as when Unger's machine had shocked her, but fluidly, like an alternating current that rejuvenated every cell. It was ecstasy.

Unger dropped to the floor and rolled into a fetal position. He was screaming now, and Reggie suddenly realized that all the noise would bring Click and Clack to the doorway. She had to shut him up.

Reggie glanced around the room for something to gag the doctor with, but when she broke eye contact with him, she lost the connection. It was like slamming a door in one's face—suddenly she was just shut out of his mind. Abruptly his screams stopped, and Reggie's heart dropped. Would he call out for help? But no, Dr. Unger continued to whimper like a baby on the floor, and Reggie remembered what it felt like when a Vour vision was pushed on you—even when it receded, it took a while to recover. Still, she had to hurry.

She winced as she ripped the wires from her skin and scalp and rubbed the permanently raw patches that they left behind. Unfortunately the orderlies had taken away the gurney, so Reggie searched for something else to use to restrain the doctor. His desk drawers yielded nothing but more legal pads and office supplies. She found masking tape, but that would hardly do. She moved to the closet in the corner of the room. Here she was more successful. Folded neatly on the bottom shelf was a straitjacket.

Reggie propped the doctor up against the couch and, with some difficulty, maneuvered his twitching arms into the straitjacket and buckled it up. He struggled slightly, but Reggie didn't think it was against her: He kept his eyes closed and, though he had stopped yelling, continued to murmur incoherently at something she couldn't see. It was taking him longer to recover than she would have anticipated, and she wondered if his age had something to do with this.

Reggie next grabbed scissors from Unger's desk and cut a couple strips of fabric from the window drapes. With one she gagged Unger, quieting his mutterings, and the other she tied around his eyes, blinding him. She stepped back and contemplated him for a moment. The once powerful doctor, now trussed up like a Thanksgiving turkey, cowed and shivering. Reggie felt a grim satisfaction, but she didn't let herself linger on it; she had to get out of there.

She gingerly turned the knob on the office door and opened it a crack. She heard nothing in the corridor outside, so she peeked her head out, swiveling it side to side. The hallway was empty and silent, lit by flickering fluorescent lights in the ceiling. She pulled her head back inside the office and glanced once more at Unger. He still twitched involuntarily, and his head lolled against the couch. Now was her chance to escape.

But as she turned back to the door, her eyes fell on the filing cabinets opposite Unger's desk. She hesitated. There could be valuable information in those files — answers as to what the doctor and the Vours were up to, what they wanted with her, and how they could be stopped. Reggie looked from the door to the cabinet to the clock on the wall: It was just after eleven. There was a shift change at midnight, when the next patrol would make the rounds and check on Unger. She had a little bit of time yet.

Reggie ran to the file cabinets and yanked open one after another. There were hundreds of files, all labeled with different names. Unger's patients and other Vours. Reggie grimaced at the hundreds of innocent people sacrificed over the years to the monsters' evils.

She certainly didn't have time to peruse them all. She would have to grab the files that seemed pertinent and take them with her. One by one she checked for relevant names. She pulled out a file for Quinn Waters and one for Keech Kassner, not that she expected these to help her much. Quinn and Keech had been foot soldiers, not privy to the Vours' bigger plans. Next she took a deep breath and opened the *H–I* drawer. Right up front was a thin folder labeled *Halloway, Henry,* and behind it, a folder three inches thick with her own name scrawled across the tab. With trembling fingers she pulled this out and held it on her lap, just staring at it.

For the first time it struck her that she had somehow developed Vour powers, that the things they'd done to her were changing her. What she was, and what she was becoming—the answers to it all could lie in these pages. She reached to open the packet, but then stopped. Her desire to see what lay in this file was almost overpowering, but her instincts warned her to keep moving. There would be time to study these pages later, if she could make it out of here. Resolved, she added hers and Henry's files to the pile on the floor and went back to her search.

She opened the *B–C* drawer and scanned the names. *Blackman, Bledsoe, Bleeker, Blighton, Blindauer, Bloodworth, Bloom.* There was no *Bloch, Eben.*

She was about to shut the drawer again when she caught sight of a file toward the back that was the size of her own. Curious, she pushed the other folders aside and gasped as she read the name. It was the last thing she had expected.

"No way," she murmured as she pulled out the file. It was marked *Canfield, Macie.*

In some ways, Macie Canfield was the person who had set the events of the last year in motion. It was her journal that Reggie had found and read, which chronicled the existence of Vours and how one had taken her brother, Jeremiah. Reggie had taken it for granted that Macie's tale was fictional and had only realized the truth after her own brother had been possessed. In trying to figure out how to save him, she and Aaron and Eben had gone so far as to track Macie down; they hadn't found her, but they had discovered Jeremiah's mummified corpse in her old house and, more frighteningly, his Vour, which Macie had managed to trap and keep imprisoned for years. The image popped into Reggie's mind as clearly as if she had seen it yesterday. It was hard to forget, the first glimpse of true evil: the monster in its black, smoky form, begging her for release. Well, she'd released it, all right. She'd frozen it and, taking literally Macie's own written advice to "devour her fears," eaten it. This was what had given Reggie the power to enter fearscapes, and it was all because of a crazy old woman's ramblings. All this time, Reggie had just assumed Macie was dead—how could Unger even know about her?

There was a groan behind her, and Reggie jumped, dropping the file. Papers scattered all over the floor. Reggie whirled around to see Dr. Unger sitting up, wagging his blindfolded head back and forth and trying to speak. She had been so absorbed with her thoughts that she had completely forgotten the doctor was still in the room.

Unger struggled in his straitjacket, and his stifled cries grew more insistent. Reggie knew she had to hurry. She bent down and began to gather up all the papers from Macie's file. There were brain scans, sheets of test results and other data, and— Reggie chilled—pages filled with a very familiar, scrawling handwriting. They had frayed edges, as if they'd been torn from a book. Or a journal.

Reggie stuffed all the papers back in the folder, and only then noticed a sheet paperclipped to the inside of the front jacket under a stamp marked *Most Recent Results*. The page was filled with numbers and scientific terms that meant little to Reggie, but what caught her attention was the date: These were results from tests done not even a week ago.

Reggie slammed the folder shut and leaped toward Dr. Unger. She picked up the scissors again and pressed them against his throat. At the touch of the cold steel, the doctor stopped his writhing and quieted. Reggie leaned toward his ear.

"Welcome back, Doc," she whispered. "Now listen up. I am going to loosen this jacket, but you are not going to struggle, no matter what, or I am going to stab you in the throat. Do you understand?"

Dr. Unger nodded, and Reggie unbuckled the back of the straitjacket. She removed one of the doctor's arms from the restraints; for a minute he resisted, but as soon as the scissor points were back against his neck again he relaxed. Reggie drew out his hand; above him, on the couch, lay the ends of the wires connected to the brain-wave machine. Reggie collected them and attached them to Unger's fingers and neck, as had been done so many times to her. The doctor stiffened as he realized what was happening. He began to cry out again.

"Hush," Reggie hissed at him, again raising the scissors to his neck. He hushed. "Very good. I'm guessing you know what you're hooked up to. And you have nothing to fear if you tell the truth. Right?" Unger didn't reply, but Reggie could see sweat forming on his brow and upper lip. "Now, I'm going to remove your gag and ask you some questions. You're going to answer honestly, because if you don't, you know what's going to happen. And if you scream, I'll be forced to remove your larynx. Are we clear?" Another nod from Unger, and Reggie untied the gag.

Dr. Unger coughed as soon as the cloth was removed, but he didn't yell for help.

"You have a Macie Canfield here in this hospital," Reggie said. "I want to know what room she's in."

Unger hesitated for only a fraction of a second, then said, "I don't recognize that name. You must be mistaken."

As soon as the words were out, he convulsed violently as the shock hit him. Reggie shook her head.

"I think you're lying to me, Doctor. Let's try again. Where is Macie Canfield?"

"Why do you care about her?" Unger croaked. Another spasm.

"I'm asking the questions now." Reggie pressed the scissors tighter against his skin.

"You're not a killer, Regina. I don't believe that you'll really hurt me."

"Maybe I don't have to kill you. Maybe I can just make you think you're dying. I can do that now, remember?"

"Yes, yes, you can. It's a miracle. *You're* a miracle!" Unger was panting now with excitement. "You have the powers of a Vour, but you're still human! I never thought such a thing was possible. You have to see the potential in this, Reggie. The things we could accomplish—"

"Shut up!" Reggie cried, then bit her lip and lowered her voice. "You are a worse creature than the monsters you serve," she hissed at him. "Now answer my question, or I'll send you back into hell. Where is Macie Canfield?"

Unger sighed. "All right, all right. She's in room 323."

He jerked as the electricity hit him. He yelped and his hand went to his heart.

"I'd pegged you as a better liar, Doctor," Reggie said. "I'm turning up the voltage now."

"Okay, okay! Wait! She's in the basement. Block four, room eight."

This time he remained still. No shock had been administered; he was telling the truth.

"Thanks for the help. You know, it's been fun, being your guinea pig and everything, but I think I'm going to have to leave the nest." Reggie ripped the wires off of Unger and tied his arm back in the straitjacket. But as she went to retie his gag, all the lights went out. Reggie stumbled backward, surprised, and tripped over the trash can, landing on her back in the middle of the room. Unger began to holler at the top of his lungs.

"GUARD! PATIENT ESCAPING! PATIENT ESCAP-
ING! HELP ME!"

Reggie scrambled up. A bit of moonlight streamed through
the window, and she could see the outline of the file cabinet and
the pile of folders she had made next to it. She felt blindly for
Unger's briefcase, which she knew he always kept next to his
desk. Her fingers touched on the leather case, and she clicked it
open, then hurriedly packed the folders inside and slammed it
shut, Unger's screeching voice behind her all the time.

"GUARD! HELP!"

BAM!

Reggie swung the briefcase at the doctor and clocked him in
the side of the head. He crumpled over, unconscious.

"That felt good," Reggie muttered. She turned, but thought
of something, and reached back toward Unger, feeling in his
pockets. She pulled out his wallet and a set of keys, stowed them
in the front pocket of the briefcase, then glanced once more
around the dark room.

Were the guards responsible for this? she wondered. Did they
know she had turned the tables on Dr. Unger and was planning
to run for it? But no, if that were the case, they just would have
stormed into the room; there was no reason to cut the lights.
That only made their job more difficult. No, something else had
caused the blackout. It was a clear night, with no storms or lightning that Reggie had noticed. A feeling of foreboding crept over
her, and as she stood with the briefcase in one hand, she clasped
the scissors in her other, holding them tightly by the closed
blades.

She quickly rifled through the doctor's desk drawers until she found a penlight, then ran for the door and threw it open—there was no time for caution now. She heard commotion down the darkened hall as hospital security rushed to check all the rooms. Beams from lit flashlights waved about, and scattered shouts echoed along the corridor. The electricity appeared to be out throughout the building.

Reggie stole out of the office and loped the opposite way down the hall, away from the lights. She stayed close to the wall, half feeling her way. Unfortunately she didn't have a sense of where she was—she was usually half out of it whenever Click and Clack wheeled her around, and all the hallways in this place looked the same to her.

She needed to figure out a way to get to the basement. She knew that she was on the fourth, maybe fifth floor because of the view from Dr. Unger's office. That meant there had to be an elevator bank somewhere. The elevators wouldn't be functional with the power out, but there would most likely be a stairwell close by for emergencies. She just had to keep following the corridor and hope it led to an escape.

Reggie's heart leaped as her fingers brushed against a button in the wall, then the closed steel door of an elevator. She clicked on the light, keeping her hand over the majority of it so only a small beam penetrated the blackness. Sure enough, she was standing in front of a bank of elevators with a large number five painted on the wall; beyond was a door marked *Stairs*.

She dared not hope too much, but at least she'd made it this far. She opened the door to the stairwell and stepped quietly inside, listening and looking. She expected any sound to echo off the concrete walls, but it was silent and dark. Reggie took a deep breath and let the door close behind her. Now there was no place to go but down.

She made her way quickly but carefully, keeping the flashlight off and using the stair rail as a guide. Still, she stumbled at the bottom of the first landing, nearly dropping the briefcase, and realized that her legs were weak from months of inaction. After that, she went more slowly, counting the steps and keeping track of what floor she was on.

At the third-floor landing she stopped again to rest. Her body was incredibly weary, and even though the briefcase couldn't have weighed but five or six pounds, her arm was tiring quickly. She switched it to the other hand, rounded the corner, and crashed straight into a solid object.

This time when she fell, she did drop the briefcase. She cried out involuntarily as she landed hard at the top of the flight of stairs, but hers was not the only sound of pain. She had run into a person coming up the stairs in the dark, and now she heard groaning a few feet below her. All her muscles tensed, and she wondered if she should flee back up, but she didn't have the briefcase, and she didn't know where it had fallen. Then she realized the flashlight was still in her hand. She clicked it on and shone it down the stairs.

"AHH!" the figure screeched. He was dressed all in black and wore night goggles, which he ripped off his head in the beam of the flashlight. He stared upward at Reggie, dazed for a moment, and fear blossomed within her. He was thinner, his hair was a different color, and he was sporting a beard, but she recognized him immediately.

Machen. The Tracer who had tried to kill her. This was the cause of the blackout—the Tracers were here now. They had found her and had come to eliminate her once and for all.

Reggie wanted to run, but she saw the briefcase at the bottom of the stairs, beyond the Tracer. And anyway, there was no escaping upward.

Reggie yanked the scissors from her waistband and dove at Machen, brandishing them. This time she knew she couldn't just threaten. This time she had to do the deed. He would keep coming after her until he had completed his mission, and as it was, in her weakened state, she had only moments before he recovered. She had to kill him first.

She raised the scissors but looked away as she brought the points down toward his head.

"Reggie, no!" a familiar voice yelled, and something caught her arm before the scissors found their mark. She struggled but the hand held her wrist firmly, forcing her to drop the weapon. The scissors clattered noisily to the ground, and Reggie felt arms wrapping around her. "Reggie, Reggie, stop, it's me. It's okay, we've come to rescue you."

It took Reggie's brain a moment to comprehend what she was hearing. She raised the flashlight to see Aaron's anxious, but smiling, freckly face.

9

"Oh my God, oh my God," was all Reggie could say. She drew Aaron to her and buried her face in his chest. He was dressed like Machen, all in black, with his goggles propped up on his forehead. His arms encircled her and held her tightly. They were stronger than she had remembered, or perhaps she was just so weak now. "How are you here?"

"Sorry it took us so long." Aaron examined Reggie's face. Even in the dim light he noticed her ashen skin, her sunken eyes, and her gaunt cheeks, but he tried not to show his concern. "They hid you pretty well."

"I knew you'd find me."

Aaron pulled her close again and kissed her forehead.

"We've got to go, kids," said Machen. He had recovered himself and was standing on the landing below them.

"What is *he* doing here?" Reggie demanded.

"He's on our side now," Aaron replied. "Trust me, Reg, we wouldn't be here without him."

Reggie looked doubtfully at Machen, but there was no time to argue. She leaned on Aaron and he guided her down the stairs.

"What's this?" Machen asked, pointing at the briefcase.

"Take it," said Reggie. "I stole some files from Unger's office."

"That's my girl," said Aaron.

Machen picked up the briefcase, and the three of them descended the rest of the way to the ground floor. But when Machen went to open the door leading out of the stairwell, Reggie grabbed his arm.

"Wait, we can't leave yet."

"Why the hell not?"

Reggie turned to Aaron.

"Macie Canfield. She's *here*. In one of the basement cells. We have to go and get her."

Aaron's eyes practically bugged out of his head.

"Crazy Macie is a patient here? She's alive still?"

Reggie nodded.

"They're doing tests on her like they did to me. Aaron, we have to get her out."

"There's no time for that," Machen hissed. "I'm sorry, Reggie, but there are a lot of patients here who are being tortured. We can't save them all."

"Macie isn't just some patient," Reggie retorted. "It's because of her that I have the power that I do. Unger wouldn't keep her here if she wasn't important somehow."

Aaron nodded briefly. "And I'm all for foiling his plans."

Machen glowered, but he shouldered his rifle and turned the corner leading down to the basement, Aaron and Reggie following.

But when Machen pushed open the door leading into the basement corridors, Reggie hesitated. The memories of Unger's dank, loathsome lab and the scent of death that permeated it slithered to the front of her memory. What new horrors awaited them down here? Then she felt Aaron's hand on her back.

"Just focus," he said quietly. "Ignore everything else. We'll get Macie and we'll get out."

She nodded, and Aaron guided her through the doorway.

The air was close and the ceilings low, but it was still a hospital, not like the cavern Unger had used before. Still, Reggie felt little relief: The moans and screams of the hospital's most damaged patients pierced the gloom. They came from behind bolted concrete doors; every now and then, they could hear sickening *bangs* as the patients threw themselves at the walls of their prisons. Reggie forced herself to block out the gruesome sounds and looked for signs pointing the way to their quarry.

They walked by blocks two and three, and Reggie pointed down a hall marked with a number four.

"This way," she said, and they passed room after room until they came to door number eight. Reggie listened, but she didn't hear anything coming from the other side. She took Unger's keys from the briefcase and began trying each in the lock, Aaron holding the flashlight for her to see. Behind her, Machen stood with his gun raised, sweeping back and forth, on the lookout for company.

Finally a key slipped into the lock and turned. Taking a deep breath, Reggie nudged the door open.

At first all seemed quiet in the pitch-black room. But then

Reggie heard a tiny voice coming from an unseen corner. It was scratchy and hollow, and it was singing:

"The dark has teeth and it will bite,
Its feast begins on Sorry Night.
When cold and fear are intertwined,
They'll chew up your heart and feed on your mind.
Where have the souls gone? What do they see?
The gateway to Hell's eternity."

Reggie's flesh crawled, and she felt Aaron tense beside her as well. The smell was terrible, like rotting meat. Reggie covered her nose and mouth with her hand as Aaron shone the light around the room. All the walls, from floor to ceiling, were covered with the nearly illegible handwriting Reggie had come to know so well. She shuddered; the letters were a deep red. They had been written in the only ink Macie had at hand: her own blood.

The flashlight beam came to rest on a gray cot in the corner and an even grayer woman sitting cross-legged on it. She looked like a skeleton, her ashy skin nearly translucent, thin white hair streaking down over her face and shoulders, almost to her waist. Her hospital gown hung off her bony frame like a doll wearing a pillowcase, and she stared at them with glassy eyes. She cocked her head, but just continued to sing her horrid little song.

Trying not to breathe in the foul air, Reggie took a few steps toward the old woman and knelt down in front of her.

"You're Macie, right?" she asked. "We've come to take you out of here."

"The dark has teeth…"

"You're going to be okay, I promise."

"And it will bite…"

Machen strode in and cringed at the smell. He looked with disgust at the corpselike woman rocking back and forth on the cot.

"This is your grand font of information?"

"Like I said, if Unger has kept her alive and is still doing tests on her, then she serves some purpose."

"Then get her up. We need to be out of here now."

Reggie stood and put her arm around Macie's shoulders. The feeling of brittle bone beneath paper-thin skin repulsed her, but she scooted the woman to the edge of the bed and helped her to her feet. Macie didn't struggle, but she made no effort to stand on her own. She fell against Reggie like a rag doll.

But then, out of the blue, her hand shot up and caught Reggie by the chin. With a surprising burst of strength, Macie swiveled Reggie's face toward her own, and the old woman peered into Reggie's eyes without blinking.

"Look who sees," she whispered, then her arm fell limply at her side again, and her head drooped. She started singing again in a low, hollow voice.

"Can you get her?" Aaron asked.

Reggie shifted her arm to better support Macie. Though she weighed next to nothing, in Reggie's weakened state it took all her effort to keep the frail woman upright.

"I think so." She glanced at Aaron and was shocked to see him holding a rifle similar to Machen's. She hadn't noticed it slung across his back before; the sight of Aaron confidently handling such a weapon didn't make sense to her, but she didn't have time to question it.

"Come on," Machen urged, already out in the hallway and heading back for the exit.

Reggie and Aaron breathed deeply when they were back in the relatively fresh air of the hallway. The sounds of the screaming patients were loud in their ears again, but they forged on, Machen a few paces ahead. And then they heard other noises: not the moans of insanity, but the commanding shouts of Vour guards. Streams from multiple flashlights bounced off the corridor walls ahead of them, and Reggie recognized one voice above the others.

"I know they're down here. They're looking for the Canfield woman. Find them!" Dr. Unger's voice had lost all its unctuousness; now it was riddled with fury and, Reggie thought, barely decipherable tremors of fear. She guessed why: If he let his most important patient escape, who knew what terrors the Vours would mine from his psyche and push to the front of his brain. Maybe they would even turn him.

"They're down here all right. I sense their fear," said a deep, accented voice, which Reggie recognized as Clack's. "Come out, Reggie, so we can play some more!"

Machen pulled Aaron and Reggie down another hallway out of the glare of the lights.

"I counted six, maybe seven guards. I doubt they'll shoot to kill—they probably have tranq guns. Still, don't get shot."

"We have tranqs of our own, of a kind," said Aaron. Something in his tone made Reggie glance at his rifle again. He was gripping it tightly. Machen leaned close to him.

"We're going to have to do this bush league. Take them out before they know what's going on. I'll lead and you cover, like we practiced. Are you ready?" Aaron didn't say anything but nodded. In the darkness Reggie couldn't see his face, but she could hear his breath coming quick and heavy. She felt Machen's hand on her shoulder. "Reggie, you stay right behind Aaron. Do not give them a shot. *You are his shadow.* Am I clear?"

Reggie's pulse was racing. She felt like she was in a video game. "I'm his shadow. Got it."

Just then Click leaped around the corner, but Machen's reflexes were faster. When he pulled the trigger, the Vour jumped away, but the dart still hit him in the thigh. He stopped momentarily as if expecting the pain from a bullet, then laughed when he realized what the projectile really was.

"I heard you had a thing about killing Vours, Reggie," he said, yanking the dart from his leg. "But tranquilizers? You think that's going to stop us? There's no way you'll win this war fighting like such a pussy."

Reggie glanced nervously at Machen, but he just waited. Click stepped forward and raised his own weapon, pointing it at the ex-Tracer.

"Not even going to run? Fine. I like a good chase, but if you're ready to give yourselves up already—" He stopped abruptly, and his gun clattered to the floor. "What the—what did you do to me?" he gasped, clutching his leg where the dart had hit him. Then he began howling, an inhuman screech, and Reggie saw that his leg was withering like a dead leaf right before her eyes. The pain quickly spread to his other extremities, and Click wrenched at his arms as if he wanted to pull them out of their sockets. His skin wilted as if the very blood in his veins were evaporating. And then it appeared that whatever poison was doing this to him had reached his heart, and he clenched his chest, his screams dying on his lips. His eyes rolled back in his head, and he fell forward onto the ground, motionless.

"What the hell is in those darts?" Reggie couldn't believe what she had just seen. Machen had rushed to the Vour's side and checked his pulse. He nodded back at Aaron.

"He'll live, painfully for a while," he said, then turned to Reggie. "It's a nitrogen cocktail. Specially designed to freeze their blood. Much more effective than bullets."

"I'll say," said Reggie.

They heard noises coming toward them—Click's cries had alerted the rest of the Vour guards, but Machen was ready for them. As each one turned the corner, a dart flew forth and struck them in the arm, or leg, or chest. Their screeches filled the dark basement as the serum coursed through their systems, turning their blood against them. But then Machen stumbled. He dropped his gun and reached for his neck, straining at something that wasn't there. He began to choke.

"That's better," said Clack, stepping out among the writhing bodies of his comrades, his gun raised. He was staring straight at Machen, and Reggie knew that he was sending him a vision. "You can expect a lot more of that in the days to come."

"I don't think so," said Aaron, jumping out from behind the

corner, Reggie and Macie just behind him. Clack whirled on him and shot; Reggie felt something *whoosh* past her ear and cried out, but Aaron already had his rifle up and aimed. He planted his feet and, with a sharp intake of breath, pulled the trigger. The dart pierced Clack in the shoulder. He brushed it away immediately, but the serum had already found its way into his bloodstream. Moments later he was a shrieking body on the ground, just like the rest of them.

"Are you okay?" Aaron said over his shoulder to Reggie. It took her a moment to respond, since she was still processing having just seen Aaron so calmly shoot someone in the chest. "Reggie?"

"Y-yes. Yes, we're both fine."

She then noticed Machen, who was kneeling on the ground and panting. She started to run over to him, but Aaron stuck out his arm to block her way. "My shadow, remember?" His voice was so authoritative that Reggie dumbly dropped back, and he led the way over to Machen.

"I'm okay, I'm okay," he said, rising. "But you hesitated."

"I got him, didn't I?" Aaron said, somewhat hotly.

"Let's get out of here," said Reggie. Macie clung to her neck, her eyes staring out like a frightened deer's. She had stopped her singing, but now moaned incoherently.

The three of them raced out the front door and into the parking lot. Reggie inhaled deeply—it was the first time she'd breathed fresh air in months. Moments later headlights peeled around the corner, and the Coles' SUV pulled to a stop in front of them. The passenger window rolled down. Quinn Waters leaned over from the driver's seat.

"Thank God. I'd about given up." His eyes lingered on Reggie and her cargo. She stared back, dumbstruck, and barely noticed Aaron taking Macie from her.

"Get in." Machen wrenched open the backseat door and practically threw Reggie inside as Aaron went to the other side of the car and strapped Macie in. Then he climbed in next to Reggie. In the front seat Machen nodded to Quinn and he hit the gas. The truck sped off into the night, leaving the dark form of the Home Institute behind.

Reggie shivered. The car's heater hadn't kicked in yet, and the flimsy hospital pajamas she was wearing weren't much protection against the November chill. Aaron noticed and quickly took off his own jacket, wrapping it around her and pulling her close to him. The weariness finally caught up to her, as well as the unbelievable reality of where she was and what she was leaving. She closed her eyes and leaned against him, her cheek burrowed into his shirt. The faint whiff of energy soda mingled with computer ink rose up into her nostrils and she smiled. It was the most wonderful smell in the world to her, one she had feared she might never experience again: the smell of Aaron.

10

Reggie felt Aaron shaking her awake. She looked out the window, expecting to see her house, her driveway, her street, but they were in a parking lot outside a roadside motel. Machen and Quinn were already leading Macie into a room a little way down the sidewalk.

"Where are we?" she asked.

"Somewhere in rural Connecticut."

"Was the hospital so far from Cutter's Wedge?"

Aaron hesitated.

"We're not going back to Cutter's Wedge tonight. You can't go home, Reggie. Not yet, anyway. It's not safe there for you."

The realization hit Reggie like ice water.

"Because of my father. He doesn't know about this little jailbreak."

Aaron shook his head.

"So what's the plan, then? Shady motels for the rest of my life?"

Aaron pulled Reggie close.

"I'll explain everything. But let's get settled first."

They got out of the car. The lot's weak lights cast dim orange pools on the asphalt. As Aaron fumbled to get the ill-fitting key into the door of their room, Reggie breathed deeply, taking in the chilled night air and exhaling it in a puff of steam. She'd never take fresh air for granted again. The lock popped and Aaron opened the door.

It was typical motel fare: dingy and dusty, two double beds swathed in well-worn comforters, and a carpet that looked like it hadn't been replaced in three decades. But it wasn't Unger's prison, and Reggie could not be more grateful. Aaron brought in two suitcases and wheeled one over to Reggie.

"Henry packed it, so don't blame me if he didn't include the right shoes or something."

At her brother's name, Reggie looked up. "Right, because that's what I'm worried about. How is Henry?"

Aaron sat down next to her on the bed.

"He's fine. Worried sick about you, of course. But he's the reason we found you in the first place."

Aaron told Reggie about his encounter with her father at the library and his subsequent attempt to visit her.

"He came to Home? He was there?"

"When they wouldn't let him in, I thought he was going to tear the place to the ground," Aaron said. "You should have seen him, Reggie. He was so upset—I know what he did was inexcusable, and I won't defend him, but after seeing him on that tape…He loves you. He really thought he was doing the right thing, sending you there."

Reggie was silent. She had taken Aaron's coat off and now

caught sight of her arms, thin and pocked with gray scars. Her trophies from the fearscapes. She knew her body was riddled with them now, and no amount of time would ever erase them. Remembering the last fearscape, she pulled the bottom of her shirt up over the waistband of her pants and looked down. A black mark ran from one side of her emaciated stomach to the other, like a horrible cesarean incision. She heard Aaron's intake of breath.

"Reggie…" He trailed off, not knowing what to say. Sympathy and rage battled inside him. But just then there was a knock on the door, and Machen and Quinn entered, carrying two large pizzas. The aroma of greasy melted cheese filled the room.

"Ahh, I forgot that smell," Reggie said.

"I can't attest to its quality," said Machen. "It was just the closest food joint."

"Where's Macie?" Aaron asked.

"She's fine. I sedated her — she should be out until morning."

Machen put the pizzas on the dresser, and Quinn produced some paper plates and napkins. He handed them around, and his eyes lingered on Reggie when he got to her. She stared back. For a moment they both grasped the plate, and Reggie noticed his missing fingers and the scar on his cheek. He, too, bore the physical souvenirs; what were his emotional ones like? Had he, like Henry, had violent outbursts? She still couldn't quite believe he was here, that he was apparently part of the gang now.

Aaron caught the exchange between the two of them and frowned.

"So it was Macie's house that you guys went to last year, where you found her brother, Jeremiah," Quinn said. "And Jeremiah was the one who Reggie…" He glanced at the pizza wedge halfway to his lips and put it back on the plate.

"It didn't taste like pepperoni," said Reggie. "But yes, I ate solidified Vour essence, and that gave me my powers."

"I can't believe Macie's still alive," Quinn went on. "How old do you think she is?"

Aaron shrugged. "I can probably dig up a birth certificate if necessary."

"I think we should be more concerned about what help, if any, that woman can give us." Machen tore into a piece of pepperoni. "I think she's schizophrenic."

Suddenly Aaron leaped to his feet.

"Sims's letter!" he cried.

"What's that?" Reggie asked.

"We found this letter in Eben's things. It was from a Tracer named Sims—he was the one who sent Macie's journal to Eben in the first place." Aaron began to pace and summarized the contents of Sims's note. "The 'establishment' that he infiltrated—it could have been Thornwood, or another hospital. Sims thought that whatever Macie knew, it was important enough to steal her journal and get it to Eben. She's obviously been a part of this for years; we just didn't know."

"There are more journal pages in her files," Reggie said. "Pages that were torn out of a notebook. I saw them. She must have some kind of information locked away in her head. It's the only reason Unger would keep her alive."

"And if she's been the Vours' captive for so long, it's possible she knows more about them than anyone," Aaron finished.

"Well, we're not getting anything out of her tonight," Machen said.

"What is the plan after tonight?" Reggie asked.

Aaron bit his lip.

"To disappear. You and me. We're going to have to stay on the run for a while, at least until after the solstice. Machen and Quinn will continue to monitor Vour activity and get any leads they can on their schemes. I've emptied out my college fund, so we'll have cash for a while anyway—"

"Whoa, whoa, whoa." Reggie jumped up. Her pizza fell on the bed, untouched. "I can't ask you to do that, Aaron."

"You didn't ask. I decided."

"No. I'm not going to let you leave your family, your friends, your *life*—everything you've worked for." Reggie tried to sound as authoritative as possible.

"Everything I've worked for doesn't mean anything if I don't know you're safe," Aaron replied.

"But...but your parents," Reggie protested. "It will kill them, not knowing what's happened to you!"

There was a thud as Quinn dropped his can of soda on the carpet.

"Sorry." He hurried to the bathroom to get a towel.

"I've written my parents a letter telling them everything. They'll believe it or not, I guess, but I thought I owed them the truth. Machen will deliver it once we're off." Aaron was so calm, Reggie could scarcely believe it. "This isn't necessarily forever, Reggie. I'm hoping we'll be able to come back before too long. Anyway, you're going to have to tie me up or knock me out to keep me from going with you, and I'm a lot stronger than you these days. So suck it up."

The emotion was beginning to well inside Reggie. Exhaustion was taking over, reality closing in. She had escaped Unger's clutches, but she still couldn't go home. Aaron was willing to sacrifice everything for her, while the people whom she should be able to count on—her parents—were nowhere to be seen. Her father…Aaron was right about her father. She hated him sometimes, blamed him for being bullheaded, for not trusting her, but he had stayed. He did what he honestly thought was best, even if that meant confining her to a psych ward. But her mother…

"If only I knew where Mom was," she said, to no one in particular, "I could go stay with her, and you all could go back to your lives."

She had meant it as a rhetorical statement, but the silence that followed was palpable. She caught Aaron and Quinn exchanging a glance.

"What?" she asked.

"Nothing," Aaron said, a bit too quickly. "This is the plan. In the morning, you and I will—"

"I can always tell when you're lying, Aaron. You're awful at it. There's something you're not saying."

"Reggie, it really doesn't matter."

"You thought of that already, didn't you? That Mom could take me in."

"It occurred to me, yes."

"And you tried to track her down." Reggie paced a few steps. "But if you weren't able to do it, then you'd just tell me. Which means—" She whirled on Aaron. "You *did* find her."

No one said anything.

"You did. You know where she is!"

Aaron looked grimly at Reggie.

"Yes."

"Then why didn't you say so? Why can't we go to her? Is she in China or something?"

"No, she's in Brooklyn. But, Reggie, she might not be your mother."

"But—" All the words evaporated on Reggie's lips, and she sank back onto the bed. The three men watched her uneasily, waiting for her reaction. She was as amazed as anyone that it wasn't rage, or shock, or even sadness. No, it was something more like relief. "But she's a Vour. Of course," she said slowly. The facts stacked up in her brain: how Mom had changed before she left, how she was distant and seemed to lose interest in the family. And then she had just abandoned them. It had never made sense to Reggie—those weren't things her mother would do. But they were very much the actions of a Vour. She grabbed Aaron's hands, and now the words spilled out. "How did we never think of this before? It all makes sense now. How did you figure it out?" Her eyes darkened. "Henry wasn't there, was he?"

"Of course not." Aaron nodded at Quinn. "We have another Vour detector now."

Reggie had forgotten Quinn was even there. Now he spoke up.

"I saw her, Reggie. I got the chills thing. That's how we knew."

"So you've seen her? You've actually seen her in person?"

"Quinn did. I was in the car."

"I have to go to her."

"No," Aaron said emphatically. "Absolutely not."

"Not absolutely not. She's my mother, and I can save her."

"This is why I didn't want to tell you," said Aaron. "Do you know how many Vours are out there looking for you right now? I'm guessing they've activated the phone tree. We can't just show up at one of their homes."

"They might even send her looking for you," Machen interjected.

"So much the better," said Reggie.

Aaron squeezed Reggie's hand.

"Look, I know you want to save your mom, but it's not going to do any good if you get yourself recaptured, right? There will be a time and a place to go to her, but now isn't it."

Reggie shook her head.

"My mother is living in a world created from her worst nightmares. I'm not going to leave her in there for one more day. I'm not going to leave her behind." Her lip trembled, and she paused. "Besides, once she's out of the fearscape, the two of us can disappear together, like your original plan. And you don't have to leave your life behind."

"I don't like it," said Machen.

Reggie sighed.

"I'm sorry, you guys. You just risked your lives to get me out of that hellhole, and I'm causing trouble before the night's even over. But you have to understand...she's my mother." She faced Aaron. "There have been so many times when I needed her over the past couple years, when I wanted her help so badly. And all this time she needed *my* help. And I can give it to her."

Aaron picked Reggie's pizza off the bed and put it back on the plate.

"When we find out what these monsters are up to, kick the crap out of them, and send their asses back to whatever hell dimension they came from, you should seriously consider law school. Okay. I'll take you to your mom."

Machen grumbled something under his breath, but Reggie didn't catch it. Louder, he said, "Well, if this is the plan, you guys are going to need some weapons."

11

Reggie tried to sleep, but the adrenaline from the escape, the anticipation of seeing her mother, and even maybe sleeping on a regular mattress for the first time in months kept her awake most of the night. In the morning Machen packed up Aaron's car with Vour weaponry.

"I gave you the subzero blanket—I think that will be the best way to incapacitate her," he told Aaron. "You'll have to charge it up first, so have Reggie keep her busy for a bit."

"What's a subzero blanket?" Reggie asked.

"A current runs through it—when it touches skin, it stimulates the nerve endings to simulate the feeling of cold," Aaron explained. At Reggie's incredulous look, he added, "Tracers may be lethal bastards, but they've got sweet gear."

"Here, take a nitro-gun, too," said Machen, handing Aaron a pistol. Reggie grabbed his arm.

"We're not going to kill her!"

"It doesn't shoot bullets," Machen said. "It has darts like the ones we used at Home—it won't kill a Vour, but it will cause enough pain to make them wish they were dead, and they'll pass out for a short time. Just take it as a precaution."

Reggie nodded, and Aaron stowed the gun and extra darts in the car.

Reggie shared an awkward goodbye with both Machen and Quinn. She barely knew them, really, and yet they'd done so much for her. Now they were going to take Macie back to Cutter's Wedge with them, and Machen promised to try to learn what he could from her.

"Thank you for everything," she said, climbing into Aaron's car.

"I did try to kill you once," Machen said. "I owed you one."

"And I owe you a lot more than one," said Quinn. "Good luck, Reggie. I mean it."

It took them the better part of a day to reach the outskirts of New York City. Aaron drove the entire way, which Reggie was grateful for. In addition to not sleeping well, she hadn't managed to eat much, despite the enticing aroma of the pizza the night before. Her stomach was so shrunken and unused to rich foods that she'd barely kept down the muffin Aaron had gotten her when he'd stopped to get an extra-large coffee for the drive.

When they started out, she caught Aaron casting furtive glances her way every couple minutes. She knew he was terribly worried about her, but she was still just too exhausted to do much besides force the muffin crumbs down her throat one by one.

She had dreamed of escaping Unger's clutches from the moment she'd been thrown in the back of that van, but those dreams had been a lot different from the present reality. Perhaps it was too much to ask that she could return to her family, sleep in her own bed, go back to school—fall back into a normalish kind of life. She had thought she would feel elation, or hope, or any kind of optimism at being out of that terrible hospital, but all she felt was an overwhelming weariness, like her organs just wanted to slow down until they stopped altogether. She supposed it was some sort of catharsis, the giant exhalation after months of worry and fear and meds had kept her adrenaline pumped to a manic level.

For now, she just let the morning sun beat down on her. She caught sight of her face in the visor's mirror and flinched: She'd showered at the motel and changed into clean clothes, but in the daylight her skin looked so pale it was almost translucent, and was certainly not helped by the shadows under her eyes and the framing of her hollowed-out cheeks. Her dark hair, at one time long and lustrous—and the one aspect of her appearance she thought beautiful—was wispy and cropped close to her scalp, like a cancer patient's. They had kept it cut short at Home since it made attaching the electrodes easier, but she had been so malnourished that it probably wouldn't have grown more than a couple inches without breaking off anyway. She was gray, and thin, and sickly, a mere shadow of the girl she had once been.

"Reggie, do you want to talk about what happened to you?" Aaron broke the silence at last. "You can tell me anything—I can help you."

It was the question she'd been dreading. She felt like she owed Aaron an explanation, but the last thing she wanted to do was willingly transport her mind back to that place.

"I—I can't. Not yet."

"I understand." He sounded both worried and dejected. "But

are you sure you're ready to do this? We can take a few days—more than that, if you want. You've been through so much...."

"No, I want to get this over with." Reggie turned to him and managed a smile. "I look worse than I feel."

Aaron was quiet a moment, then said, "Don't start lying to me now."

Reggie was momentarily taken aback.

"Well, let's pretend I look worse than I feel."

"Okay, then."

It wasn't the only thing they were pretending, and they both knew it. They were also pretending this was just some normal road trip a couple of friends were taking, that everything was just as it had been, that there wasn't this new, invisible wall between them.

"Look, I don't feel like talking, but I'd love to listen," Reggie said. "Tell me a story. What important stuff have I missed?"

"Oh, all kinds of things. Your best friend, Nina Snow, won a grueling battle for Homecoming Queen last month. A bunch of basketball players got caught cheating on the SATs, and now there's no way we're going to State. They put a new soda machine in the cafeteria."

"I'd actually like to hear about your new part-time gig as Universal Soldier."

Aaron's cheeks colored.

"Oh, that. Yes, I have some new skills to go along with the computer hacking and the ability to multiply big numbers in my head. And yet, I'm still afraid of water. Go figure."

"But seriously, how did all of that happen?"

"How did Machen and Quinn and I become a little team, do you mean?" Aaron asked wryly.

"Yes, that's what I mean."

Aaron launched into an account of the last several months, starting with the day after Reggie was taken. He told her about Machen quitting the Tracers and enlisting others' help, including his own. He told her about Quinn seeking him out and proving himself to be, as Aaron grudgingly put it, "reasonably useful." Reggie didn't interrupt, but sat back and listened, melting into the car seat, soaking up the heat emanating from the dashboard vent and the overhead sun on her face. After a while, her eyes slipped closed.

When they opened again, Aaron had stopped the car along a tree-lined street, opposite a four-story brick apartment building. It was flanked on either side by similar structures, with a fruit market and a non-Starbucks coffee shop in the nearby storefronts. People who had just gotten home from work were walking their dogs, and young mothers strolled along, pushing high-end strollers. It was a thoroughly quaint little block, straight out of a New York–based romantic comedy. With dismay, Reggie realized she was half-expecting zombies to emerge from the alleyways, or demon babies to start crawling out of those strollers. Would she never be able to enjoy a tranquil scene again?

"So that's it? That's where she lives?"

"Yep. Second floor." Aaron pulled into an alley next to the building and clicked on his flashers as he turned off the engine. They both got out of the car. Aaron removed the duffel from the backseat and slung it over his shoulder. "Remember how we're going to play this? She won't be expecting you, so she probably won't realize right away that you know what she is."

"I know," Reggie said, a bit testily.

"I know you know," Aaron said. "But I just want you to be prepared. It's going to be tough for you to see her after all this time. You have to be the scared, overwhelmed, maybe even angry teenager for a bit—"

"Trust me, it won't be hard to pull that off."

"But you have to stay in control," Aaron continued. "Make her think that you trust her while I charge the blanket. Then I'll be there to—"

"Yeah, I got it. Let's do this."

Reggie strode around the corner of the alley and up the front stoop, Aaron close on her heels. Reggie scanned the names on the buzzer, then let out a mirthless chuckle. Of course there was no Halloway.

"I don't even know what she's calling herself these days," she said.

"It's Stroud," said Aaron. "Rebecca Stroud."

Rebecca. It was her grandmother's name. Reggie didn't know where the Stroud came from. She pressed the appropriate button and waited.

"Maybe she's not home yet?" she said after a few minutes of silence, but then the lilting, singsong voice that she hadn't heard in so many, many months sounded out of the speaker.

"Hello? Who is it?"

Reggie had prepared herself for the moment when her mother opened the door to her, the moment she saw her again for the first time. But she hadn't anticipated this, hearing the disembodied voice that sounded so much like her mother's but had been stolen by the Vour. There was still time to run away, to jump back in the car and take off for anywhere, anywhere but here.

She felt Aaron's fingers encircle hers. "You can do this," he mouthed to her.

"Is someone there?" the speaker asked.

"M-Mom?" Reggie stammered. "It's me. It's Reggie."

There was another long stretch of silence. Then the static of the speaker squeaked on again.

"Reggie? Is that really you?"

Reggie had to hand it to the Vour—the voice sounded teary now.

"It's really me, Mom. Can I come up?"

"Oh my God, of course. Of course! It's the second floor."

A buzzer sounded, and Aaron pushed the door open. He and Reggie walked through the vestibule, past a short line of mailboxes, and up a twisty staircase lined with green carpet. They heard a door slam above them and footsteps descending, and then suddenly Reggie was in her mother's arms, swaying back and forth as the older woman clutched her tightly.

"Oh, Reggie! I can't believe it's really you! Here, let me look at you." Mom pulled away and cupped her daughter's face in her hands.

The emotions flooded through Reggie too quickly to even register—anger, hate, wonder, grief, longing—so she just stood there and tried to stifle the primal scream she felt rising in her throat. Here was her mother; here was the Vour, just like in

Henry's fearscape. The porcelain skin, the lovely dark hair—she was the same, but for the stylish, minimalist clothing that looked much more chic than the mom clothes she used to wear. In fact, she was more beautiful than Reggie had remembered. Turning into a Vour and abandoning her family seemed to suit her.

Tears were wet on Mom's cheeks, but Reggie knew not to trust them. Vours couldn't cry, but they were masters of trickery: A few eyedrops in each eye would produce the same effect.

Mom drew her slender fingers down Reggie's sunken cheeks and over her shoulders, as if trying to warm her. A spark of worry seemed to flit across her face as she examined her daughter's sallow complexion and gaunt features. Reggie knew she looked like a heroin addict, but, in one piece of good fortune, it wasn't like she needed to explain herself to the Vour. She could handle any fake concern it threw her way.

Mom glanced behind Reggie at Aaron, standing a few steps below.

"You remember Aaron, right, Mom?" Reggie asked. "He came with, to make sure I got here okay."

"Of course I remember Aaron," said Mom, beaming down at him. She extended her hand and shook his. "Now," she continued briskly, wiping her eyes and turning back to Reggie, "you look exhausted. Come in, come in."

She clasped Reggie's hand and led her up to a doorway on the second floor, Aaron following behind.

"Let me hang up your coats," said Mom, opening a closet just inside the front door. Reggie and Aaron obediently handed over their jackets, and Mom set them on hangers, but Aaron politely declined to turn over his duffel. Mom then ushered them into a large living room. Reggie stared around her; the apartment was open and light-filled, with white walls and stained hardwood floors. The furnishings were simple but tasteful, with minimal knickknacks disturbing the dust-free surfaces. Framed posters of old movies and mid-century art hung on the walls, but there were no photographs around that Reggie could see.

So this was the life her mother had been leading since she'd left. No, Reggie reminded herself, not her mother, the Vour. It was the life the Vour had chosen. Reggie had to admit it looked better than the messy, cluttered version back in Cutter's Wedge. Once Reggie had actually saved her mother, would she even want to come back when her existence here was so much cleaner, so much simpler, so much more *Vogue*-worthy? She forced such thoughts out of her head.

"Come sit down, you two," Mom said, crossing over to the plush white sofa. Reggie sat down gingerly, as if she was afraid she would stain it. She did not feel comfortable in this home. It was too sterile, like the hospital she'd just escaped from. She tried to calm her racing nerves.

Mom sat in a high-backed wing chair next to the couch, but Aaron remained standing awkwardly in the doorway.

"You guys have stuff to talk about," he said. "I'll just amuse myself in the kitchen or something."

"Oh, of course," said Mom, and she pointed to another doorway leading off from the living room. "In there. Help yourself to whatever you like. Reggie, are you hungry? Do you want anything? Water? Soda?"

A reset button that will give me a new life where my mother isn't a monster from a hell dimension? Is that really too much to ask?

Reggie shook her head.

"I'm fine."

Aaron disappeared, still holding the duffel bag, and Reggie and her mother stared quietly at each other for a few minutes, neither knowing what to say. Finally Mom broke the silence.

"Reggie, you must have so many questions," she began. "I don't know if I can give you answers, but I'll try."

"Well, if you're in a sharing mood, let's start with *why*. Why did you leave? Why didn't you try to contact us? Why did you just disappear?" Reggie didn't mean for the bitterness to seethe out so, but there was no stopping it.

"Oh, Reggie, that's the most difficult answer, and I don't know if you'll understand."

"Try me."

Mom drew a throw pillow onto her lap and began fingering the fringe border. It was a nervous habit Reggie remembered. This Vour was very good.

"Life was getting…tough…for me," Mom stammered.

"Life is tough for everybody," said Reggie. "Life was pretty damn tough for me after you left. But I guess you didn't think about that."

"I left *because* I didn't want things to be hard for you. I honestly thought it would be better—things between your father and me were getting to such a point that I was worried how it would affect you and…and Henry." Her voice broke a little as she said her son's name.

"There's this thing called divorce, where you end a marriage in a legal fashion and can continue to be a part of your children's lives. It's all the rage these days."

"I deserve all of your anger, Reggie. I know I do. But it wasn't just your father. I was feeling, I don't know, trapped, like I was locked underground, suffocating in my life. Being a wife, being a mother, I felt like I was in prison."

This is it, thought Reggie. The wiliness of the Vour beginning to show itself. Preying on Reggie's private fears that she was the reason her mother had left, that her mother didn't love her, that it was all her fault. But she wasn't going to let it wreck her. She kept her gaze steady.

"Go on."

"So I left before I broke, before I did something that I couldn't take back."

Mom knelt down in front of Reggie and took her hand. She stared pleadingly up into her daughter's eyes.

"I want you to be able to forgive me," she said.

Reggie saw movement in the doorway behind her mother.

"Can you? Can you ever forgive me?"

Reggie took Mom's hands in her own, pressing her thumbs against her wrists.

"I love you, Reggie."

"NOW!" Reggie shouted.

Aaron burst through into the room and threw the blanket over Mom's head, wrapping her tightly in it.

"What the—?" Mom yelled, but stopped as the charges began to lick her skin. Then her yells turned to wails. "Ow! Ow, help! Get this off of me! Oh, it hurts!"

"You're not going to torment my family any longer, you

soul-sucking bitch," said Reggie, squeezing the Vour's pulse. Its arms were twitching violently from the pain of the cold shocks. Reggie shut her eyes and waited for the blackness to close in.

But it didn't. The Vour kept seizing, kept shouting and thrashing against Aaron, who tried to keep the blanket touching its skin.

"Help me! I'm being attacked! Reggie, please, make it stop! *Make it stop!*"

Reggie opened her eyes and looked at Aaron, horrified.

"It's not working," she said.

"I gathered," said Aaron through gritted teeth. "The blanket must be malfunctioning, or I didn't charge it long enough—"

The Vour screamed in agony.

"Let her go," Reggie shouted above the shrieks. "She's weak at least. We'll tie her up and figure out something else."

Aaron loosened his grip, and the Vour whipped off the blanket, then lay huddled on the floor, wailing and continuing to twitch periodically. Reggie had expected the shocks to leave black marks, but the Vour's skin was covered in red welts. Tears streamed from its eyes, across its face, into its hair. Real tears.

"Oh, no." Reggie cupped her hand over her mouth. Her brain was like mush—she couldn't be seeing this. This couldn't be true. "No, it's not possible...."

"What? What is it?" Aaron rose and followed Reggie's gaze. He caught her meaning immediately.

"Reggie, I—"

"She's not a Vour. She wasn't taken."

"Reggie, maybe you should sit down." Aaron reached for Reggie's arm but she shook him off.

"I was so stupid. I wanted to believe that she...but she's not..."

"Reggie, please."

"She's human."

12

Reggie continued to stare at her shaking mother, and Aaron continued to stare at Reggie. They remained like that for a long time, until Mom's spasms and her breathing relaxed. Slowly she pushed herself up into a sitting position, using the couch for support. Her eyes were bleary with tears and smudged makeup, and she looked at her daughter with a mixture of horror, fear, and repulsion.

"What did you do to me?" she gasped. "Did you try to electrocute me? Did you come here to kill me?"

Reggie couldn't reply. She gaped at her mother, the comprehension of reality still working its way through her mind.

"Answer me!" her mother screamed, and she burst into a fresh round of tears. Aaron knelt by her side.

"No, we weren't trying to kill you. We thought you were a—" But his explanation was cut short as Mom shoved him away with such ferocity he nearly smacked his head on the coffee table.

"Get away from me!" She scrambled up onto the couch and folded herself into its farthest corner.

Finally Reggie seemed to snap to attention.

"I'm sorry, Mom. We made a mistake. We thought you were something else."

"You thought I was something else? What does that mean, Reggie?"

"It means, we thought you were a monster, or possessed by one anyway…a demon. I'll explain, but—"

Mom stared incredulously at her daughter.

"Are you on drugs, Regina?"

Reggie couldn't help exhaling a laugh.

"You know, sometimes I wish I were."

"It's true, Mrs. Halloway…er, Stroud," Aaron cautioned. "Some pretty crazy stuff has gone down since you left."

"That I can see. Reggie, did your father put you up to this? Has he done something to you?"

Reggie sank back down onto the sofa.

"No, this isn't about Dad. And I'm not crazy, or high, I promise." She turned to Aaron. "But something's wrong—if it's not Mom, who's the Vour?"

"Quinn could have been wrong," Aaron offered.

"Maybe. But I think we should get out of here. I have a bad feeling."

"You're not going anywhere, young lady, until you tell me what the hell is going on."

Reggie wheeled on her mother.

"Don't you dare 'young lady' me. Clearly my emotional maturity level is higher than yours."

"Is that what this is about? You want revenge because I left? You *are* on something, aren't you? I didn't want to say anything when I first saw you, but your appearance…"

"I told you, we thought—"

"Yes, I heard you. You thought I was a demon."

"Possessed by a demon," Aaron corrected. "But, uh, that's really neither here nor there...."

"You're both insane." Mom looked from Reggie to Aaron and back. "I don't know what's going on. I think I should call a doctor. Or the police."

"Mom, I will tell you everything you want to know, but we need to get out of here."

"I'm certainly not leaving this house with you."

"Is everything all right, darling?"

Reggie and Aaron whirled around to see a tall, well-dressed Indian man in the entranceway. He hung his overcoat in the hall closet and strode into the living room. Reggie didn't know how long he had been standing there.

"Oh, Avi, thank God you're here." Mom stood and ran around the side of the couch into the man's arms. He kissed her warmly on the lips, at first ignoring the two teenagers standing there. He wore a trim three-piece gray suit and silk silver tie; next to Reggie's pencil-skirted mother, he was like the other half of a salt- and pepper-shaker set, and the apartment around them was the tastefully set table.

Mom was still visibly shaken, and the man regarded her uneasily.

"You've been crying, Rebecca. And your face is all red. What's the matter?" His voice was velvety and had just a twinge of a British accent. He pulled a handkerchief from his inner jacket pocket and wiped the tears from Mom's cheeks. It was a tender, intimate gesture, Reggie noted, and not one she could ever recall having passed between her two parents. Some of Mom's tension seemed to ebb away at the man's touch. So, Mom had a boyfriend.

He now turned to Reggie and Aaron, looking them up and down suspiciously. Reggie felt a prickle at the back of her skull under his cold gaze.

"Avi, this is my daughter, Reggie," Mom said. "She—she found me."

"Oh, I know who she is." Avi gave Reggie a twisted smile. She and Aaron began to back away.

"What? How can you know that?" Mom asked.

"The resemblance, of course." His answer was easy, but his voice had lost its creaminess, instead now sounding cold and malevolent. He folded his arms close around Mom's waist, keeping her firmly between Reggie and himself. The prickle intensified: Reggie was sure this was a threat, even if her mother didn't realize it.

"Avi, listen, something has happened. My daughter is very sick—I think I need to get her to a hospital."

"Yes, I know the perfect place to take her. It's a bit of a drive, though."

Reggie felt the familiar sensation of fear and adrenaline pulsing within her, and she knew Aaron was feeling it, too. When Quinn had shown up here a few weeks earlier, it hadn't been Mom that he had sensed; there had been someone else in the apartment. Someone who, perhaps, had been keeping tabs on her mother. Someone who *was* possessed by a demon.

"So you've been holding her here this whole time?" Reggie asked.

Avi laughed at her, a thin, weaselly chuckle.

"Hardly. She's stayed of her own volition. I mean, who wouldn't? Great apartment, great city, great boyfriend, great life. Certainly much better than the one she had before."

"What are you talking about, Avi?" Mom asked.

"But why?" Reggie continued. "Why bother? Surely Vours have better things to do than play house with desperate, middle-aged women."

"Reggie!" Mom exclaimed. She tried to disengage herself from Avi's arms, but he kept hold of her. Still, she seemed unaware of the danger she was in.

"You know, we were afraid it was going to be hard to find you again," Avi replied. "It was so considerate of you to deliver yourself right to us."

"Would someone please tell me what's going on?" Mom demanded. "Ow, Avi, you're hurting me."

"Let her go," Reggie said.

"Sure. If you come quietly, I'll let them both go." Avi's eyes flicked toward Aaron.

Aaron tensed, but said nothing. Mom sputtered more questions, but Reggie saw the confusion and fear begin to register in her face as she struggled against Avi's strong embrace. Reggie had no doubt he would kill her mother if it came to it, but for right now he still needed her as leverage.

"When have I ever gone quietly?" she seethed.

Immediately she felt the pull in her mind as the Vour searched for her fears and attempted to push them to the surface. But she was not a victim any longer. She pushed back and closed her mind, locking the Vour out.

Aaron was not so lucky. He crumpled to the ground as the visions swept into his consciousness. Reggie turned her gaze for only a second, but Avi used the distraction. Pushing Mom away, he dove at Reggie and caught her about the waist, but his momentum sent them both careening across the floor. Momentarily stunned, Avi lost his grip on her, and Reggie scrabbled backward to the other side of the couch. Her fingers closed around the subzero blanket as Avi lunged at her a second time, his hands going for her throat. But as he landed on top of her, she whipped the blanket over his head, smothering him with it.

The reaction was immediate, despite the blanket's low charge. Avi jerked violently, and she could hear muffled screams coming from under the blanket, then he went limp.

Reggie stared upward at the ceiling, trying to catch her breath. Avi, whether unconscious or just dazed, was lying on top of her, and his body was heavy. She tried to push him off, but she didn't have the strength. Just then, Aaron's face appeared above hers.

"Kinky," he said.

"Shut up and help me."

Aaron knelt down beside her and rolled the Vour over onto the floor.

"Good work. Are you okay?"

Reggie nodded as she sat up. She saw that Aaron had retrieved his duffel bag from the kitchen.

"You?"

"I've seen a lot worse. I'll deal with him—you should check on your mom."

Reggie had almost forgotten about her mother. She leaped up and saw her slumped in the doorway to the foyer. There was a bloody smear on the doorframe, and blood was flowing down her face from a gash in her forehead.

"Mom!" Reggie ran toward her, and Mom hazily lifted her head. "Mom, are you all right?"

"I think I hit my head," Mom said. She put a hand to her cheek; when she drew it away again, it was stained red. "I'm bleeding."

"Come on, we need to clean that cut." Reggie helped her mother up.

"He pushed me." She sounded dumbfounded. "I can't believe he pushed me like that. He's never done anything like that before. He's not a violent man."

"Sure." Reggie did her best to keep the sarcasm from her voice.

"Did he—did he hurt you?" Mom looked up at Reggie, genuine worry in her eyes.

"I'll be fine. But he tried to, Mom, he tried to hurt me."

Mom shook her head.

"I don't understand...." She caught sight of Avi's legs sticking out from the other side of the sofa, and this seemed to focus her attention. "Oh my God!"

Before Reggie could stop her, she ran around the side of the couch and knelt by Avi. He was lying on his stomach, and his head was still wrapped in the blanket. Aaron was in the process of restraining his hands behind his back, using handcuffs he'd pulled from his duffel bag.

"Is he...dead?" she asked.

"No, just stunned," Aaron replied. As if to prove it, Avi's body twitched suddenly, and a muffled moan came from within the blanket. Mom jumped back.

"Should we call the police?"

"No." Reggie came up beside her. "Aaron, take off the blanket."

"Are you sure?"

"She needs to see."

Slowly Aaron unwrapped the blanket and pulled it off of Avi's head. At first, nothing seemed out of the ordinary, since he was facing the floor, but when Aaron rolled him over onto his back, Mom let out a cry of astonishment.

His skin had been drained of color, except for the black veins that streaked up his throat and across his cheeks, and the inky stain that covered his lips, eyelids, and the area around his nostrils. The once-handsome face now looked ghoulish and inhuman.

"What...what...?" Mom stuttered.

"Your boyfriend isn't who you thought he was." Reggie watched her mother carefully. She could practically see the neon sign in her head flashing *My daughter is nuts*, but she continued anyway. "He's a demon called a Vour. Most of the time he looks human, but that blanket is specially designed to weaken him. That's why he looks like that."

"This isn't real. This can't be happening." Mom's expression was twisted with horror, but she couldn't tear her eyes away from the grotesque sight before her.

Aaron got up and quietly disappeared into the kitchen; moments later he returned with a steak knife and a couple of ice cubes. He rolled Avi back over onto his stomach and took one of his cuffed hands in his own. Slowly and calmly, he sliced through the skin on Avi's palm.

"What are you doing?" Mom yelped. She tried to grab Aaron's arm, but Reggie pulled her back. Red blood seeped from the cut.

"It looks normal, right?" Aaron said, looking at her. "Now watch." He put the ice up against the cut, and immediately the broken skin began to turn black, and dark marks like the ones on Avi's face began to creep across his palm. "They can't handle cold temperatures."

Mom cupped her hands over her mouth and gaped at Avi's blackening hand. Reggie knew what she was feeling—the rational brain trying to reconcile the eyes' impossibility. But right now, she didn't have time for coddling.

"When did you meet him?" she asked.

Her mother turned away from Avi abruptly, startled.

"What?"

"When did you first meet Avi?" Reggie repeated.

"It was over the summer." Mom spoke distractedly, and her eyes kept darting around as if she expected a television host to pop up out of nowhere and tell her she was on a hidden-camera show.

Reggie caught Aaron's eye.

"When over the summer?"

"Um…" Mom paused, thinking. "It was the beginning of July. At a coffee shop. Our orders got mixed up and we started chatting."

Reggie had to stifle a gag.

"Right after the solstice," Aaron muttered. "It was definitely a setup. They grabbed you, and they sent him after her."

"Mom, this is important. Since you've been with Avi, did you ever get any visions? Scary ones? Like nightmares, but you were awake?"

Mom looked at her blankly.

"No, of course not."

"You're sure? Nothing out of the ordinary?"

"I'm positive. I used to have nightmares sometimes, when I was asleep, but that was months ago. Actually, they stopped after…after Avi and I started seeing each other."

Reggie and Aaron swapped another glance. They were thinking the same thing: Avi hadn't tormented her, and Vours always inflicted misery on those close to them. There must have been some specific reason why he'd resisted—some order from on high, perhaps?

Mom started to sway on her feet, and she put a hand out to steady herself. Reggie realized she was still losing a lot of blood from the gash on her forehead.

"Mom, we need to get that cut cleaned up."

"But what about—?"

"I'll keep an eye on him," Aaron said.

Reggie led her mother to the bathroom. Like the rest of the apartment, it was modern and spotless, as if it had just been photographed for a design catalog. Mom sank into a chair at a vanity mirror. She looked shell-shocked. The blood had gotten in her hair and dripped down her cheeks onto her beautiful clothes. There was so much of it, red and sticky and glistening.

Reggie wet a washcloth and began to wipe the blood away. A memory popped unexpectedly into her mind of when she used to sit like this in the bathroom at home, and Mom would cut her hair and they would talk about all sorts of things. Of course, her mother never looked like Carrie after the prom then.

"What is all this?" Mom asked. "What happened to Avi?"

"Like I said before, Avi isn't Avi. He's a monster."

With that, Reggie told her mother all about her travails with the Vours. The woman sat in stunned silence until her daughter had finished.

"This is completely insane," she said finally.

"But true," Reggie said. "The proof is lying right there on your floor."

"But…but there has to be some other explanation…."

"Are you saying that you don't believe me?"

"No…I don't know….You can't exactly blame me for not believing in monsters."

Reggie fetched some antiseptic from the medicine cabinet and rubbed it on the gash.

"Because he wasn't a monster," Mom continued. "He was…he was perfect. Everything I'd ever wanted. Funny, charming, attentive." Reggie noticed that she didn't explicitly say "Handsome, rich, and cultured," but Reggie could read between the lines. "He'd bring me flowers for no reason. He'd take me to the symphony and galleries, and he introduced me to so many interesting people. He was exactly the person I had been looking for."

Exactly the person who wasn't Dad, thought Reggie. *Exactly the person who didn't have kids to feed and clothe and listen to.*

"Right. Who'd want to deal with all that tedious parenting crap when you had gallery openings to go to?" she snapped.

"Reggie, I…I don't know how to say this, to tell you, after all that's happened…"

In all the chaos of the day, adrenaline had pushed away the hurt, and confusion, and anger from Reggie's mind. But now it was boiling back into her.

"If you're going to tell me that you're in love, I might vomit."

"But we are, honey." Mom rose and slowly approached her. "I can't explain what that is lying on the floor in there, but it's not my Avi. It's hard for you to hear, I know, after everything, but he makes me happier than I've ever been in my life. We've even talked about moving in together, getting married…."

"Yeah, it's a regular Hallmark card, Mom. Except for the part where your one true love isn't human. You saw what happened to his body—to his skin. Did that look like a human reaction to cold?"

Mom had no answer to this, and returned meekly to her chair. Reggie was slightly gratified to see the seeds of doubt blooming in her eyes.

"You can deny it, Mom. You can ignore it, or pretend like it doesn't exist, like you've done with everything else that you don't like. Or you can act like a goddamned adult for once in your life and accept that these horrors are real, that you got conned, that everything in your life is a lie."

Mom looked up at her daughter.

"Excuse me if it's hard to accept that my boyfriend is a…a *demon*."

"At least he has an excuse."

Mother and daughter glared at each other.

"I see," Mom said at last. "You thought I left because I was one of them."

"Yeah. Well, who knew the truth could be worse," said Reggie. She didn't want the tears to come, she didn't want this woman to see her cry, but they came anyway, traitorous droplets with minds of their own. "You just walked away and didn't look back. *You* did that. Did you think, did you think at all, what would happen to us?"

"Reggie, I—"

"Did you think that Henry might turn into a basket case, afraid of the dark, afraid of everything? Did it occur to you that you were condemning me to the life of a teenage mother? I turned fifteen and got a household to take care of as a birthday present. Oh, and then, as a bonus, my little brother got possessed and I got sucked into a living horror film. So tell me, Mom, please, what were these terrible issues that caused you to abandon your family? Because I'm dying to know."

"Reggie, I'm sorry."

"Your apology is shit, Mom."

"You certainly have the right to think that." Though the bleeding from Mom's wound had slowed, it hadn't stopped entirely. Now she took another, clean washcloth and pressed it to her forehead. "You're so much better than I am, Reggie. I was a bad influence in that house. I was so messed up, and I didn't want it to infect you and Henry. No mother wants to see her daughter looking at her the way you're looking at me now."

"Now's your chance to make up for it."

"What do you mean?"

"You can come back with me. Come back to Cutter's Wedge. Talk to Dad. See Henry—God, if you only knew how much good that would do." Reggie's voice had gone from angry to pleading. She felt like a six-year-old asking for a puppy.

"It's not that simple, Reggie...."

"Why not? Why can't it be that simple?"

Mom's eyes swept over to the bathroom door. Aaron had appeared. He looked apologetic.

"I'm sorry, but his breathing's evening out. I think he's going to come around soon."

Reggie sighed. The debate about Mom's returning would have to wait.

"What are you going to do?" Mom asked.

"We have to find out what Avi knows."

"You think he's just going to tell you?"

"Yes," Aaron said simply.

He headed back to the living room, and Reggie and Mom followed. He had managed to get the Vour onto the couch and had bound him to it using duct tape. He had removed his shirt and cut off his pant legs so that Avi's arms, legs, and chest were exposed. He looked to be in extremely good shape—other than his blackened face—and Reggie wondered if extracting information from him would be as easy as Aaron seemed to think.

Her gaze fell on the coffee table, on which Aaron had placed a series of small, Band-Aid-like adhesive patches that had wires protruding from them. Reggie assumed these were more of Machen's "sweet gear." She wondered what they did.

Like Aaron had said, Avi's breathing had slowed considerably, though it was still shallow. A few minutes later he groaned, and his eyelids fluttered open. Black ooze seemed to float across the whites of his eyeballs. Mom winced and turned away.

Avi blinked a couple of times, discombobulated. But when he saw Reggie, he began to struggle violently. He looked down and realized he was half-naked and taped to the couch.

"What is this? What have you done to me?"

"Surprised?" said Aaron. "Didn't think a couple of kids could take on a big, bad Vour like you?"

Avi glared at him for just a moment, then relaxed. The mellow fluidity returned to his voice as he spoke, but his eyes darted about, taking in the details of the scene, belying his calm demeanor. He saw the wired strips on the table close to this head.

"On the contrary. I heard you both were crafty. But I thought these kinds of extracurriculars went against your high moral standards."

"We're not going to kill you." Aaron spoke very matter-of-factly. He picked up one of the patches.

"What is that?" Mom asked tremulously. "What will it do to him?"

"It's called a nerve pad." Aaron held the patch up with one finger in front of Avi's face. "The electrified gel simulates the feeling of cold, like that blanket did. It fools your nerves into thinking that you're being exposed to freezing temperatures, but only at the point of contact, as if you were holding an ice cube against your skin. To humans the nerve pads are merely uncomfortable. But to Vours..."

Avi was breathing more heavily now. He looked like a cornered animal, searching for escape.

"What do you want from me?" he asked.

"Just tell us what you know."

"Can you be more specific?"

"Why were you with my mother?" Reggie demanded.

"Because of the scintillating conversation." Avi's voice dripped with sarcasm. "Oh, and she wasn't a half-bad lay."

Reggie heard her mother sniffle. Aaron leaned over the Vour and planted the nerve pad on his shoulder. The reaction was immediate. Avi cried out in pain and his arm convulsed, but after a minute he forced himself to regain his composure.

"You Tracers have some good gadgets," he said through gritted teeth.

"I'm not a Tracer," Aaron said, preparing another pad. "Answer Reggie's question."

"I'd rather face you than them, thanks very much. I think you've seen what they do at that institute."

"Have it your way." Aaron placed the pad on Avi's other shoulder, and again he moaned in pain but was able to control it.

"I can...do this...all day."

"So can I."

A sob racked Mom, and the Vour heard his opportunity. He turned feverish eyes upon her.

"Rebecca, help me! Make them stop, make them stop!"

"Her name isn't Rebecca," Reggie said coldly, but Avi kept his gaze fixed on Mom's tear-streaked face.

"Rebecca, I love you. From the moment we met, I've loved you. We can be together, forever, away from all this."

Reggie grabbed her mother's hand.

"They're all lies, Mom. Everything. He can't feel love."

"Don't listen to her, Rebecca. I've given you everything you wanted. We can live any life you desire!"

Mom shook her head, backing away. She pulled her hand from Reggie's grasp.

"I—I can't deal with this!"

She ran from the room. Aaron glanced questioningly at Reggie.

"It's okay. Let her go." She turned back to Avi. "She believes me. She's not going to help you. Help yourself and tell us what you know."

In response, Avi spat at Reggie.

"Have it your way," said Aaron, and he continued placing the nerve pads on Avi's skin, one by one—on his chest, his wrists, his thighs, his stomach. The Vour howled and writhed but still refused to speak. Reggie was surprised to see how calmly and methodically Aaron conducted the torture. Despite her abject hatred of the Vours, it was hard for her to listen to the agonized screams. She had to keep telling herself that this was the monster, and the human body would be fine.

As the Vour's yells grew louder, Aaron paused.

"We should amp up some music or something to cover his screams. We don't want the neighbors to hear."

"Right." Reggie looked around the living room. She saw

speakers but no tuner, and figured the apartment was wired for sound; she just needed to find the receiver. "I'll be right back."

She headed through the kitchen to the bedroom, where her mother had gone.

"Mom? Where's your stereo?" Reggie called as she walked through the open door, but she was surprised to see that the room was empty. "Mom?"

She wasn't in the bathroom, either. Reggie even looked in the closets, but there was no sign of her mother. Feeling apprehensive, she crossed back through the kitchen, and only then noticed a piece of paper taped to the back door. Her trepidation grew when she saw that it was a letter in her mother's handwriting, and it was addressed to her. She stripped it off the door, already knowing what it would say.

Dear Reggie,

You were right about everything—about Avi, about me, about my life. I know that you want me to come back with you, but I just can't. My world is entirely changed now, and I need time to process what you've shown me. I'm weak. I know I am. I know you probably won't believe this, but I do love you, with all my heart. I'm so sorry that I can't be the mother that you need. You'll be better off without me in your life. Take care of yourself—you can do that much better than I ever could.

I'm sorry.

Mom

Reggie read the letter again and again. It said nothing and it said everything. The words she used were excuses and clichés, but it showed exactly who she was. She was a coward, she was selfish, she was content to run away when things got rough. *She* was, not a Vour.

And she could run away, because she didn't claim responsibility, and she didn't care. And Reggie was left to pick up the pieces once again.

Rage suddenly tore through Reggie. She ripped the letter into pieces and stormed back into the living room. She stalked past a surprised Aaron and grabbed the steak knife that was sitting on the table.

"Bad news?" Avi grunted.

Reggie brandished the knife in his face.

"You're going to tell us what you know."

"Oh, am I?"

"Reggie, what—?" Aaron began, but Reggie pushed him aside. In a quick motion she swiped the blade across Avi's chest, slicing open a six-inch cut. Blood spurted up.

"Now we'll see how tough you are." She picked up a nerve pad from the table and stuck it over the gash like a Band-Aid. Avi howled in agony, his shrieks more inhuman than any he'd uttered yet. Black streaks spread out from the wound, covering his chest like inky veins. Reggie leaned in close to Avi's face. His temples were lined with sweat, and his lips were turning black. "I don't even care what you wanted with my mother. I want to know what the Vours want with me. Why I was a lab rat for five months. Tell me!"

"Okay…okay…" Avi panted between yowls. "Take that thing off!"

Reggie removed the patch, and Avi's screams quieted.

"Tell me," she repeated.

Gradually Avi's breathing slowed and his writhing stopped. He spat again, and his saliva was stained with dark spots.

"Your mother…was just a pawn," Avi panted. "Insurance for a rainy day. It's always been about you."

"What's so special about me?"

Avi choked out a laugh.

"What *isn't* special about you? You travel between the worlds, seemingly at will. How?"

"I ate one of you guys."

"Do you know what happens to most people when they're fed Vour? They die a horrible, painful death. But you not only survived, you also gained a unique ability."

"And the tests were supposed to show why that was?"

"In part."

"What's the other part?"

Avi hesitated, and Reggie started to reapply the nerve pad.

"No! Don't!!" Avi thrashed his body, but the tape held him firmly. "Unger thought it had to do with your body chemistry. Distinct DNA markers."

Aaron tapped his foot sporadically on the floor. Reggie recognized the sign that his brain was whirring through some problem. She was glad—this was starting to go beyond her level of understanding.

"Why send her into all those fearscapes, though?" he asked.

"Unger fancied himself a modern-day Doctor Frankenstein," said Avi. "For years he's been obsessed with creating a new species, one that retains both human and Vour qualities."

"And the fearscapes?" Aaron said darkly.

"The greatest irony of all." Avi chuckled, then coughed in pain. "When she beats a fearscape, the Vour isn't destroyed. It becomes *part* of her. Every time she wins, she gets a little more Vour in her."

Reggie stared in horror at the Vour as his expression alternated between agony and humor.

"*I'm* the new species?"

"That you are, my dear."

"Liar!" Reggie swung the knife down toward Avi's throat.

"Reggie, stop!" Aaron grabbed her arm, and the knife fell from her hand.

"Why should I stop? Aren't you the one who's the expert on killing now? What's the point? He's evil!"

"He is, but you're not. You don't kill, remember?"

"Then what do we do?"

Reggie trembled in fury. Aaron let go of her arm but spoke softly and firmly, as though he were trying to calm a wild colt.

"Well, you're not going into his fearscape, obviously, just in case there's some truth to what he says. I'm not saying that there is," he added, catching Reggie's horrified look. "We'll take him to Machen. He'll know what to do."

Reggie nodded and stared icily at the Vour.

"You're going to die very soon."

"Let's get him up," said Aaron.

He began to rip off the duct tape binding Avi's body to the sofa. Avi yelped as the adhesive tore away from his skin, leaving rough red patches. Reggie picked up the knife again and held it to his throat.

"Don't try anything," she said, but the warning was unnecessary. Avi's hands were still cuffed behind him, and he was too weak from the nerve pads to do more than squirm.

"It doesn't matter what you do to me," Avi snarled. "We've been here since the beginning of the world. You can't beat us. You can only last until we beat you. The fear always wins."

"Shut up." Aaron propped Avi's arm around his shoulder and stood him up.

And then, several things happened at once. There was a *bang* and the crinkling sound of broken glass, and Avi's face contorted in shock and pain. He let out a gasp and looked down at his chest, where a dribble of red was leaking out of his left pectoral. Reggie stared at it a moment as well, not, at first, comprehending what had happened. There was another burst of glass, and Avi fell backward onto the couch, his eyes opened wide, and between them, a small red hole.

"Get down!" Aaron yelled, and he pulled Reggie to the floor and flattened himself over her. She heard a series of *pop*s, and the window exploded inward under a shower of bullets. "The back door! Stay low!"

Reggie nodded and began to belly crawl toward the kitchen. Aaron swiveled around and linked his arm through the strap of his duffel bag, which still lay on the floor by the coffee table, then followed Reggie, dragging it along behind him. Bullets careened into the furniture and the far wall; Aaron and Reggie were in greater danger of being hit by a ricochet than a direct shot.

A crash came from the street below as the Vours broke through the building's entryway. Moments later they were thudding up the stairs and banging on the door to the apartment. Reggie heard splintering wood as they tried to wrench it from its hinges.

They had reached the kitchen when the door broke. Reggie threw open the back door as Aaron pulled the gun Machen had given him from the bag.

"What about your mom?" he called.

"She's gone already. Come on!"

Vours dressed all in black, like SWAT members, poured into the kitchen, but jumped back as Aaron fired blindly at them, giving Reggie and himself just enough time to plunge down the fire escape. He smiled smugly as he heard one of them shriek and hit the ground.

Luck was finally on their side: This was the alley Aaron had parked in, and his car was just yards away, the flashers still blinking. Reggie was about to get in the passenger side when she felt a tight grip on her arm.

"Let me go!" she yelled, spinning around. She came face to face with Mitch Kassner.

She hadn't seen him since the night at the high school when she'd gone into his brother Keech's fearscape. He was the last person she expected to see now.

"What—what are you doing here?" she asked dumbly.

Mitch was leaner than she remembered, but more muscular.

His hair was buzzed into a crew cut. He looked like a marine. His face was unhappy but resolute.

"I'm sorry, Reggie, I've got to take you in," he said.

"I think not." Aaron cracked the butt of his gun against the back of Mitch's head. Mitch grunted in pain and dropped to his knees, releasing Reggie. She swung the car door open, slamming him in the face with it and knocking him backward. Seconds later both she and Aaron were in the car; Aaron gunned the engine, and they sped out of the alley, only narrowly missing Mitch as he threw himself after the car.

13

"Aaron, that was *Mitch Kassner*."

"I saw."

"What does it mean?"

"I'm not sure." Aaron kept his eyes on the road as he wove in and out of traffic.

"He said he needed to 'take me in.' You don't think he's a Vour now, do you?"

"No. Sorry Night is still the only time Vours can inhabit people."

"Mitch *hated* the Vours," said Reggie. "I refuse to believe he's in league with them now. It makes no sense."

"It makes sense if he's a Tracer," said Aaron.

"*What?*"

"I don't think those were Vours at your mom's apartment. I think they might have been Tracers."

"But, how would they know—?" Reggie broke off.

"I don't know. We've got to get back to Machen. This has taken on a whole new complicated level of bad."

"At least they'll probably take care of the body," Reggie

muttered. She rubbed her arms, trying to get warm. Her and Aaron's coats were still hanging in the closet in Mom's apartment.

"Reggie, do you want to talk about your mom?"

"There's not much to say. She left. Again."

"She probably just wanted to get out of the house for a bit. We *were* torturing her boyfriend."

"She left me a note," Reggie said. "'I'm weak,' 'I'm sorry,' 'You're better off without me,' blah blah blah. She wasn't coming back."

"I'm sorry, Reg."

Reggie shrugged. She would have preferred that the conversation end there, but a few minutes later Aaron spoke up again.

"About the other thing…what Avi said…"

"About me being some new species?"

"He could have been lying. You are not a different person than you were." His words were carefully chosen, but even as he said them, Reggie could hear the doubt in his tone.

"But I am a different person," she said. "That's exactly what I am. Day after day seeing people's worst fears, a series of endless nights—of course I'm different now."

"No, I didn't mean—" Aaron protested. "Not that it didn't affect you…I didn't mean it that way…."

"I know you didn't." Reggie sighed. "But I don't just mean that I'm emotionally different or whatever psych euphemism you want to use for 'screwed in the head,' though I'm sure that's valid, too. I discovered something the other day." Reggie told Aaron about her encounter with Dr. Unger in his office and how she had managed to see and push his fears to the forefront of his mind.

At this new news, Aaron turned toward her so abruptly that he nearly steered the car off the road.

"Christ, Reggie! Are you telling me you have a Vour power now?"

"Bully for me, right? So I don't think Avi was that far off base."

Aaron exhaled deeply and tapped his fingers on the steering wheel.

"We'll figure it out. I promise. This doesn't prove anything. You had a special power before—now this is just a new one."

Reggie just looked out the window. She was surprised that she wasn't more upset—perhaps she was just too exhausted at the moment, or maybe she was in some kind of shock, or maybe it was just too much to wrap her head around. This last one seemed the most likely. They both fell back into silence, which lasted most of the trip. Reggie offered to drive, to give Aaron a chance to rest, but he refused, claiming he was too wired to sleep. They drove through the night and arrived at Machen's doorstep at a little after four in the morning.

Machen opened the door to them with a look of shock and ushered them inside. Reggie noticed that he had a gun tucked in his waistband; she wondered if it contained tranq darts or bullets.

"What's happened?" he asked. "Are you both all right?"

"It turns out my mother's boyfriend was actually the Vour," Reggie said.

"He must have been inside when Quinn was at the door," added Aaron. "The chills thing isn't a foolproof detector."

"The Vours sent one of their own to date your mother? For what purpose?"

"I think as an insurance policy," Aaron said. He relayed what Avi had told them.

Reggie felt restless, and while Aaron was talking, she rose and walked around the room, examining various of Machen's possessions. The apartment was small and sparsely furnished, but neat. The map that he and Aaron had been using to mark Vour activity hung on the wall, and papers were spread out across a desk in the corner.

"Is it okay if I get some water?" she called over.

Machen only nodded and waved her toward the kitchen, keeping his attention focused on Aaron. Reggie wandered back and found a clean glass in a cupboard above the sink. As she was filling it from the tap, she saw another door off to the side and slightly ajar.

She went to it and nudged it open a few more inches. Inside, Macie lay stretched out on what Reggie presumed was Machen's bed. Her chest rose and fell in even breaths, and her eyes were closed. Machen must have kept her sedated; in that moment Reggie envied her—she actually looked peaceful. Looking at her this way, the possibility that she could be of any use to them seemed remote, even absurd.

As she was about to return to the living room, she noticed that Aaron's and Machen's voices had dropped low. She paused behind the door and strained to hear them.

"I'm worried about her," Aaron was saying. "I've never seen her that way. What she did to him to get him to talk—she never would have done that before. And then, I had to stop her from killing him...."

"I'm sure that she wouldn't really have done it."

"I don't know. There was something…deliberately cruel about her. Machen, what if there really is something inside her, something that's changing her?"

There was a pause, then the sound of shuffling papers.

"Is this what I think it is?" Aaron asked.

Reggie couldn't bear it any longer.

"Is what what you think it is?" She strode into the room. Machen and Aaron had moved to the desk and were looking at the papers that she had already seen strewn across it. Before they could remove them, she swiped them up and perused them. They appeared to be copies of lab results. "What am I looking at?"

Machen and Aaron eyed each other, but at Reggie's expectant and impatient look, the former nodded and took the papers from her.

"So this Avi claimed that the Vours think your DNA has something to do with your ability. I found something in Unger's files that suggests the same thing."

"What?"

Machen spread the papers back on the desk.

"These are test results from a blood workup they did on you. Specifically DNA. It looks like they analyzed samples of your blood and DNA on a weekly basis and recorded the…" Machen hesitated. "The changes."

"So it's true. I am some kind of new half-breed freak."

"Let's not jump to any conclusions. From what I can tell, certain chromosomes in your genetic code are, well, they're turning on."

"Turning on?"

"Becoming active. But it doesn't necessarily mean anything bad—all the chromosomes that make you who you are are still functioning normally. Now you just have some...extras."

"Like a souped-up car. Great."

The resignation she'd felt earlier seemed to be morphing into something else. Perhaps despair? When it had just been the word of a Vour, it had been possible to believe that it was all a lie, and there was some less horrific explanation for her newfound powers and the cruelty streak Aaron had pointed out. But now scientific proof was staring her in the face. She was physically altered.

"Like I said, there are any number of explanations for this, and you turning into some kind of Vour-human hybrid is far down the list," Machen said. "I'm going to get into it, but I don't want you to worry until there's something concrete to worry about. In the meantime, let's get back to Avi. Where is he now? Did you defeat his fearscape?"

"Well, a sniper shot him in the head, so, no."

"What?"

"That's the other thing," Aaron said. "We were attacked. At first I assumed they were a Vour hit squad, but now I think they were Tracers. I think they'd found Mrs. Halloway already, too, and had been staking out the place just in case Reggie came calling someday."

"Why do you think they weren't Vours?" Machen asked.

"They were trained like soldiers...and Mitch Kassner was with them."

Machen whistled.

"So they recruited Mitch, did they?"

"They've completely brainwashed him," said Reggie. "He was going to turn me over to them."

"Of course he was, if he's really a Tracer," Machen said. "You know this part. This is where they get the new guys—people whose lives have been damaged by Vours. His certainly qualifies. And with his size and determination and tendency to obey an alpha figure, not to mention a certain comfort with violence and an ax to grind, he's an excellent new hire for them."

Reggie shivered.

"They were so brazen—they just stormed in, guns blazing. Completely unconcerned about any innocent bystanders."

"That's how they operate. Quick, dirty, brutal. They don't fear repercussions because, like the Vours, actually, they have members in high places. FBI, CIA, even Congress—they'd never face prosecution."

"Were you like that?" Reggie asked.

Machen's eyes widened in surprise.

"Yes, I suppose I was."

"And you just...changed?"

Machen contemplated Reggie for a moment, then crossed the room to a cabinet near the entrance to the kitchen. From it he withdrew a small bottle of bourbon and a glass, and poured himself a slug. He returned to the sofa and sat down. Reggie and Aaron followed suit, both watching him carefully.

"My story is different from yours, Reggie. It wasn't that someone close to me became a Vour." He took a long sip of his drink. "I was a reporter in my former life. I found out that Vours existed and was trying to figure out a way to expose them, and to discredit me, they murdered my family and framed me for it. I spent two years in prison before the Tracers came to me. When they did, I was in a rage. I didn't care what happened to me, I just wanted revenge, and they gave me the window to do it. They got me out of jail, erased my identity, trained me, and in exchange I joined their ranks. I first tracked down the Vours that had killed my family, and I made them pay. And the bloodlust... it fueled me for years. Until I first met you. Until I saw what you could do."

"Why?"

"Killing Vours contains the problem—it's not a solution for it. We don't know how yet, but I truly believe that your ability will lead us to that solution, to the complete destruction of the Vour world. How could I sabotage something like that? I always thought that my role was a necessary and righteous one, but the truth is, killing Vours is cowardly. It's easy. My anger was all about me; it wasn't about helping others, and it wasn't going to bring my family back. And I saw you, a fifteen-year-old girl, making the choice to stand and fight, to sacrifice yourself. I did change, Reggie. What happened to me changed me for the worse and turned me into a monster as bad as the Vours. When I met you, I wanted to change back."

"I wish the rest of the Tracers felt that way."

"So do I. And it concerns me that they actually saw you," Machen went on. "They know you've escaped Vour custody and are out in the open. They'll be hunting you—all of us, possibly."

"What can we do?" Aaron asked.

Machen put his hands on his knees and stood.

"First, we need to find a place to hide Reggie. I think it'd be a mistake for you two to go on the run now. I want you someplace close so I can keep an eye on you. Aaron's is out—that's the first place they'll look."

"I…I have an idea," Aaron said, though he spoke so slowly it was like the words wanted to stay in his mouth.

"What is it?" Reggie asked.

"It's remote, and spacious, and the last place someone will expect you."

"Sounds great. What is it?"

Aaron could not have looked less enthused.

"Quinn's house."

14

The Waterses' place was on the other side of Cutter's Lake, a sprawling old farmhouse set on several acres of land. Mr. and Mrs. Waters had apparently made their money in New York real estate some years earlier and, upon moving to Cutter's Wedge, had become one of the wealthiest families in town. Reggie had never been to Quinn's house, but she'd certainly heard the stories; the parties Quinn's older brothers, and then Quinn himself, had thrown over the years were legendary. Neither Reggie nor Aaron, of course, had ever attended one, but Aaron had been over a couple of times since teaming up with Quinn.

"Are you sure it will be okay if I stay here?" Reggie asked as Aaron took the drive past the lake. "His parents won't have a problem with a known psych case shacking up with their son?"

Aaron seemed to choke a little at the words *shacking up*.

"I think we won't exactly tell them."

"Their house is so big they won't notice another person living in it?"

"You'll see."

Aaron turned the car onto a gravel driveway that wound

through rolling fields. After about a mile, they came upon the house, a charming old home with a wraparound porch, painted gray with lavender shutters and surrounded by flower beds. Reggie guessed the gardens were lovely in the spring and summer, but now they were browned and emptied. Still, the scene was like a Winslow Homer landscape. But Aaron didn't stop the car; instead, he followed the driveway back around the house to a similarly painted barn situated on the opposite side of a swimming pool. Aaron parked behind the barn so that the car was out of view of the main house.

"They converted the barn into a guesthouse, but it's mostly where Quinn lives," Aaron explained.

"He has his own *house?*" Reggie asked, incredulous.

"It's nice to be a Waters," said Aaron, somewhat ruefully.

The dashboard clock flipped to 6:00 AM, and the sky was growing lighter. Aaron and Reggie got out of the car and walked to a side door. Aaron knocked, waited a bit, then knocked again, louder this time.

"Quinn! Quinn, it's Aaron! Open up!"

After another several minutes, the knob clicked and Quinn opened the door, clad only in plaid flannel boxers. His hair was tousled, and his eyes were still half-closed with sleep.

"Aaron, what are you doing here?" he mumbled, then noticed Reggie standing a few feet behind. "Reggie! What—"

"Can we come in?" Aaron didn't wait for an answer but pushed past Quinn. The surprise of seeing Reggie woke him up more fully, and he suddenly seemed aware of his half-nakedness as he stood aside to let Reggie pass. She herself was quite aware of it.

Turning back into a human had done nothing to lessen Quinn's fairly amazing physique. He still looked leaner than he had a year ago, but this only seemed to emphasize his muscular arms and chest. Even so, his skin was very pale, and Reggie thought she saw a few faint black etches crisscrossing his pectorals—scars that remained from injuries he'd received as a Vour.

Don't stare, she screamed at herself. *For God's sake, stop staring at him, you perv.*

Seeing him like this, Reggie couldn't help but think of the day they'd gotten trapped in the culvert, back when he was still a Vour. Back when he was evil, playing her. The things he'd said to her that day—she hated to admit it, but they'd stuck with her. Even then, though it had all turned out to be a con, she had felt some spark between them, and it both thrilled and repulsed her. He had told her that he was the only one who really knew what she was going through, what she was dealing with, and that hadn't been a lie. And now here he was before her, the same but different. Once her enemy, now her teammate. She didn't quite know how to feel about it.

Quinn shut the door, and the three of them stood awkwardly for a moment. Reggie tore her eyes from Quinn's chest and glanced around the room: It was a neat little house that preserved much of the feeling of the original barn, including the vaulted ceilings and loft rooms at either end. They were currently in the main space of the barn, which had been converted into a living/rec room complete with a large flat-screen television and multiple video game consoles.

"Uh, come on in," Quinn said quickly, gesturing to a couch.

"Just give me a sec." He crossed to a ladder leading up to one of the lofts and disappeared up it. Reggie and Aaron sat down, and Quinn reemerged shortly, wrapped in a robe.

Aaron cut to the chase.

"Things didn't go quite as planned with Reggie's mom," he said, and jumped into an account of the past twenty-four hours.

"God, Reggie, I'm so sorry," Quinn said when Aaron was finished. "Of course you can stay here."

Reggie flushed.

"I know it's a terrible thing to ask. I really don't want to drag you back into all of this, but we…well, we just don't have any other place to turn."

"Reggie, are you kidding? You're not dragging me anywhere—I'm already up to my neck in this. It's like I told Aaron: I want to help."

"No one can know she's here," said Aaron. His tone was cool and businesslike. Reggie knew that he was not pleased with the arrangement, even though he'd been the one to think of it. "Not your parents, not anyone."

"My parents never come in here. I go up to the main house for meals and everything, so they have no reason to. And that loft there is another bedroom." Quinn pointed to the other side of the room. "So if someone does happen to pop in, you can just stay up there and they won't see you." He paused. "We will have to share a bathroom, though."

"I think I can manage," Reggie said.

"So we know you'll be safe here," said Quinn. "What's the rest of the plan?"

"Figure out what the Vours are plotting, stop it, save the world," said Reggie.

"So no biggie, then."

They were all quiet, but the silence was soon broken by an alarm sounding from Quinn's room.

"Crap, I've got to start getting ready for school," Quinn said.

"Yeah, I guess since I'm not going to be on the lam anymore, I should head home, too." Aaron stood reluctantly. "Quinn, it's important that you and I keep up the appearance of leading normal lives. We can't miss school or be seen talking to each other. The only way this will work is if it seems like you have no connection to me, or Reggie, or the Vours. Hang out with your usual friends, do your usual thing. It's too bad you quit all sports, really...."

Quinn stared quizzically at Aaron.

"Maybe I wouldn't have if you'd been straight with me from the beginning and I knew it was going to be an issue."

Tension suddenly seemed to descend upon the room. Aaron hadn't told Reggie much about how Quinn had come to be part of the group, and now she realized there was more to it than she knew. She could guess, though.

"I've got to shower," Quinn said at last. Giving Aaron one last, cool look, he went into another room at the far end of the barn and closed the door. They heard running water a few minutes later.

Aaron and Reggie walked to the door. Aaron hesitated on the threshold, obviously reluctant to leave.

"Are you sure you're going to be okay?" he asked.

"This was your idea, remember?" Reggie smiled at him.

"I know, but I don't have to like it," Aaron grumbled.

Reggie hugged him tightly.

"Of course I'll be all right."

"Just be careful. No going outside, no matter how stir-crazy you get. No one can see you here."

"Believe me, I'm not going to stick my neck out."

"I'll check in tonight."

"I'll be fine, Aaron, I promise."

Reggie watched Aaron pull away from the barn, then crossed over to the far loft. She climbed the ladder and surveyed her new room: It looked comfy, with a double bed, nightstand, dresser and dressing table, and a plush armchair in one corner. A skylight in the ceiling let in the morning light, which shone brightly off the whitewashed walls and hardwood floor. After the nightmare of the Home Institute, she could not imagine a more perfect place to make her new home, even if it was temporary.

"Reggie?" Quinn called from downstairs.

"Up here. Hang on, I'm coming down."

She swung herself down the ladder and met Quinn in the middle of the main room. He was dressed in dark jeans and a button-up, his hair shaggy and wet. He smelled wonderful.

"So, what do you think?" he asked.

"It's perfect," she said. "Seriously, Quinn, thanks so much for this. I really owe you one."

"I swear, it's no trouble. I'm just glad you're okay." He reached out and put a hand on her arm. Reggie flinched automatically, and he pulled away uneasily.

"Sorry," she said quickly. "I guess I'm still a little jumpy." What she didn't say was that the last time he had touched her like that, he had been a Vour.

"No, I'm sorry. I shouldn't have — I should probably get going. Mom expects me for breakfast about now."

"Yeah, of course, go. I'll be fine."

"I put out some extra towels. And there's a small kitchen on the other side of that wall." Quinn gestured to a doorway beneath his loft bedroom. "It's stocked with some basic food, bread and peanut butter, chips, snack stuff. I'll try to smuggle some better things over after school."

"I'm sure whatever's there is just fine. A peanut butter sandwich sounds like heaven after the gruel they fed me at Home."

She saw the pity fly across Quinn's face.

"I can't believe what you had to go through," he said.

"It's not like your life's been some kind of picnic." Reggie forced a smile. "But we heal, right?"

"Right."

Neither of them sounded particularly convinced.

———

Reggie stood in the middle of the room for several minutes after Quinn had left. She closed her eyes and wrapped her arms around herself, embracing the silence. She was alone. For the first time in months, truly alone. At Home, even when she wasn't being pricked and prodded, when she was left by herself in her cell, someone was always watching. She had lived in a constant state of trepidation and anxiety, wondering what new nightmare she'd be thrust into, what new pain would be inflicted on her, how she could possibly survive this. There, silence was the calm before the storm, filled with anticipation of the horrors to come.

But now, here—well, she wasn't safe exactly, what with both demons and assassins after her—but it was the closest she'd felt to it in a long time. Here, the quiet was just that—quiet.

And yet, the peace couldn't last long. There was still the mystery of what the Vours wanted. There was still the question of what she was.

She opened her eyes and shivered. The barn was cool. Clouds were rolling in overhead, and the air had the tinge of snow in it. It suddenly occurred to Reggie that what she wanted most right now was a hot, relaxing bath. Maybe for just a little bit she could wash the present away.

Reggie went to the bathroom and turned on the tub faucet full blast. In minutes the small room was filled with steam. Reggie undressed and was careful not to look at herself in the mirror; she didn't want a reminder of how altered and scarred her body was, a physical embodiment of how she might be changed on the inside, too.

She found some body wash under the sink—presumably for when guests stayed here, for she didn't think "lily of the valley" was Quinn's scent of choice—and poured a few drops into the water. As the soap bubbled up, she lowered herself into the tub and breathed in the aroma of flowers. The water was scalding, but to Reggie it felt wonderful. It was like melting a chill that had been growing inside her for months.

She lay back, the suds hugging her, the pounding of the running water in her ears. She was so sleepy, and her eyes dropped shut as she exhaled all the air from her lungs.

If only she could forget everything, even for just a little while. It was almost laughable that she had once been a normal teenage girl whose biggest drama was making a fool of herself in front of heartthrob Quinn. Worry meant wondering if she was going to pass her geometry final, not if demonic fear monsters were going to take over the world. What a difference a year made.

Now that blessed feeling of aloneness was transforming into a darker loneliness. Yes, Machen had pledged to help her, and Quinn had sheltered her, and Aaron, of course, would do anything for her, but there was nowhere she belonged anymore. One by one, her family had been stripped from her. She was a threat to her brother, her father didn't trust her, and her mother…

Mom. Reggie had been willfully pushing the encounter with Mom from her mind, but now her hurt and anger propelled themselves to the surface, mingling with the sweat and steam that coated her skin. Mom had left. Reggie had thought she had come to terms with that long ago, but now it was apparent she had just been waiting for an excuse to justify her mother's actions. She had been so ready to accept that her mother was a Vour. It made everything fit; it tied everything up with a little bow and erased all of the doubt and regret and pain that Reggie had tried to ignore for so long. But now there was a crack in those defenses; Mom wasn't a Vour. Her choices had been her own. She had gone off to find a new life because she couldn't take the one she'd had.

Reggie had no time for self-doubt or self-pity, but it took only one crack to bring down a dam. All of the questions that had plagued her when Mom first disappeared came flooding back. Had it really been so terrible? Were she and Henry really so difficult to care for? Why didn't Mom love them enough to stay? There were no satisfactory answers.

There were no answers to any of it. What did Unger want with her? How did she figure into the plan? Was her own blood turning against her?

Her skin began to prickle in the sweltering heat, and her head swam. Sorry Night was in a few weeks, but she wanted it all over with now.

Suddenly the water went frigidly cold as a hand slapped down on her forehead, and Reggie felt herself plunge down into the bath. The hand held her firmly, and she felt another wrap around her throat, keeping her underwater. She thrashed about but could get no purchase on the slippery porcelain tub. She had little breath in her lungs and in her panic felt herself exhaling even more. Her hands found the ones that held her, and she yanked fruitlessly at them as she kicked her legs to and fro, arching her back and trying to wriggle out of the viselike grasp.

She knew she had only a few seconds before her aching lungs forced her to inhale, but at this point time seemed to slow. Instead of her life flashing before her eyes, she thought how humiliating it was that her body would be found drowned and naked, that Quinn, and maybe Aaron, would see her this way. Either a Vour or a Tracer had located her. She wondered which it was, and if she'd even be able to tell the difference.

She opened her eyes. They burned in the soapy water, but she was able to see up through the surface to the face above hers so bent on taking her life.

In her shock, Reggie almost gulped down a mouthful of water.

It was her own — her own face; her own hair, long again now, and dark and lustrous and hanging so its tips swirled in the water; her own dark eyes staring blankly down, neither filled with malice nor with glee, but with a kind of empty determination. Black scars traced down her pale skin from the corner of her eyes like permanently etched tear tracks, but she was not crying.

Reggie wanted to scream with her last breath, but her other self's fingers tightened on her throat, choking out the sound. They were so strong, those hands, and now they pressed harder, forcing her down farther so the back of her head smacked against the bottom of the tub. With one last effort, Reggie reached up and pushed at her double's face, grasping for her neck, her nose, poking at her eyes, anything that would put her off. She tore at her double's lips and felt the skin break; instead of blood, black, wet smoke gushed out of the wound and clouded the air.

Through the smoke, Reggie glimpsed her other self's teeth through her parted lips. They were blindingly white and filed down into spikes like sharp fangs. Then Reggie felt a searing pain as those teeth chomped down on her index finger. They sliced through her skin and bone as though they were no more than gelatin; Reggie instinctively yanked her hand back, and it came away without her finger attached. The double spat it out, and it landed in the tub by Reggie's head and sank to the bottom, blood flowing out of it and turning the bathwater red. The pain was too intense, and Reggie screamed.

As she felt the water flow into her mouth, the pressure on her disappeared. Reggie shot up and gasped for breath, simultaneously spewing water from her mouth and trying to draw air into her lungs. Half the water in the tub had sloshed out onto the floor, but it was hot again, and there was no sign of blood, or smoke, or the other Reggie. She looked at her hand: Her finger was intact.

She leaped out of the bathtub, spilling more water over its sides, and scooted across the floor to the corner of the bathroom. She sat huddled there for several more minutes, coughing up water until her throat ached, staring with horror at the tub.

Reggie had no idea what had just taken place. Had she fallen asleep and dreamed it all, accidentally slipped under the water? There were no such things as accidents or innocuous dreams in her world anymore. Had it been a more nefarious vision sent by a Vour? Some instinct told her that it wasn't that, either. She'd become used to the nuances of those, which felt like pressure on the mind as the Vour propelled fear to the front of the brain. This had been something different.

Despite the steam hanging in the air, Reggie was cold again. She reached for the towel folded on the sink and wrapped it around herself. If what she'd just experienced wasn't a Vour-induced vision, and it wasn't a simple dream, what could it be?

She'd splashed so much water out of the tub that it sat an inch deep on the floor. There were more towels hanging from a rod by the door, and Reggie took these and began sopping it up, crawling on hands and knees. The towels were soaked through in no time, but she at least was able to clean up most of the mess. When she got near the tub, she hesitated, then swooped her hand in to unplug the drain and skittered back across the floor again as quickly as she could. But no other specter attacked her, and the only sound was the *glug glug* as the remaining bathwater swirled away.

On shaking legs she rose and wiped the steam off the mirror.

Her reflection was crisscrossed with black lines, and her eyes were hollow sockets that leaked inky smoke.

Reggie shrieked and thrust her arms out in front of her face. Her hand punched the mirror and it shattered. She dropped to the floor again and was soon racked with sobs.

"What is happening to me?" she wailed, over and over, but there was no one to answer her.

She lay huddled in the fetal position, letting the tears flow. This wasn't the work of an outside Vour — this was coming from within. Her own mind was turning against her, making her see the thing she feared. Suddenly it was becoming clear: Earlier, when she had wanted it all to end, that was the moment her figment had tried to kill her. She had done it to herself — the Vour in her trying to kill the human.

The thought popped in her brain like a corn kernel: Perhaps that wasn't so terrible. She was going insane, turning into some kind of freak of nature, a creature never meant to exist, and she posed no end of danger to everyone she loved, and maybe even to humanity itself. Even her own mother had turned away from her. Perhaps death was the answer to all of her questions. The final test: She, who could never take a life, would have to take her own. For her own sake, and yes, for the greater good.

Reggie opened her eyes and sat up. Her hand really was bleeding now, and red streamed from cuts in her knuckles that were laced with shards of mirror. Larger fragments lay sprinkled across the sink. She rose, calmly this time, her sobs having mostly abated, and carefully chose the largest and most jagged of the pieces.

Just do it, she thought. *End it now, before any more damage can be done.*

She closed her eyes.

Just one more bit of pain, and all the pain will stop. Forever.

She put the shard to her throat and pressed it against her skin.

Where do the souls go? What do they see? The gateway to Hell's eternity…

For some reason the last bars of Macie's new song jumped into her mind. What had Macie called her that night? The girl who sees? Well, she did, and Macie had somehow known that she'd already seen so many gateways to hell. One slice and the memories of them would vanish.

Macie had known.

Reggie's eyes shot open once more. Macie, who had started her down this path. Macie, who had figured out how to imprison a Vour, a feat that had shocked even the world-weary Eben. Macie had knowledge, had made discoveries, that no one else had—was that why Unger had captured and tortured her, to unlock the secrets she possessed? What if those secrets were a threat to the Vours now, and held the key to their ultimate undoing?

Macie, who had lived for who knew how long in Unger's clutches but had not killed herself. Against all odds, had not given up. Surviving was fighting. By writing that journal, she had unwittingly made Reggie her successor in the fight. Who could take up that mantle if Reggie now checked herself out?

Suddenly Reggie had the strongest sensation that Macie still had knowledge to share. What it was and how to get it she didn't know, but if there was the possibility, she had to try. Surviving was fighting.

She exhaled. She was soaking, and shivering, and bleeding, and tired, and starved, and maybe even part monster, but something inexplicable had found root in her dark and hardened heart. It was tiny, no more than a speck, but it was enough to make her drop her hand away from her neck and sweep the sharp edges of mirror into the wastebasket. It was hope.

15

When both boys strode through the door that evening, it was clear they'd been arguing. Aaron was scowling and Quinn just looked supremely annoyed.

"I really thought we had covered the whole 'we're not friends and we don't socialize' thing," Aaron was saying. "I didn't realize I had to write you a manual about how to pull it off."

"Don't be such a bitch, Aaron. I gave us the perfect excuse to be seen together, so you don't have to sneak around."

"What's going on?" Reggie asked.

"Brainiac over here got Ms. Crenshaw to pair us together for a project."

"And it was a brilliant idea," said Quinn. "Now you can come over here in the open, and I can talk to you at school, and I'll just say that it's because we're working on this lab."

"You were hardly subtle about it," Aaron countered. "Yelling out in the middle of class that you wanted to partner with me. I saw your friends give you a weird look. *Any* behavior that's out of the ordinary could call attention to us—I thought I'd been crystal clear about that."

"Oh, give me a break, Cole. Everyone knows you're a genius—what, aren't you in like three AP classes and you're only a sophomore?—and I need all the help I can get to pass. Obviously I'd want you as a partner."

"It actually doesn't sound like such a bad idea, Aaron," Reggie offered in her best peacemaker voice. Aaron turned his glower on her.

"That's great, take his side. I'm only trying to keep you safe."

"I'm not taking anyone's side. But it doesn't sound as dire as you're making it out to be."

"*Thank you,*" said Quinn. "Besides, it's done, so we might as well make the most of it. And now you don't have to sneak over here on your bike in the twenty-degree weather, which was your original genius plan."

"Fine," Aaron said, though Reggie knew he was still pissed off. "How was your day?" he asked her.

"Slept a lot." Reggie had decided not to share her rock-bottom episode with either Aaron or Quinn, though Aaron looked askance at her when she tried to explain away the broken mirror by saying she'd stupidly tossed her hairbrush on the sink and had overthrown it, shattering the glass. She tried to keep her cut hand in her pocket as much as possible.

"Are you sure you're okay?" he asked her warily.

"It could be better timing for seven years of bad luck," she replied. "Other than that, I'm fine. But listen, I want to talk to Macie again. She responded to me in Home. Maybe if I talk to her again, under better circumstances, I can get something useful out of her."

"Okay," Aaron said slowly. "But you know that having you two meet is dangerous. She and Machen can't very well show up here."

"I'll go to them, then," Reggie said.

"If I think it's safe," Aaron replied.

Reggie was surprised by the finality of Aaron's tone. She again wondered at the change he had undergone in just a matter of months. Ever since they'd discovered that Vours were real, he had been the sidekick, the tech geek, the loyal follower—indispensable, of course, but a support player. Though she hadn't wanted to admit it to herself, that was how she'd always seen him. Even the Vour Quinn had recognized that, and he'd played upon her arrogance to fool her into thinking that he was actually her best ally. But now she and Quinn were damaged goods, and Aaron was the one standing there, coolly and calmly calling the shots. He was physically different, too. His clothes didn't droop off him the way they used to—now she could see the outline of muscle along his arms and chest. He no longer stooped, and when he moved, the discombobulated awkwardness he'd always possessed had been replaced with a certain grace. While she had been wasting away at Home, Aaron had turned into a leader.

"Righto, Captain. When you think it's safe."

That turned out to be two days later, when Quinn told his mother he'd run an errand for her in Wennemack after school. Because Aaron was concerned about tails, Quinn was to drop Reggie off at a market a few blocks from Machen's apartment, and Reggie was to take a series of alleys to get to his back door. Reggie felt a bit ridiculous, especially when Aaron presented her with a wig to wear, but she didn't protest, except to sarcastically ask if there was a secret knock she needed to learn, too. Aaron's dour look had curbed her humor.

The walk to Machen's was chilly but otherwise uneventful. The old Tracer ushered her in, and she found Macie sleeping on his couch, snoring just slightly.

"Have you gotten anything from her?" Reggie asked. He shook his head.

"Babbling. Mostly I try to keep her calm."

Euphemism for "keeping her in a drug-induced haze," Reggie thought.

Machen went to her side and nudged her shoulder. Macie's eyes shot open.

"It's okay. Macie, it's me. It's Arthur," Machen said soothingly. He glanced at Reggie. "She can get a little edgy. I'll get her some juice. You make friends."

Machen disappeared into the kitchen while Reggie approached the sofa and sat down. The old woman blinked rapidly at her but said nothing. Reggie felt very foolish all of a sudden: She didn't even know what questions she should ask.

While she was considering, Macie leaned toward her so that their faces were only inches apart.

"There's blood in the pudding," Macie said confidentially.

"Oh...really?"

"Blood pudding is guts, you know," Macie went on. Her voice was raspy, like nails on sandpaper. "That's what they do to you. They pull out your guts and feed them to the pigeons."

"Who pulls out your guts, Macie?"

Macie glanced back and forth, as if checking to see if anyone was listening.

"The shadow hands," she whispered hoarsely. "They pull them out and twine them up like ribbon. Gut ribbons to tie up their presents."

Reggie sighed. This was going exactly nowhere.

"They have to give their presents to the girl who sees," Macie went on. Reggie's head shot up.

"Yes, what about the girl who sees? Who is she?"

Macie let out a cackle so loud Reggie was surprised it could come from such a frail person.

"Don't you know who you are, girl?" she asked, laughing hard enough to bring tears to her eyes. It was very off-putting.

"So I'm the girl who sees? And someone's going to give me a present? Do you know what it is?"

"Don't you see? Your present is *not* to see."

"My present is not to see," Reggie repeated. "That follows, sure. So what can't I see?"

Macie stopped laughing abruptly and tilted her head upward.

"Tut-tut, such a gift not to see what the others do," she said to the air behind Reggie's right shoulder.

"The others? The Vours, you mean?"

Macie cocked her head at Reggie again and began to chant in a low voice:

> *The dark has teeth and it will bite,*
> *Its feast begins on Sorry Night.*

When cold and fear are intertwined,
They'll chew up your heart and feed on your mind.
Where have the souls gone? What do they see?
The gateway to Hell's eternity."

They were the same lyrics she had sung over and over again when they had rescued her from Home.

Machen returned with a glass of orange juice and handed it to Macie. She took it eagerly and drank.

"I read your journal," Reggie continued. "I found your brother under your house. You tried to save Jeremiah, didn't you?"

At the mention of her brother's name, Macie hurled the glass away and began to scratch violently at her arms, emitting little shrieks of pain. The glass shattered against the wall, leaving a swath of orange liquid dripping down it.

Machen leaped at Macie and tried to pin her arms to her sides.

"Whoa, calm down, calm down."

"No, Macie, don't, I'm sorry." Reggie grabbed the old woman's hands as well, in an effort to stop her from clawing at herself. As she did so, she saw long, thin scars reaching all the way up Macie's arms. More remnants of Unger's torture.

Macie would not calm down. She continued to thrash about, shaking her head back and forth and singing the song at the top of her lungs. Machen vanished for a second and reappeared with a syringe, which he injected into Macie's forearm. Reggie watched ruefully as the serum entered her system, and soon Macie dropped back onto the sofa with closed eyes.

"Sorry that didn't go better." Machen clipped a cap on the syringe and pocketed it. "Anything useful?"

Reggie shrugged.

"Nothing that I understood. But I did get the feeling that she wanted to help me, that she was trying to tell me something important. I just have no idea what it is."

Machen got a towel and began to clean up the spilled orange juice and broken glass, and Reggie moved to a chair on the other side of the coffee table.

"She said I'm the 'girl who sees.' But then she told me that some shadow hands are going to give me a present, and that present is *not* to see."

"So, to see or not to see," said Machen.

"Shakespeare humor from the fake English teacher. Hilarious." Reggie paused. "Has she been singing that song this whole time?"

"On and off."

Machen grabbed a notebook from the desk and handed it to Reggie. The lyrics were scrawled across it. They scanned it for a few minutes, then Machen said, "Well, this mentions 'seeing,' too. The lost souls see a gateway into hell."

"Maybe she means a fearscape?" said Reggie. "They can see their own personal hells?"

"But you can also see those," said Machen thoughtfully. "According to Macie, there's something that you *can't* see. And she thinks of that as a gift—a good thing that you can't see it. Which must mean that it's pretty terrible."

"That's assuming she's not just spouting crazy."

"Assuming that, is there anything you can't see?" Machen asked.

Reggie considered this.

"There is one thing," she said slowly. "Whenever I helped someone beat their fearscape, it would kind of melt away and leave us in an empty space. There was always some kind of visible exit that we used to get out, but a few people have seen something else. A kind of cloud or spiral in the distance." She sat up in her chair. "Quinn saw it. I'd forgotten until now."

"But you've never seen this... this cloud?"

Reggie shook her head.

"Never. But I never thought much about it, either. The victims who noticed it weren't afraid of it, just curious, but not curious enough to investigate. It would only appear after a fearscape had been destroyed, and that was about the time we ran like hell."

"So we can probably assume that only the person who just beat their fearscape can see the cloud," Machen concluded.

"But like I said, it never seemed to be something horrible," Reggie pointed out. "I don't know why it would be a 'gift' that I can't see it."

"If it's in a fearscape, it's probably horrible, Reggie. But as you said, maybe she's just nuts. I'm afraid we'll have to try again another time."

16

The next several days were routine, as the calendar ticked down toward Sorry Night. Quinn would leave in the mornings for school and return in the evenings, sometimes with Aaron, often bearing leftovers from dinner and other food he pilfered from the main kitchen. Mrs. Waters, the mother of four boys, thought nothing of this.

Reggie's desire to talk to Macie again was foiled, however. The old woman's body had gone through such abuse at the hands of the Vours that she was in danger of total organ shutdown. After a week she had lost consciousness, and Machen had been forced to call in a favor with a discreet physician friend and hospitalize her. They hid her under a false name in an intensive care unit in a hospice, where Machen visited her every few days, posing as her grandson. But so far she had remained in the coma, and it was too dangerous for Reggie to try to visit, not that it would have done any good.

In Macie's absence, Reggie turned to the ripped-out journal pages she had found in Macie's file. They were disjointed and sometimes even seemed to be told from different points of view, as if Macie had had various personalities surface and take hold of the pen. It wasn't a far-fetched possibility.

I have to swim forward. I have to keep swimming, but the water turns to blood, and it's filled with parts. Human parts. Legs and arms and hands and feet and ears and noses and fingers and toes. I have to push through them, but they start grabbing at me. And they pull me under, and my arms are so tired, and my legs can't kick anymore. Their flesh is so rotted it falls off the bone, and then the bones stab me, tearing off my own skin so I'm a skeleton swimming through....

And everywhere I look there is black, except for the eyes, the red and yellow eyes that are always staring at me, even when I close my own eyes. They burn me, they burn into my heart! I can feel the fire burning me from the inside out, until I am just charred and black...a roasted pig....

The words swam together before her eyes, a jumble of loops and ink blots. Reggie could picture the visions all too well, even though they weren't her own — they appeared in her head and rolled over her consciousness. The dark, the smoke, the bodies, the insects, the fire — she'd seen versions of all these things in the different fearscapes. They were so real....

Reggie stopped looking in mirrors, because like as not, when she did, she saw the vision of herself staring back with empty, smoky eyes and black-pocked skin. The immersion in Macie's journals seemed to prompt hallucinations of her own, flashbacks to the fearscapes she'd already visited, like the ones that had begun in Home.

Cold air seemed to be the best defense against these figments, but Reggie dared not go outside during the day. Ice compresses on her temples and the back of her neck had to suffice to clear away the nightmarish cobwebs that clogged her thoughts. She also tried to focus on pleasant sights, like the views from the barn windows. To the north were apple orchards and rolling fields, one of which still had a scarecrow up on a post, though the crops were long dead. She'd also look at the main house for long stretches of time, watching Mrs. Waters come and go throughout the day. Quinn's mother was a holiday-decorations person, and as Christmas neared, swaths of green garlands and holly wreaths bedecked the house. Reggie started to feel a bit like a girl from a fairy tale, locked in a tower and forced to watch the goings-on in the world from afar, never to participate in them. She wasn't counting on any Prince Charming to come and rescue her, however.

Soon, she found herself listening for the crunch of gravel in the late afternoons that signaled Quinn's arrival home from school. The arrangement had been awkward at first, them sleeping in the same house, though in separate rooms, but soon enough they fell into a comfortable routine. As lonely as Reggie was during the days, she was glad to have company at night. And, of course, Aaron would come by when he could.

As she read more, what didn't make sense to Reggie was why Unger had torn out and kept these particular pages. It seemed probable that whatever assignment the Tracer Sims had had, it had concerned Dr. Unger, and Sims had gotten his hands on the journal and sent it to Eben. But she still didn't understand why Unger would have ripped out certain passages for safekeeping.

That is, until a little over a week later, when Aaron and Quinn arrived home from school fraught with nerves.

"You were right," Aaron announced as he withdrew a pile of papers from his backpack and spread them out on the table. "Macie has everything to do with this."

Reggie stared at the papers. They appeared very similar to the ones Machen had shown her, the ones that most likely proved she was some kind of hybrid creature.

"I've seen these already, Aaron."

"You've seen *these*." Aaron pointed at the top row of papers. "These are your results." Then he gestured to the bottom row. "These are Macie's."

"*Macie's?*"

"Dating back years, but they're the same tests. And they show extremely similar results."

"How do you mean?"

"Macie's DNA mutated in much the same way yours is doing."

"Okay, first, can we not use the word *mutate*?" said Reggie. "And second, you're telling me that Macie and I have the same DNA?"

"Not exactly. It's still different in the way your DNA and my DNA are different, but some of the same chromosomes that are now active in your system are also active in hers."

Aaron looked at her expectantly. The pieces were beginning to click in her mind. The same tests, the same results. The same experiences.

"She went into fearscapes," Reggie breathed. "Like me, she went into fearscapes and helped people."

Aaron nodded.

"She had your power, Reggie. That's why Unger wanted her. That was the power Sims was talking about in his letter to Eben. The power of the fearscape."

"And it's why Unger kept those specific journal passages," Reggie said. "They're not visions that she had—they're fearscapes! She wrote down the fearscapes that she visited."

"But there's something else," Quinn said, nudging Aaron.

"What? What else?" Reggie asked.

Aaron bit his lip.

"Your results are similar, as I said, but only up to a certain point. For a while—years ago—there was a period of dramatic alteration in her code, but then it plateaued. Her genes stopped mutat—er, changing—and yours...haven't."

Reggie felt the cold swarming over her again. The sensation that her body was betraying her, morphing into something that she couldn't stop, and she couldn't control.

"We were both experiments for Unger," she said, looking at the ground. "But what you're saying is that maybe I am the more successful result."

"That's...one possible interpretation," Aaron said.

"But what that could also mean is that, locked in her head somewhere, Macie knows what Unger's end game is." Quinn put a hand on Reggie's shoulder. "Maybe that's why he wanted to keep her locked away—because she knows something."

"But we can't get it from her," Aaron said shortly.

They were all silent for a minute.

"Macie cracked under the pressure," Reggie said at last. "That's what happened. Her mind couldn't take all the horrors, and it finally went bonkers. She lasted longer than some of those other poor souls that the Vours have experimented on, but in the end the result was the same: Her mind split."

"What are you thinking, Reg?" Aaron asked.

"I have the ability to go into people's consciousnesses now. Not just their fearscapes—like Vours, I can burrow into their heads and poke around their thoughts. Maybe Macie still has some sanity in there somewhere, tucked away, buried deep down. If I can get at it, communicate with her that way, maybe she can give us the answers we need."

"Reg, that's brilliant!" Aaron exclaimed. "It's a long shot but certainly possible. With her in a coma, it might even be easier, since the crazy part of her is silenced. I'll call Machen—we're going to the hospital as soon as possible."

Hopefully it's soon enough, Reggie thought. It was already December sixteenth, and they had less than a week before a new wave of Vours would descend upon the world, and who knew if Reggie, in her current state, was supposed to be a part of it?

———————

Reggie woke in the night to a bloodcurdling scream. For a moment, glancing around the dark, she thought she was in a fearscape, but as her eyes adjusted, she saw the green numbers on the bedside clock and realized she was still in Quinn's guesthouse. The clock showed 3:17. She blinked; all was silent—had she dreamed the scream? But then it came again, an animalistic shriek from the other side of the house. Quinn.

Reggie leaped out of bed and almost fell down the loft ladder in her haste. She sprinted across the room—the screams were definitely coming from Quinn's room. She scaled the ladder and burst into the bedroom, switching on the light as she ran to the bed.

"Quinn!" she shouted.

He lay rolling on the bed, his sheets tangled about his body, his face drenched with sweat. His eyes were screwed closed, and Reggie saw his eyeballs roving madly back and forth behind his eyelids.

"Quinn!" she yelled again, grasping his shoulders and trying to hold him steady. But the nightmare had him, and he did not wake. He continued to thrash about, too violently for Reggie to control. She jumped on the bed and straddled him, using all her weight to try to pin him, shouting at him all the while. "Wake up, Quinn! It's a dream. *Wake up!*"

She saw a half-drunk glass of water on the bedside table and snatched it up, then dumped it on Quinn's head. His eyes flew open, wild with terror. She was sitting on top of him, her hands on either shoulder, staring down at him.

It all happened in an instant. The world washed away in a wave of swampy, wet blackness. Reggie stood alone, surrounded by ink-colored vapors that undulated with a soft, sickening *squish*. The clouds that swirled slowly around her coated her bare skin with a heavy and cold film. It took her a moment to realize that she provided the only source of light in this place. Her flesh emanated a dull glow that lit the immediate grayness around her.

By now Reggie had gotten used to passing into otherworldly realms, but this place was quite unlike either fearscape or subconscious. It was just…empty, murky space.

"*Who are you?*" asked a hollow voice from the miasma.

"I'm Reggie," she called out. The sound of her own voice was like flat soda, syrupy and heavy. "What is this place? Where am I?"

"*It is the void.*"

"The void?" Reggie moved in the direction where she thought the voice was coming from. The glow of her body brought a small shard of light to even thicker clouds of black. Something began to solidify in the dark.

At first it was a distorted oval, stretching and pulling in all directions like oily taffy in front of her. Two slits opened in the top portion, another at the bottom, taking the crude shape of a face. Slowly the vapors pulled into greater detail—eyes, nose, mouth, ears—and Reggie recognized the face of Quinn as a young child. He was the same age as she remembered from her harrowing journey into his fearscape, a boy no more than eight years old.

"*Gone…*"

Reggie stepped toward the face and pushed a finger into the swirling cloud. It quivered like not-yet-cooled pudding and started to fall apart into dozens of floating globules.

Other shapes drew together from the vapors around her: a large bear; a medicine ball with tortured faces; another little boy, with his intestines spilling out of his body. The images could only maintain themselves for a few seconds before ripping apart like wet tissue and returning to the gloom.

"They're like memories...." Reggie murmured. "Memories of the fearscape..."

As she walked through the dark clouds, the glow from her skin lighting her way like some freakish candle, Reggie saw what she could only conclude were *walls* of some sort. There were aspects of this place that had become completely solid, marked periodically by horrific but frozen images. She ran her fingers across them. Cold and forgotten.

"They're like scars, aren't they?" she said, and it struck her. Reggie knew exactly where she was. The contact with Quinn during the struggle had transported her unexpectedly into his mind, and she had projected herself into the lost space that was once occupied by his fearscape.

Fearscapes took up physical space in the mind, but Reggie had never given much thought to what happened to that space after a fearscape was destroyed. She had assumed the space ceased to exist as well, but this was like an empty apartment. The fearscape had moved out, leaving a shabby shell of a home behind. This was psychic scar tissue, like a *scarscape*.

Suddenly Reggie couldn't breathe, and she felt herself yanked away. The mists disappeared, and she was back in Quinn's room, sprawled across his bed. He was on top of her, and his fingers encircled her throat, pressing into her, squeezing the life out of her.

She batted frantically at his hands as her vision filled with black spots.

"Quinn!" she choked out. "It's…me. It's…Reggie. Stop…"

It was only seconds, but to Reggie it felt like eons. Then the pressure around her neck eased, and the weight lifted off her. She lay there for a minute, coughing, trying to regain her breath. Vaguely she heard someone saying her name.

"Reggie, oh my God, oh my God, I'm so sorry, I'm so sorry."

The words repeated over and over again. Reggie opened her eyes. The spots were gone. She felt her throat—it was sore, but her breathing was evening out.

Quinn was kneeling next to her, but when she sat up, he scrambled back to the other edge of the bed.

"Oh my God, Reggie, I am so sorry. What can I do? I'm so sorry."

His brain seemed to be on a loop, rerunning the same words and phrases, not sure what to do next. He was soaking wet, both from the water Reggie had poured on him and his own sweat. Water dripped from his hair, over his cheeks and neck, and onto his bare chest. He was wearing only flannel pajama pants, and his body was racked with shivers—Reggie wasn't sure if it was from the cold or the horror at what he'd almost done.

"It's okay, Quinn," Reggie said calmly. She was surprised when her voice came out like a croak, but she persisted. "It's fine. It's not your fault."

"I almost killed you," Quinn whispered, wide-eyed. He looked at his hands as if they were sentient objects that had betrayed him. "I can't believe I…Are you all right? Should we go to the hospital?"

"No, of course not." Reggie sounded more confident than

she felt, but it wasn't like they could stroll into the emergency room anyway. Besides, she needed to tell him where she had been. "Quinn, listen to me. I think I went inside your head."

Quinn was silent for a moment.

"I think you did, too. I think I felt you in there and something in me...freaked."

"It was an accident. I didn't mean to."

"Reggie, don't apologize. I'm not the one who almost got choked to death. Are you sure you're okay?"

"I think I just need some water."

They headed down to the kitchen, Quinn helping Reggie down the ladder as much as he dared without touching her too much. He filled a glass with water and handed it to her; she drank eagerly, and the coolness felt good going down her throat. She noticed that Quinn was still half-naked and looking like a drowned rat. He caught her staring at him and absently grabbed a dish towel, drying off his face and slicking his hair back.

"You're going to catch pneumonia," she said.

"I'm not so concerned about that right now," he replied. "We have to call Aaron. You need to go someplace else. It isn't safe here...with me."

Reggie scoffed. "Don't be stupid. Of course I'm safe here. It was an accident, Quinn. I just won't go skipping around in your brain anymore without your permission. Lesson learned."

"How can you joke about this? I could have *killed* you."

Reggie didn't have a good answer for this. It wasn't funny, of course. Quinn was experiencing aftereffects of the Vours, much like Henry had: visions and nightmares that were more powerful than the average person's, that caused reactions more unpredictable and dangerous.

"But you didn't kill me, Quinn. Because you're not a killer."

"How can you be sure? I've been having the nightmares for a while, and they're getting worse. Tonight I was in my fearscape again, but it was mixed with things that I think were real. You were there. I was…God, I was trying to kill you."

The horrible irony sat in the air between them. He was right—she couldn't be sure he wasn't damaged now, somehow. She suddenly felt the need to do something with her hands, any kind of busy work that would exempt her from the guilty stare Quinn turned on her.

"I think I could use some tea. You?"

She grabbed the kettle off the stove, filled it with water, and turned it to high heat. The flame from the burner was welcome warmth in the cool kitchen.

"I think I could use something stronger," Quinn murmured, but he retrieved two mugs from the cabinet.

"Look," said Reggie, opening a tin of Earl Grey. "You were a Vour then. Trust me, there were a couple times when I almost killed you, too."

"But I'm not a Vour now!" Quinn slammed the mugs down on the counter. "It's like parts of my mind and body are working against me. Doing things I can't control. Seeing things that shouldn't be real, but they are; they happened. Is that what you saw when you were in my brain just then?"

Reggie turned back to him. He looked defeated, yet wild at the same time.

"No. I think I went to the place where the fearscape used to be. It's empty now, but…scarred." She stepped toward him and held out her forearm, pointing at the black marks etched across her skin. "We'll always have these, inside and out. It's sick, and twisted, and it isn't something anyone should have to deal with. Maybe neither of us has an answer how to do it yet, but we will. *We* will. You're not alone here, Quinn."

Quinn's fingers brushed his own scar on his cheek, and he touched the two stubs on his right hand.

"I don't want you to leave," he conceded. "I know it might not seem like it after tonight, but things changed for me when you moved in. They got easier, because I finally didn't feel like such a freak."

Reggie let out a short, bitter laugh.

"In comparison to me?"

"No! No, that's not what I meant. When I came back, everyone expected me to be this guy, this guy who I didn't know at all. At first I was just a seven-year-old in the body of a seventeen-year-old, which was weird enough, but then when the memories started to return and mix together—I didn't know how I could go out in the day, how I could talk to people without screaming or curling into a ball or…or even hitting them in the face. It's like sometimes I still feel this sludge inside me…."

"Like it's infecting you? Making you a different person?"

"Exactly. Do you think it will ever go away?"

"I don't know," said Reggie. "Too bad they don't make soul colonics."

They both smiled grimly, and the teakettle began to whistle.

17

Quinn and Reggie strode down the sterile white hallway. It had been a couple of days since Reggie had discovered Quinn's scarscape, and now she was going to try to enter another mind.

"I really hate hospitals," Reggie muttered.

"No kidding," Quinn replied.

They reached the room the nurse had directed them to. Aaron was pacing back and forth, and Machen sat in a chair by the window. He got up when he saw them.

"Hey, guys, come on in." He hurried over and shut the door behind them.

Both Reggie and Quinn gawked at Macie lying in the hospital bed. She was so frail that her body barely left an outline beneath the blankets. Her face was covered with wrinkles and liver spots, and an oxygen tube was shoved up her nostrils.

"She's dying, isn't she?" Reggie asked.

"I'm afraid so. The doctors say it's only a matter of time."

"So you should get in there while you can," Aaron said. "What do you need from us?"

"Just some quiet, and if you can make sure there are no interruptions…"

"No one will interrupt."

Reggie nodded and sat down next to Macie's bedside. She glanced back at the three anxious men hovering behind her.

"Well, here goes nothing."

Reggie took Macie's hand, concentrated, and pushed into the old woman's subconscious. The familiar tunnel opened, and she traveled down it, farther than she'd ever had to go before. It got very dark, and very quiet, and it felt a bit like she was floating in some kind of inner space. There was the feeling of emptiness all around her, as though she were traveling through a land that had been erased. Macie's consciousness was buried deep.

And then, in the distance, she saw a spark. Where before it had felt like she was drifting in nothingness, now the air grew cold, a biting winter cold, as she neared the flash of light. It rose in the darkness, bright and orange, flaring and flickering, but it was not a friendly fire. The tongues of flame lashed out like angry, cracking whips, lacerating the black, scarring the night.

She felt solid earth beneath her feet—very solid, frozen solid, in fact. Ice coated the ground, glinting off the dancing firelight ahead. A chill that had nothing to do with the temperature speared up through her body. She thought she knew where she was.

The fire was eating up a huge cross that stood in the middle of a cornfield. And then a piercing shriek filled the air. A body was tied to that cross, and it screamed into the dark.

"Macie! Macie! Cut me down! They're coming! They're coming for me!"

Smoke as black as the night around it billowed up, swirling around the boy, quenching the flames. As the fire died, the smoke seemed to take on its violent nature, moving like a living beast.

"They're coming!"

The smoke attacked the boy, surging into his mouth, smothering his words. It flew into his nostrils and out of his ears, in through his lips and out from his eyes, choking him, blinding him. It enveloped his skin like an oily blanket, seeping into his pores and turning his veins black. His skin withered and wrinkled like a prune until it was no more than a flaky casing for his bones. His eyeballs gorged with black fluid until they exploded out of his eye sockets. His brain turned to mush under the devouring vapors and leaked out of his ears onto the ground. He no longer screamed, his tongue now eaten away completely by the toxic smoke.

After all this time, after all the horrors she'd seen, Macie's greatest fear was still the sight of her brother, Jeremiah, being taken over by a Vour. In a fit of drunken rage, her father had strung the boy up on a scarecrow's perch one Sorry Night, and his terror had called to the Vour like a siren song. Unable to help him, she had watched the transformation happen. This was how her mind had corrupted the scene, into a gruesome snuff film.

Reggie heard a wail, higher and weaker than Jeremiah's had been, and saw a tiny lump on the ground near the base of the cross. It was a small girl lying in a heap, weeping softly.

"Macie?" Reggie said. Her voice echoed in this psychic space, and the girl looked up, shocked and terrified. Only it wasn't a girl after all. It was an old woman, wan and wrinkled, with long, straggly gray hair and limbs so emaciated they looked like toothpicks.

The woman scrambled backward, but Reggie held out her hands.

"Don't be afraid. I need to talk to you."

"Who are you?" Macie asked.

"My name is Reggie. Are you always here? Do you always have to watch Jeremiah?"

"Always. It's always the same. I can never save him. But how did you know—?"

"I read your journal. It told me all about Jeremiah, and the Vours, and how to defeat them. How to devour my fear."

"You read my journal?" Recognition seemed to dawn in the old woman's eyes. "You're *her*. The one who sees."

Reggie nodded.

"You see, too. You went into fearscapes, too, didn't you?"

Macie cringed.

"A few. I couldn't take it. And now I'm trapped here. Is this my fearscape? Am I a Vour?"

"No, no, you're not a Vour. I think the tests that Dr. Unger did on you split your mind. He tortured you, Macie. He forced your conscious mind deep inside. I think you were trying to hide from the evil outside, but somehow you're tormented here as well. I'm sorry."

"Why are you here?"

"I need your help. You told me that I shouldn't look. What did you mean by that? Shouldn't look at what?"

Macie began to wag her head back and forth.

"No. No. You don't want to know these things."

"I do, Macie. I have to."

"How do you think I am the way I am?" Macie demanded, grabbing Reggie's arm. Her grip was like cold stone. "I looked. It drove me here. It split me in two. Do you want to end up like me?"

Reggie took Macie's hand in her own.

"I have to try. I have to see what they don't want me to see. Macie, Sorry Night is almost here. We're running out of time."

They had wandered away from the cross a bit, and now Macie stopped. Reggie tried again.

"Does it have something to do with the cloud? That cloud that some people see when they defeat their fearscapes?"

Macie sighed and seemed to make up her mind. "It's your sanity, girl. Yes, it's a portal. A portal to their world."

"To the Vours' world?"

"It's how they get in. It's the back door. It leads to a hub that connects all the fearscapes. It's the birthplace of fear."

Reggie felt the excitement growing inside her.

"But how do you know this? How could you see it? I can never see them."

"When a fearscape crumbles, it leaves a void."

"Yes, yes, I've been there! Afterward. But it's different."

"Yes. The void rots away, like a house that no one cares for. The white walls you see when you first demolish a fearscape are just a façade, a coat of paint hiding the scars left over. But that paint chips away with time. The scars are revealed, and so is the portal."

"So if I go back into a scarscape, I'll be able to see this back door?"

"But why would you want to, girl? Listen to me—it will drive you mad. It is terror and despair and all the things that drag us into hell. Look at me."

"Surviving is fighting," Reggie said. "It's my turn to fight."

"Then good luck to you, girl."

Macie began to shrink away, back toward the cross. Reggie looked up and saw that Jeremiah was freshly hung on it, and the fire was just starting to spark.

"Macie, no, come with me! You don't have to fear this!"

But Macie had crouched back down by the cross, weeping and wailing for her brother and trying desperately to undo the knots that bound him. Reggie could do nothing to move her.

———

Reggie blinked and found herself back in her body. Aaron was by her side.

"What happened?" he asked.

"It is the cloud," she said breathlessly. She explained what Macie had told her about the portal to the Vours' world. She looked up at Quinn. "I have to go back to your scarscape."

"No. No way," Aaron said. "Macie's right—it's too dangerous."

"I have to see it, Aaron. I have to see if it's a viable way in. Don't you realize what this could mean? An entrance to their world. We could take the fight to *their* world."

"I'm all for new ideas, Reggie," Machen said, "but I have to agree with Aaron. We have solid evidence that even just looking at this thing could hurt you."

"This will be a fact-finding mission only," Reggie said. "I won't try to go into the Vour world by myself or anything stupid like that. Look, I've been there already and I was fine. I just need to go a little further."

All three of them could see that there was no arguing with her. Aaron knew better than anyone that when Reggie made up her mind to do something, she did it. Finally they relented.

"Fact finding *only*," he said to her.

"Are we doing this now?" Quinn asked.

"Yes, immediately. It shouldn't take long." Reggie pulled Quinn down onto one of the visitors' chairs and knelt beside him.

"You said you could feel me in there before?" she asked.

"I think so, yeah."

"I won't trash the place, then." She took his hand and gazed into his eyes, and soon she was back in the cloudy realm of the scarscape.

This time she knew where she was, and she had more purpose.

"Hello?" she called out. Her voice was swallowed up by the churning walls. But then one of the clouds reassembled into a childish face with cherub cheeks and blank eyes.

"*Hello again,*" it said, sounding like wind through reeds.

"I'm looking for something," Reggie said.

"*What would you look for here?*"

"A cloud," Reggie said at first, then realized that this whole world was clouds. "I mean, a window, a door, some kind of passage."

"It closed, along with the rest."

"Can you show it to me anyway?"

The face said nothing more, but pushed along the wall in front of Reggie. It left a trail of vapor, a desperate string winding through a deep labyrinth. It beckoned Reggie to follow.

She did, half walking, half floating along through the ethereal landscape, for what seemed like a long time but could have been only seconds. Time wasn't a factor here. But as she progressed, her feet felt heavier, and it took more effort to move them forward. She felt pressure in her chest, as though her heart were actually sinking. Finally she heard the voice again.

"There…"

It dissipated once again in front of what appeared to be a grayish window.

Reggie approached slowly, laboring.

The opening throbbed, a gray maw with a heartbeat all its own. As she peered closer, Reggie noticed that the breach was sheathed in a gauzelike film. She pushed a finger into the film, and a stab of cold ran up the length of her arm like ice through her veins. She drew her hand away but tried again, determined. It gave a bit, stretching like a thin latex membrane. She tried to pull at it, tear it a little so she could see through, but the strange fabric was deceptively strong.

However strong it was, it was translucent enough that she could see through to the other side. Something was beyond.…

Reggie ignored every instinct that screamed for her to back away, to leave this place. She needed to *see*.

With supreme effort, as though she had to fight her own muscles, she pressed her face to the gauze, keeping her eyes open, ignoring the stabbing cold pricks that seemed to freeze her in place. She pushed until she could see details, something to give her a sense of what lived beyond this forsaken place. Nothing moved, but Reggie could feel that the space was alive.

Everything was blurry, but she could see grayish, cavelike corridors extending in all directions. Lining these were doorways—these were the back doors Macie had spoken of. These were the Vours' access to fearscapes. A shudder racked her body like a seizure as more of the hub came into focus.

A line of shadows reached as far back down the corridors as she could see, each one waiting by a door. Thousands and thousands of them, lingering, waiting, wanting. Malice radiated from them like steam off a morning pond. They were the Vours, and they were preparing for Sorry Night.

Her brain was alive with feelers of fear. Since developing some of the Vours' powers, it was like she had an extrasensory perception for terror, and it was on high alert now. Not here in the scarscape, but in that corridor beyond. Fear emanated from all those doorways, every kind of fear imaginable. Every kind of fear that one might see in all the fearscapes of the universe.

Now she wanted to run, but she was frozen in place. It was like a black hole had opened in her gut and was slowly drawing the rest of her body into it. It was as Macie had said—overwhelming terror and despair, eating at her like a thousand black worms. Tinges of visions from the world beyond swam scattershot through her mind. Tentacles of blood reached out for her; monstrous claws that dripped black bile tore through the tissues of her brain; and spiders—spiders were everywhere, crawling up across her lips, into her nostrils, laying eggs in the nooks of her ears. And yet she was paralyzed, held in place by the very fears that tormented her.

Bit by bit she felt herself slipping away. Her mind began to crack.

And then, faint as a moth's wings, she heard a voice.

"*Reggie. Reggie, come back. Come back. Follow me back,*" the childlike Quinn whispered.

With all her effort, she focused on the voice, and it grew louder.

"*Reggie, follow me back.*"

She regained feeling in her limbs, and the monsters tearing at her brain withdrew. She stumbled backward, away from the portal, and a little bit of warmth returned to her body.

"*It is closed, you see.*"

"This one is. There are many that are not."

Reggie floated back out to her own body.

"Are you okay?" Quinn asked worriedly. "I could feel you… slipping. Like you were leaving us."

"I almost did," Reggie said quietly. "But I saw it. I saw them. They're gathering. They're waiting for Sorry Night, just on the other side of that wall, they're ready to pour through. And I don't know what to do about it."

She looked from one of them to the next with abject despair.

"I guess you can't really bring explosives in there and blow the whole thing up," said Aaron. "Although psychic C4 would be pretty awesome."

"It's not funny!" Reggie leaped to her feet, and she could feel tears coming to her eyes. The dread from the place she'd just visited clung to her like filth.

"Of course not, I didn't mean—"

"Reggie, you need to rest now," Machen said.

"No, we need a plan—"

"Tomorrow. Your body and your mind need a rest after what you've been through. Aaron and I will talk about it tonight, and Quinn will take you home."

18

Reggie sat silently in the car, staring out the window at the darkness whizzing by.

"Are you okay?" Quinn asked.

"No. No, I'm not okay."

"No. That was a stupid question. I'm sorry."

Reggie shook her head.

"I thought I could deal with anything they threw at me—the visions, the tests, the torture, the constant hells I traveled through. I even took a kind of pride in it." She spoke softly, almost to herself, and Quinn had to lean toward her to hear. "My whole life I doubted myself, until I started fighting Vours. And then I started to believe, just a little bit, that there was something in me that made me special. That I had what they lacked, and that gave me this power—and it's a power that I've cursed, but it's also become a part of who I am. And I thought that it had to do with courage, and honor, and all those other things that make humans great, but now…now I know it was the opposite. *They* became a part of me. Or I became a part of them. I became less human, not more.…" Her voice broke, and she trailed off.

"That's not true."

"Isn't it our DNA that makes us different from spiders or cats or monkeys? Now my DNA makes me different from humans—whatever's in their cells is in mine, too. *I'm part Vour.* And, Quinn, what I saw in there, what I felt, I don't know how I can fight that, especially if it's in me already."

"Reggie, there are plenty of people out there with one hundred percent human DNA who do very inhuman things. It's your actions that determine who you are, not your blood."

"Until you have no control over your actions. I look at Macie, and it's like staring at a mirror that reflects the future. I can feel the darkness around me all the time now, closing in like fog. Every day there's a little more in my head." She swiped at her eyes. "I'm sorry, Aaron's usually the lucky one who gets to listen to my sob stories."

"I don't mind," said Quinn. "But would you rather be talking to him?"

The question caught Reggie off guard.

"No—I—I don't know. I don't know why I started telling you these things."

"He loves you, you know."

"Of course. I love him, too."

"I mean, he's *in love* with you."

Reggie didn't respond. How had the conversation turned to Aaron? She felt the color rising in her cheeks and was thankful for the black cover of night.

"He and I have our differences," Quinn continued, "and I get why he'll never really trust or like me. He's honorable, and smarter than all of us, but there are certain things that he won't ever fully understand."

"That's not his fault."

"Maybe not, but it's how it is. He hasn't been on the inside. And it's good that he hasn't, because at least one of us should have a clear head. But maybe that's why you're talking to me." Quinn steered the car onto the exit ramp and left the highway. "I know what it's like to live in a nightmare, to question what you're seeing, what your brain is telling you is real, to wonder if you'll ever be normal again."

"It's a terrible way to live," Reggie whispered.

Quinn put his hand on top of hers.

"But you don't have to live it alone."

The car crunched on the gravel of the Waterses' driveway, and the shape of the barn loomed ahead in the gloom. No lights were on in the main house, either; Quinn's parents had told him they'd be out for the evening. Quinn turned off the engine and faced Reggie. She smiled ruefully at him through her tears.

"So the best-case scenario is I just totally lose my mind and go insane, and…well…I don't know about the worst-case scenario. I turn into a Vour? I turn into something worse?"

"Or…" Quinn reached out his hand and touched her cheek, gently wiping the tears away. "You turn into something better. Maybe you become a new kind of being that's stronger and better equipped to fight the Vours. Maybe you become the secret weapon the human race needs to survive. Maybe you become a superhero."

Quinn leaned toward her, and Reggie felt a chill start at the top of her head and race down her spine to her toes. Unlike many of the sensations she'd been feeling lately, though, this was a good kind of chill.

"As long as I don't have to wear a leotard and tights."

"I don't think that'd be so bad."

He pulled her to him and kissed her tenderly, cupping her head in his hands. The thrill went through her like a firecracker, and for just a second she wondered if this, too, wasn't some skewed vision. But his lips, warm and soft, were real enough. She closed her eyes and let herself fall into him, heart pounding, skin tingling, a fiery ball of delight building inside her. He tasted like coffee and something sweet. Gum, maybe, or candy? The image of a purple sucker flashed through her mind.

Reggie abruptly pulled away, her head swimming.

"I'm sorry," Quinn said quickly. "I shouldn't have—"

"No. No, it's not your fault. That was really…unexpected."

Quinn swallowed. "Okay. Not exactly the adjective I was going for…"

"I mean, a good unexpected. A *great* unexpected." Reggie felt like a complete moron. Was she still talking? Why was she talking when she could be kissing him? "I'm sorry, leave it to me to spaz and ruin the perfect first-kiss moment."

Quinn seemed to relax.

"*Perfect* works. But what is it, Reggie? What's wrong?"

Reggie hesitated.

"You taste like lollipops."

At this a laugh burst from Quinn's lips.

"Lollipops, huh? Yeah, I had one earlier. I admit it's not very manly, but it's probably better than the garlic pasta I had for dinner."

"It's just that…when you were a Vour…you were always eating candy and chewing gum. Your breath always smelled sweet."

It was like Quinn wilted in his seat before her. He pulled away and avoided her eyes.

"Right, no more candy, then."

"Quinn, I'm sorry. I shouldn't have said anything. It just surprised me, and made me think—"

"Made you think of me as the Vour," Quinn finished. His voice was laced with disgust.

Reggie placed her hands on either side of his face and forced him to look at her.

"I was reminded of time I spent with *a* Vour. I never confuse that monster with you." And now she leaned toward him and pressed her lips to his. She had no idea where this rush of confidence was coming from, but she figured she'd go with it. Within moments Quinn was kissing her back, and that feeling of warmth and giddiness returned as they remained locked together.

After a few minutes they slowly pulled apart but stayed inches from each other's faces. Reggie giggled.

"I think if you had asked me an hour ago how I thought I was going to end my night, this would have fallen somewhere after 'reality dating show marathon' and 'sprout wings and fly to Tahiti.' I mean, what are we doing here?"

Quinn smiled and brushed away a piece of her hair that had strayed across her nose.

"I honestly don't know. But I'm okay with it."

"You and Nina aren't—?"

"No. She wants things to be the way they were and they just aren't. They can't be. You and Aaron?"

"Oh, no. He's my best friend in the world, but…" Reggie suddenly felt guilty. She didn't want to be thinking about Aaron right now. This had nothing to do with him. She wasn't betraying him, not this time. Was she?

"Come on, let's go in," Quinn was saying. They got out of the car, and Quinn grabbed her hand, squeezing it as he led her to the side door of the barn. Before turning the knob, he leaned down and kissed her again. Reggie thought she might melt into those strong arms wrapped around her. When they separated, she stared at him, wide-eyed.

"What is it?" he asked.

"I just don't think I'm allowed to be feeling this happy when the world's probably coming to an end."

Quinn laughed and put an arm around her shoulder, then pushed the door open. They stepped into the dark guesthouse.

The lights flew on and there seemed to be a hundred people standing in the room.

"SURPRISE!" they all yelled.

19

Reggie nearly bolted out the door, but Quinn, in his shock, had instinctively pulled her closer to him. They stood huddled together, and for a split second Reggie's bewildered brain thought she was facing a Vour army, but then she began recognizing students from school and Quinn's parents. Balloons floated on the ceiling, and the card table was stacked with gifts. And, of course, there had been the jubilant shout of *Surprise!* that had just as quickly died on the lips of the shouters. Indeed, they all seemed as surprised as Reggie and Quinn, and everyone gaped at each other. Reggie disengaged herself from Quinn's arm as quickly as possible, took a few steps away from him, and prayed for a hole to open in the earth and swallow her. It didn't.

"You didn't tell me it was your birthday," she muttered at him through her teeth.

"I didn't want to make a big deal of it," he muttered back. "Guess that didn't work out so well."

Mrs. Waters was the first to react. She stepped forward and hugged her son.

"Happy birthday, darling!" she exclaimed.

"You threw me a surprise party?" Quinn was apparently still catching up.

"I know you said you didn't want to do anything, but really, Quinn, you only turn eighteen once."

"That's right." Mr. Waters strode up and shook his son's hand. "So don't get upset with your mother. Besides, Nina thought it was a great idea."

"She did most of this, in fact." Mrs. Waters cast a suspicious glance in Reggie's direction. "Aren't you going to introduce us to your friend?"

Every pair of eyes in the room had been glued on Reggie with various degrees of astonishment and uncertainty. Quinn's parents might not have recognized her, but all her old class-mates did.

"Um, sure," Quinn stammered. "Mom, Dad, this is Reggie."

Mrs. Waters started.

"Reggie? As in...Reggie Halloway?"

Reggie could practically see the rumor mill scrolling through Mrs. Waters's mind: Reggie Halloway, the loner girl from the dubious family, the crazy girl who'd been shipped off to an asylum, and now, the slutty girl who'd just been making out with her darling son.

"Yes, ma'am." She remained pinned to the wall, and then, upon reflection, stuck her hand out. Mrs. Waters took it.

"It's...er...very nice to meet you, Reggie. Glad you could make it to the party."

There was a noise that was halfway between a sob and a cry of rage from the middle of the room, and Reggie caught sight of the figure of Nina Snow pushing back through the crowd. She disappeared and there was the sound of a door slamming.

There was an awkward silence, then Mrs. Waters clapped her hands.

"All right, everyone, don't worry, the adults aren't staying. There's cake and refreshments in the kitchenette. Everyone be safe." She winked at Quinn, hugged him again, and kissed him on the cheek. "Have a very happy birthday, sweetie," she said, then she and her husband left the barn.

Within moments music was blaring from the speakers, loosening up the dumbfounded party guests. Red plastic cups filled with beer began to appear from the patio outside, and kids swarmed around Quinn, wishing him a happy birthday. Reggie recognized most of the members of the football, basketball, and baseball teams, as well as the majority of the cheerleading squad (except for Nina, who had not returned).

Reggie was about to disappear herself amid the reveling—where to, she wasn't sure—when Kip Larson, the Cutter High shortstop, handed her a beer.

"Reggie Halloway, no shit," he said, cheersing her cup with his own and sloshing some of his beer on the ground. "Were you really in a mental hospital?"

"Um, yes?" Reggie took a sip of her beer to avoid having to answer any more questions.

"That is so *cool*. Rodney!" he called across the crowd. "She totally was. I told you! You owe me a burrito."

"What was it like?" asked Shelley Amberson. "Did they do, like, tests and stuff on you? Like, electroshock therapy?"

"Don't be an idiot, Shelley, this isn't the nineteen hundreds," said Michaela Flowers. She leaned in toward Reggie conspiratorially. "My therapist has been wanting me to go to this retreat thing that's like half Eastern philosophy relaxation techniques, but with a specific focus on meditation to reduce my stress levels. Was the place you went to like that?"

"Kind of. I did spend a lot of time in a dream state."

Michaela nodded.

"I knew it had to be something like that. You have to tell me all about it."

"Yeah, sure. But, uh, we're not really supposed to talk about what happens…doctor/patient confidentiality…" Reggie sputtered. Michaela gave her a quizzical look, and Reggie was thankful that Quinn chose that moment to appear at her side again. They seemed to be surrounded by kids dying to hear about her stay in the loony bin.

"Are you okay?" he whispered in her ear. Reggie nodded, a fake smile plastered across her face.

"So, are you guys a thing now?" Shelley asked doubtfully. Reggie remembered that she and Nina were best friends. "How did you even know that she was back, Quinn?"

Quinn and Reggie glanced at each other, neither ready with a good cover story. This was not a scenario they had prepared for. But luckily, at that moment a shout went up, and then Kip was dragging Quinn toward the door. Quinn grabbed Reggie's hand and pulled her along with him through the crowd.

"Quinn, man, you'll never guess who's here!"

Reggie felt a blast of cold air as the door opened wide, and suddenly she and Quinn were face to face with Mitch Kassner.

They just stared at each other for a moment, until Mitch's old teammate Rodney Perez came up and slapped him high five.

"Mitch, you made it. Good man. Hey, how's your brother?"

"Doing well. Couldn't make it out tonight, unfortunately, but I'll tell him you said hi."

"Definitely. Beer's out back."

Rodney moved on, and Mitch turned his stony gaze back on Reggie and Quinn.

"Happy birthday," he said.

"What do you want, Mitch?" Quinn asked.

"I need a smoke. Why don't we talk outside?" He held the door open for the two of them. It was the front entrance, and Quinn's car was on the other side of the barn. Mitch seemed to guess Reggie's thoughts. "Don't do anything stupid. There are others watching this place, and if I give the signal, they'll burn it to the ground."

"And you'd let them? What happened to you?" she asked.

"You know what happened to me," he answered simply.

They walked out into the frigid air, and Reggie huddled in her coat. Luckily she hadn't had a chance to take it off inside.

"How could you become a Tracer?" she asked. "After you saw me save Keech—you know there's another answer, but you became an assassin anyway?"

Mitch pulled out a pack of Camels and lit one.

"There's one of you. Millions of Yours. You do the math."

"So you would rather Keech had been murdered?" asked Quinn.

Mitch took a long drag on his cigarette and contemplated Quinn.

"You look like you've readjusted pretty well to human life." Reggie caught a hint of disdain in his tone.

"I have good days and bad days," Quinn answered, equally coolly. Glancing from one to the other, Reggie felt like she was missing some kind of invisible macho signal that was transmitting between them.

"Keech just has bad days." The smoke Mitch exhaled mingled with his steamed breath. "He's pretty much a raving lunatic when he's not catatonic. He spends twenty-three hours a day in a padded cell in a hospital in Boston. The other hour he gets meds, and doctors look in on him. One time a brain-dead med student wasn't paying attention, and Keech got hold of his pencil. He stabbed out one of his own eyes before they got it away from him. So, you know, I think maybe death wouldn't have been so bad in his case."

Reggie knew the horror she felt was palpable. Mitch's sentiment was not foreign to her—she had asked the same question herself early on, when she had wondered if Henry could recover from his experience in the fearscape. And now Keech had tried to blind himself to block out the terrors he still saw in his mind. Was dying really mercy for these victims? For some of them, maybe, yes.

"I'm sorry," she said.

Mitch shrugged.

"It's done. I was emotionally involved then, but I see things more clearly now."

"You mean you see the things the Tracers implanted in your head," said Quinn.

"What about the things this one implanted in yours?" Mitch gestured at Reggie with his cigarette. "You're going to stop the Vours from taking over? Save all the Vourized humans? How? You've got one soldier. Our solution may be messy, it may be hateful, but it's scalable. It's tactically sound. And it has a chance in hell at success. In war there are casualties, and you have to think about—"

"If you say *the greater good*, I'm going to ash that cigarette on your face," said Reggie. "Look, this is ridiculous. We should be pooling our resources, working together. We'd have such a better chance at defeating the Vours."

Mitch laughed, a mirthless chuckle.

"Reggie, *you* don't even understand the extent of your powers, or what will happen if the Vours use them to their advantage."

"What do you mean, 'what *will* happen'?" Quinn asked. "What do you know, Mitch?"

But Mitch only shrugged, keeping his gaze on Reggie. "I'm sorry. You risked everything to help me last summer, but we're talking about saving the human race now. You're too big a risk."

"So you're taking me in?" Reggie asked. "This is a kidnapping?"

"I don't think so," said Quinn. He shuttled Reggie behind him protectively and stepped between her and Mitch.

"Don't do this, Quinn," Mitch warned. "We don't want you. You can go back to your life." He nodded toward the noisy partiers laughing and drinking and dancing inside the barn, oblivious to the potential danger lurking in the dark outside.

"My life's not in there anymore."

They each tensed, then dove at each other. Mitch got in the first punch, striking Quinn in the jaw. Quinn doubled over, but it was a feint; when Mitch went in for another blow, he left his lower half exposed, and Quinn sprang at his midsection, knocking him to the ground. He kicked Mitch in the groin, and the Tracer growled in pain, but he started to get up again almost immediately.

"Reggie, get out of here!" Quinn cried.

But Reggie stared intently at Mitch, concentrating. More experienced now, like the Vours themselves, she didn't need physical contact to enter his thoughts. Slowly the tunnel between her mind and his began to open, as it had with Dr. Unger in his office. But this time Reggie knew what to do. She accessed the deep parts of his brain, the places where the horrors lay buried. What she saw there almost snapped her back to her own body: The scene was so realistic, and so terrible. Had this actually happened?

She forced herself to focus and lassoed the image.

Mitch had recovered and was on his feet, ready to attack again. Quinn's nose was bleeding and he was panting, but he still put himself between the Tracer and Reggie. She heard a whistle somewhere in the darkness and knew that the signal had been given: The rest of the hunters would be on them in moments.

She mentally gathered Mitch's fear and thrust it into the forefront of his mind just as he lunged at them. Quinn swept her out of the way with one arm, but Mitch flopped to the ground, screaming in terror and covering his eyes with his hands.

"No! We couldn't stop it! We couldn't stop it!" he howled.

Quinn fell back in shock.

"What's happening?"

"He's seeing his darkest fears," said Reggie, keeping her eyes locked on Mitch. She let him writhe on the ground for half a minute, then broke the connection. "Was that real?" she demanded.

Mitch shuddered, his hands covering his eyes. "You...have... their powers," he gasped.

"Was that real? Answer me! Or I'll send you back in!"

"Yes, it's real," said Mitch through gritted teeth.

"What's going on, Reggie?" Quinn asked, but Reggie gestured for him to wait. She leaned over Mitch and grabbed his hands, wrenching them away from his face.

"How do you know this?"

Mitch stared back at her, furious but fearful.

"We got Unger. We made him talk. He was easier to crack than a walnut."

"And that's what he was planning to do?"

Mitch nodded. "And now you understand the stakes."

Reggie's head was reeling, but just then figures emerged around the side of the barn, descending upon them in a swarm. She thought she saw the glint of a pistol in one of their hands.

"RUN!" shouted Quinn, and he dragged Reggie off into the fields behind his house, leaving Mitch collapsed in a heap. Soon they were beyond the light emanating from the party, and they tripped along the uneven ground. At least the darkness kept them hidden from the Tracers, but Reggie knew they were making a tremendous amount of noise as their feet trampled and snapped the dead cornstalks lying in the dirt. Their pursuers would overtake them before too long.

Suddenly Reggie noticed a reflection of light, and she realized with some surprise that they were running past a parked car. And then there was another, and another. It was as if they had stumbled into a parking lot. This was where all the kids had left their cars, away from the house and barn so Quinn wouldn't be suspicious when he got home. They both started trying door handles. Finally Quinn found one that was open, and he and Reggie leaped inside. Quinn yanked out some wires under the steering column and within a couple minutes had hot-wired the car. The engine roared to life.

"Muscle memory," he said in response to Reggie's questioning stare. "Quinn the Vour apparently did this pretty frequently."

"Glad he was good for something."

There was a shot, and the back window exploded in a shower of glass.

"Reggie!" yelled Quinn.

"I'm all right, I'm all right." Reggie slumped forward, keeping her head down. "Just go."

"You're bleeding!"

Reggie put her hand to her forehead and felt the sticky drip of fresh blood.

"It's just a cut."

Another gunshot rang out. Quinn slammed on the gas and the car hurtled forward. He threw the steering wheel back and forth, trying to avoid the other cars parked around theirs. There was a screech of metal as he sideswiped one, and the side mirror popped off.

"Keep your head down as best you can," Quinn said. He swiveled in his seat and looked behind them, but didn't see any headlights following. "Their cars must be on the other side of the property. That's good. They'll have to take the long way around on the driveway, and we're already almost to the main road."

"Where should we go?" Reggie asked.

"We shouldn't stay on the main roads for too long or they'll catch up to us," Quinn answered. "What's close but not obvious?"

"I have an idea," said Reggie. "Not perfect, maybe, but it's the best I've got."

"Where?"

"Something Wicked."

20

Quinn looked surprised, but nodded.

"Good as any place right now, I guess."

The moon was bright enough to see by, so Quinn drove with the headlights off to make their car more difficult to follow. Fifteen minutes later he pulled into the alley behind the bookstore that had once belonged to Eben Bloch. The building looked dark and unfriendly; after Eben had died, there had been some dispute as to who actually owned the property, and no one had taken over the premises yet. Paper lined the interior of the storefront windows, one of which was cracked. The sign letters that had spelled out *Something Wicked* had been removed but left weathered outlines on the building's exterior surface.

"Good hiding spot," said Quinn. "Looks like a crack den."

They walked hesitantly up to the front door; the latch was damaged, and Reggie was able to push it open without too much trouble. The bell that hung from the top of the door jangled, and she and Quinn stepped inside.

It was pitch-black, but the smell of mildew and must filled her nostrils, and the memories flooded back. It had been almost a year since she'd been here, but before that, she had spent so many hours in these rooms, talking with Eben, confiding in him, and reading her favorite stories. Scary stories. The irony was as stifling as the shuttered air.

She instinctively reached for the light switch, but it didn't work. That made sense. No one had been paying the electric bill for quite some time. She took out the disposable cell phone Aaron had given her and turned it on, flashing its dim light around the room. The place was a disaster—it had been ransacked long ago. Display tables were overturned, the wallpaper had been torn from the walls, and Reggie saw piles of broken glass from shattered lamp bulbs. And the books. All the books that Eben had lovingly collected now littered the floor, having been dumped unceremoniously from their shelves. Reggie felt a pang in her heart: It wasn't that many, or even any, of these books were very valuable in the marketplace, but they had been like Eben's children. And now the moisture and mildew and mold were destroying them.

"Let's go up to Eben's apartment," Reggie said to Quinn. "Hopefully it's in better shape." But she didn't feel very hopeful.

They walked up the stairs that led to the apartment above the bookstore. The door here was unlocked, too, and as Reggie shone the phone light around, they saw that it was only slightly less destroyed. In the kitchen the shelves and drawers had been emptied, the floor was covered with broken glass and china, and someone had sliced open the sofa cushions in the living room. But the dining room furniture, while disarrayed, was still in one piece. And in Eben's office, the most sparsely furnished room in the house, there was little to destroy. Someone had taken all the files from the filing cabinets, and the computer was gone, but the desk and chair were still there.

"Why don't you call Aaron, and I'll try to find some light," said Quinn. Reggie nodded.

Aaron picked up on the second ring, and Reggie told him what had happened. Before she had even finished, she could hear him running out the door.

"Don't do *anything*," he directed. "I'm on my way."

Quinn had found some candles and matches among the clutter in the kitchen and was in the process of setting them up around the apartment. The light flickered eerily on the walls; the emptiness of this place was profound, but Reggie pushed it from her mind.

For lack of anything better to do, Reggie and Quinn began to clean up the debris in the kitchen. Reggie found a broom and dustpan, and they took turns sweeping the floor, being careful not to cut themselves on all the broken dishes. They had a garbage bag mostly filled when they heard thumping up the stairs, and Aaron burst in moments later. He ran to Reggie and hugged her.

"Thank God you're okay. Sorry I didn't get here sooner—I wanted to make sure I wasn't being followed."

"It's okay. We've been keeping busy."

"They really did a number on this place, didn't they?" Aaron asked, glancing about.

"The Vours?"

"The Tracers. Machen and I came here after you were kidnapped and took away as much stuff as we could that we thought might be important. But a few days after that, I came back and it looked like this. I think the Tracers were trying to find any evidence Eben might have left behind."

"Lucky you got here first," Quinn said.

Aaron put a large duffel on the counter and unzipped it. He pulled out a few flashlights and an electric camping lantern. He switched the lantern on, and ghostly white light filled the kitchen.

"Okay. Tell me everything."

They took the lantern to the dining room and sat at the table. Reggie took a deep breath before she began.

"I know what Unger wanted to do. I know his plans. For me."

"How?" Aaron and Quinn both asked.

"When I was looking into Mitch's fears tonight, I saw it. His worst fear is that Unger's plan might come true."

"But how did he know what Unger was plotting?" Aaron sat forward in his chair.

"They kidnapped him," said Reggie.

"That's right. Mitch said the Tracers found Unger and tortured him to get the truth," Quinn added.

"Avi was right," Reggie said. "I am a kind of hybrid now, half human and half Vour. Unger was trying to turn me into a new being, and he succeeded. Or, at least, he thinks he succeeded." She hesitated. She saw Mitch's fears as clearly as if they were in her own head. Really, now they were. Aaron and Quinn waited for her to go on, tension etched across their faces. "Every time I defeat a fearscape, the energy that gets released—the black smoke, I guess, the Vour 'essence'—it doesn't just float away. It goes back inside me. That's what infected me. That's what changed me. Killing the Vours has made me one of them."

The words hit the air like the beats of war drums.

"Don't say that," Quinn insisted. "You may have some of their powers now, but you're *not* one of them."

"Semantics, really," Reggie said bitterly.

"So Unger sent you into all those fearscapes because he wanted you to defeat them," Aaron said slowly. "And that's what he did with Macie before you, but she stopped being able to beat them. That's why her tests plateaued. You were stronger. But why does he want to make a hybrid?"

"Because he wants to Vourize one on Sorry Night," Reggie answered.

"Of course. Of course, that's it!" Aaron tried to take her hand, but Reggie pulled away. She didn't want anyone to touch her.

"He was planning to turn me into a Vour this Sorry Night," Reggie went on. "But I wouldn't be just any Vour. With my altered DNA I'd be a—"

"A super-Vour," Quinn finished. Reggie nodded.

"With who-knows-what kind of abilities. That's why the Tracers are desperate to kill me before the twenty-second. And frankly, I don't blame them."

"Don't think like that, Reg," said Aaron.

Reggie peered at him.

"I saw it, Aaron, in Mitch's mind. I saw myself, killing people at will, causing mass delusions that drove the entire town crazy. I turned this world into a kind of hell, a fearscape that no one could escape from."

"*You* didn't do any of that," Aaron said. "It's just a fear, like the hundreds of others you've seen. It isn't reality."

"But it could be!"

"Not if you're not turned into a Vour," said Quinn. "Sorry Night is four days away now. All we have to do is keep you safe and fear-free until it passes."

"Right, until next year."

"Let's jump off one bridge at a time," Aaron said. "Quinn's right. If we can make it through the next ninety-six hours, we'll have quelled the most immediate threat. The Tracers have Unger, so he won't be launching an attack. The bigger danger are those would-be 007s. But if we can evade them, we'll have at least bought ourselves some time."

It all seemed too big. Too many enemies, and now Reggie could count herself among them. She leaned forward and laid her head on the table.

"Mitch was right. I'm the biggest danger of all. If one thing goes wrong, it could mean the end of everything."

"Reggie, I can't imagine what it was like to see those things in Mitch's head." Aaron rose and began to pace. "But you have to remember that it's not a prophecy. It's a possibility. One of millions. We can't base our actions on one guy's fears. Look, you're exhausted, and it's been a rough day. Let's all get some sleep and we'll see things more clearly in the morning."

Reggie didn't have the energy to argue. She let Aaron lead her to the couch, where he flipped over the sliced cushions so she could lie down.

"Eben's mattress is in even worse shape—torn to shreds," he said.

"I wouldn't want to sleep in there anyway," Reggie said. She stretched out on the couch, and Aaron spread a blanket he had found over her.

"We're going to get through this, Reg," he whispered to her.

But Reggie wasn't so sure.

Reggie had been afraid she wouldn't be able to sleep, but as soon as she closed her eyes, she fell into a deep slumber. She woke once or twice during the night to see either Quinn or Aaron sitting awake with the lantern in his lap, but each time she drifted back into unconsciousness almost immediately. The next time she opened her eyes, the sun was streaming through the windows, and she heard noises coming from the kitchen.

Still a little groggy, she got up and went to investigate. Machen was there with Quinn and Aaron, and steaming cups of coffee and bagels covered the counter. It was almost like a normal breakfast among buddies, except that they were discussing how they were going to prevent their friend from turning into a horrific monster and causing the end of the world.

"How are you feeling?" Aaron asked her.

"Better," Reggie responded, though that was a lie, and they all knew it.

Quinn passed Reggie a cup of coffee and a bagel.

"Compliments of our esteemed former English teacher."

"Thanks, but I'm not that hungry," Reggie said. "You guys have everything figured out yet?"

She meant it as a joke, but the three men exchanged dubious glances.

"Kind of," Aaron said. "I'm not sure you're going to like it, though."

"Just lay it on me."

Machen cleared his throat.

"I think Aaron and Quinn are right—we should try to keep you off the grid until after the solstice. It's risky, but trying anything else might be riskier. However, that means taking certain…precautions."

"What kind of precautions?"

Machen hesitated. "I want to keep you on a regimen of sedatives for the next few days."

"You want to drug me?"

"It's imperative that you not experience any kind of fear on the solstice. Sedating your brain will help accomplish this. If the Vours are trying to track you by sensing your fear, it will help with that, too."

"If I'm asleep, I can't be afraid? What about nightmares?"

"The medication I have will put you in a deep enough sleep that you won't dream," Machen explained.

"So you want to induce a coma. Excellent."

"I know it's not ideal, Reg, but if it's the best way of keeping you safe…" Aaron broke off.

"I get it. I do. Hell, maybe a dreamless sleep isn't the worst idea anyway. At least I won't have to remember what I've seen."

"Exactly," said Aaron.

"I also think that it's best that you all stay here," Machen went on. "Mitch knows that you're now aware of the danger you pose and that they're after you, and he'll have reported this to the Tracers. Especially if the three of you have disappeared, they'll assume that you skipped town, trying to get as far away from them as possible. They'll be sending their feelers outward, not in."

"So we'll be hiding in plain sight, as it were," said Aaron.

"Right," Machen replied. "I brought enough supplies to last you the next several days. Water, dry food—I'm afraid it's nothing gourmet, but it will tide you over."

"We'll be fine," Aaron said. "What are you going to do?"

"It's better if, once I leave here, I don't come back, just in case someone is watching," said Machen. "I'm going to try to keep on top of what and where the Tracers are, maybe even set a few false leads if possible."

Something occurred to Reggie.

"Your parents are going to flip when you both just vanish," she said to Quinn and Aaron. The latter shrugged.

"It can't be helped. We'll be gone only a few days," he said. Quinn looked more unsettled but didn't say anything. Reggie guessed that while he was just as willing as Aaron to make this sacrifice, his situation was much different. His family had already been put through hell because of a disappearing act on his part. Plus, it was Christmas.

"Thank you. Both of you. For doing this," she said.

"Eat your bagel, Reggie," Machen said, breaking the awkward silence that followed. "You need some nourishment before we put you under."

Reggie knew Machen didn't mean anything by it, but the words *put you under* made her shudder. Still, she spread some cream cheese over her bagel and forced it down. When she was finished, she followed Machen back to the sofa. As she lay back, Machen brought out a pouch. He withdrew a tourniquet and a syringe filled with light, golden liquid.

"Give her one of these every twelve hours," he told Aaron and Quinn. "She'll begin to wake up around then, so make sure she eats and drinks before you put her under again. You need to ensure she stays hydrated." He took the tourniquet and tied it around Reggie's upper arm, then tapped the vein in her inner elbow.

"So this is something of a crack den after all," she said drily.

"You're going to be fine, Reggie," Machen told her. "This is going to put you right to sleep. When you wake up again fully, all of this will be past us, and you'll still be you."

"I feel a little bad about it, actually," Reggie said. "You all are doing all the work, and I get to take a nap."

"A well-deserved nap," said Aaron.

Reggie looked away as Machen stuck the needle in her arm. She felt the surge of medicine as it entered her bloodstream, and within minutes her eyelids became heavy. The last thing she saw were the three of them standing around her, concern laced in their eyes. They were willing to sacrifice everything for her. Her heroes, all of them.

21

The medicine worked as Machen had said it would. Reggie slept for almost a full twelve hours without dreaming a single thing, and when she opened her eyes again, she barely realized she was awake. Aaron made her drink several cups of water and fed her some chicken soup, and after she made a groggy trip to the bathroom, the boys helped her back to the couch.

"You all are sssso great," Reggie mumbled, slurring her words. Aaron wrapped the tourniquet around her arm again and took out one of the syringes. Reggie only half-understood what was going on, and their voices sounded very far away.

"I hate this," he said.

"Do you want me to do it?" Quinn asked.

"No, I got it."

He plunged the needle into Reggie's vein, and she drifted off again.

The routine continued, morning and evening, for the next few days. Reggie only vaguely remembered the brief periods when she was awake, and other than that all was blessed blackness. She had long ago lost track of the date, but one morning, as she was falling back into unconsciousness, she heard Aaron whisper in her ear.

"Almost there, sweetie. We're almost there. You're doing great."

The words were a comfort, and she smiled.

She didn't know why, but the next time she came out of the dark, it seemed like less time had passed. The bronze light of the setting sun dazzled her eyes, and it took her a moment to realize that she wasn't in Eben's apartment. She was in a car, speeding along past the fields outside Cutter's Wedge. She tried to turn her head, but it wouldn't move, nor could she speak. *The medicine must still be wearing off,* she thought, but she wasn't particularly concerned. It was kind of nice, looking at the scenery in the sunset. The golden light sparked off the icy rime that covered the dead fields, looking almost like flame.

The car slowed to a stop at a four-way intersection, and something in the field caught Reggie's eye. A huge cross rose up out of the ground, and something was strapped to it. She peered at it, trying to see what it was, and her breath caught in her throat. Arms, legs, a torso, a head. It was a *body*, and it was crying out, pleading with someone unseen.

"Pa, please. Not tonight. Any night but tonight!"

She'd heard those words before. Who had spoken them?

"Can you see it? The shadow…"

The sun hit the very edge of the horizon, and its red light glinted off the brown fields like a match striking flint. Suddenly the earth was ablaze with angry flames, and it licked the edges of the cross. Black smoke billowed up into the sky, and all Reggie could hear were the shrieks coming from the body as the smoke and fire engulfed it.

The fear blossomed in Reggie like the inferno before her. It was unlike anything she'd ever experienced: pure, hateful, manic fear that twinged every nerve in her body, fear that almost blinded her for its power. Her mind couldn't handle the pressure, and she thought it might burst. But then, in the background, a familiar tune played out to the beat of her pounding pulse:

"Your body's here but not your soul."

And then, all of a sudden, it was gone. The fear, the dread, the worry—gone, as was the fire and the smoke and the screaming. The "body" on the cross was only a scarecrow, left to hang there long after the crops had been harvested. *Of course*, thought Reggie, *it's the same scarecrow I saw from my room at Quinn's.* Now she felt very stupid for having overreacted so.

As this understanding set in, she realized that she *felt* different. It was like her eyes had been opened for the first time, and everything was crystal clear. She was invincible, unable to be countered or conquered, and anyone who stood in her way would crumble before the terrible visage that was she.

But when she turned her head, she felt a pang of alarm. Mitch Kassner was in the driver's seat.

Reggie wanted to scream, but her lips were unresponsive. So was the rest of her body. She tried to move her arms, to hit him, to grab the steering wheel, to open her own door and jump out of the moving car—anything—but it was like she was paralyzed. Maybe he'd given her some kind of drug.

What had happened? The Tracers must have found them at Eben's and taken her. And if that was the case…

Oh, God, thought Reggie. Aaron, Quinn, Machen. They could all three be dead right now. But why wasn't she? Why hadn't

Mitch killed her? If he was taking her someplace, it was probably because the Tracers wanted to interrogate her, and they would use any method to get her to cooperate.

Reggie turned her head involuntarily, and she suddenly realized that her thoughts were turned outside the moving car. Like hatching spiderlings escaping their web, they flew out in many directions, seeking something, but she didn't know what, nor could she control them. They drifted out over town, some of them landing on people having dinner, or watching television, or reading to their children. But most of them soared past Cutter's Wedge to the surrounding areas, so many thoughts, so many webs, Reggie couldn't keep track of them all. They pulled at her consciousness, making her dizzy and confused. But still, something drove them forth, something she couldn't identify.

But Reggie began to sense motivation behind all these threads of thought and, what was more, malice. They were searching, searching desperately for something, driven by a singleness of purpose and an overwhelming hate. Reggie felt a bitterness enter her headspace like black bile. She wanted to pull them all back, but they were too far gone.

And then one of them *blipped*—it was the only way Reggie could describe it—one of the thoughts had found its mark, and it was as though it sent up a flare to the others. Immediately the rest surged toward the one, yanking Reggie's consciousness far, far away. She was no longer seeing the car or the road or Mitch; she was soaring over the land, past housing developments and farms, until she was swerving among the dilapidated buildings of a town she didn't recognize. She entered a broken top-floor window in one of these and zoomed downward, passing straight through floor after floor until she got to the basement, and only here did she finally slow down. It was dark, but she could see without difficulty.

The basement seemed to be a collection of cells. A guard patrolled the entrance, but he was of little interest to the thousands of thoughts converging on this spot. They all entered one particular cell, and Reggie was astonished to see Dr. Unger, asleep on a cot.

This was a Tracer hideout, the place where they were keeping Unger, and maybe where Mitch was taking her right now. But Reggie had barely had time to note this before, like parasites, her thoughts attacked Unger. They swarmed over his body, pricking his skin, and flooded into his nostrils, his mouth, his ears, and even under his closed eyelids to get to his brain. Unger woke with a start and began to scream as the thoughts probed his mind.

Reggie didn't understand what was happening. She was seeing into his inner psyche like she had before, viewing his deepest fears, but this was all wrong. Unger was feeling *physical* pain from the mental invasion. His body jerked about as though he were being electrocuted. Then Reggie felt the strain as Unger's fears were pushed to the front of his mind, but she was not doing the pushing. He screamed as his fears came to life before his eyes, his victims cutting into him, sawing off his limbs one by one, splaying open his abdomen and removing his guts.

They were the same images Reggie had witnessed when she'd gone into the doctor's mind in his office, but something about them was different. They were pulpier, somehow more real, as if they had depth and form and weren't just hallucinations. Unger was seeing the lacerations appear on his skin; he saw the cuts deepen until the bone showed through. All the while, Reggie's thoughts pounded away at Unger's mind, but she was not controlling them. The visions expanded in his head until the blood vessels in his eyes burst, and blood and brain matter began dripping out of his ears and down his nostrils. He screamed in agony and terror, having lost control entirely of his seizing body.

And then his brain popped. The frontal cortex simply split apart like a runny yoke, his eyes rolled back, and he was dead.

Reggie couldn't believe what she was seeing. What had just happened? What had she done? She had killed this man with her mind, she was sure of it, but she hadn't wanted to. It was as though her thoughts were being controlled by someone else.

Unger lay still on the bed, his limbs jutting out at odd angles, his face a mess of blood and sweat and tissue. She heard the Tracer guards throwing open the door to Unger's cell and shouting in confusion at the sight before them. She could feel the fear growing in them as they wondered what could have done such a thing.

But then she was being pulled back again, back out of the building, up and over the hills and fields, past rows of homes, down the highway, and into the front seat of Mitch's car. Once again she was gazing out the car window at the frozen fields, though it was darker now and harder to see.

What had just happened? What had she done?

Mitch! she wanted to say. *Mitch, something terrible is going on!* But her lips wouldn't move, and her voice wouldn't work. Instead, her head lifted and her eyes turned upward. The sun visor was down, and she saw her reflection in its mirror. Staring back at her was the wrinkly, pale, and sunken face of Macie Canfield.

22

"NO!" Reggie screamed, sitting bolt upright on Eben's couch. She almost smacked heads with Aaron, who had been trying to shake her awake.

"Reggie, what is it? Are you okay?"

Reggie was panting hard, and her eyes darted about the room. Aaron took her face in his hands.

"Look at me. Reggie, look at me. It's Aaron. You're in Eben's apartment. You're safe."

Reggie touched Aaron's hands with her own.

"You're real?" she whispered.

"I'm real. This is all real."

"It was a nightmare, then?" she pleaded.

Aaron frowned.

"I don't know. You're not supposed to have nightmares."

Reggie took a few deep breaths, trying to control her heartbeat. She still felt discombobulated.

"It must have been a dream," she murmured. "Because it was impossible. But it was so *vivid*...." She paused. "What day is it?"

"It's the solstice." Quinn walked into the room, carrying a tray laden with a glass of water and a bowl of soup. "Sorry Night. Less than an hour to—"

Suddenly, in the middle of his sentence, Quinn dropped the tray and fell to the ground. The dishes crashed everywhere, and he began convulsing. Reggie and Aaron were caught so off guard that it took them a few seconds to respond.

"Grab his legs! Hold him down!" Reggie yelled at Aaron as she tried to pin Quinn's shoulders to the ground. "Quinn! Quinn, can you hear me?"

"What's going on?" Aaron asked, but a moment later he, too, toppled over and started to seize. Reggie looked with horror from one to the other of them as they thrashed on the ground.

"No, God, no no no. Why is this happening?"

Reggie raced from the room in search of Machen's supplies. She found them in the kitchen, including the syringes filled with the sedative. She grabbed two and returned to the living room; both Aaron and Quinn were still shaking uncontrollably, and saliva foamed at their lips.

She looked fretfully at the syringes; she had no idea if the drugs would stop the seizures, but it was all she could think of. She was about to plunge one of the needles into Aaron's arm when there was a sharp knock at the door. Reggie looked up. The knock came again, louder this time, and Aaron and Quinn suddenly lay still.

Reggie stood and faced the door.

"Reggie, I know you're in there," said a scratchy voice. She had heard it before. "Let me in, Regina, or I'll fry your friends like I did the good doctor."

Reggie hesitated for just a moment, then strode to the door, unbolted it, and opened it. The woman looked scrawny and thin, still clad in hospital scrubs, her white hair falling down past her shoulders. But there was undeniable malevolence in those eyes that had not been there before.

"Aren't you going to invite me in, dear?" she asked.

"You're not a vampire. I assume that if you want to come in, I can't stop you."

"True, but there are such things as manners, you know." Macie's arm shot out and pushed Reggie out of the way. Her strength was remarkable for how frail she appeared. Reggie stumbled back into the kitchen, and Macie entered the apartment.

"So you...you're a Vour?" Reggie asked.

"Not just any Vour," Macie retorted.

"What happened to Dr. Unger—that was real? You did that?"

Macie nodded her head once, smiling smugly.

"But why? How?" Reggie stammered.

"Because I could. I had to try out my abilities, didn't I? He seemed as good a test case as any. And it seems to be one of the by-products of becoming a hybridized human, that I can seek out people at will, discover their fears, and incite such fright that it kills them. Isn't that marvelous?"

"In the car—it was you. How did I see all that?"

"I sent you the vision so you could see my handiwork personally. Yes, it was me in the car. Fate is a funny thing, you know. That Tracer found Macie and kidnapped her, never imagining that Macie would wake to see—or think she was seeing—the thing that frightened her most. On Sorry Night, no less!"

"She thought she saw Jeremiah on the cross."

Macie nodded.

"Leaving the door wide open for me."

"But Macie's chemistry stopped changing," said Reggie. "She was a failure."

"That dolt Unger just gave up on her," Macie snapped. "True, you appear to be the stronger specimen. And that is, of course, why I had to come and see you."

"You're going to kill me?"

"Oh, heavens no, dear. Sorry Night is nearly over, and I don't want to wait a full year to see what kind of amazing fiend you'd be. I'm going to turn you into one of us, of course."

"No, you're really not." Aaron strode into the room holding one of Machen's nitrogen pistols and pointed it at Macie's chest. Quinn was right behind him. "There's enough serum in one of these darts to freeze you from the inside out, super-Vour or not."

Macie's blackened lips stretched out in a wicked grin, thin wisps of dark smoke threading out between her decaying teeth. Her wild eyes darted from Aaron to Reggie to Quinn.

"Shoot her!" Reggie yelled.

But Aaron hesitated. The old woman didn't look so old anymore—in fact, her skin began to smooth out, her hair darkened, and her eyes grew into large, brown orbs. She looked just like Reggie. And the girl he could have sworn was Reggie was old and decrepit now, a withered woman with yellowed teeth and skin. He turned the gun on this new Macie.

"No!" Quinn jumped in front of Reggie, shielding her from the nitrogen pistol.

The gun shook in Aaron's hand as he saw black lines begin to crawl across Quinn's skin, and his anxious expression seemed to morph into a sneer that Aaron knew all too well. He leveled the weapon at Quinn.

"Yes, he's the one you really want to hurt," said Macie. "He says he's human now, but you know differently. There will always be evil inside him. It's just a question of when it shows itself again. He'll steal her away from you, and then he'll destroy her."

"Aaron, don't listen to her—whatever you're seeing, it isn't real!" Reggie tried to push Quinn out of the way, but he held her back and stayed between her and Aaron.

Aaron blinked several times, unsure whether to trust his eyes. But it was so real....

"That's right," Macie taunted. "You have to kill him to protect her."

Reggie whirled on Macie. "Stop this! I'm the one you want!"

"But I can have three for the price of one," the monster replied. "You fear more for them than for yourself. It's delicious."

Aaron's thumb touched the safety and unlocked it with a cold click.

"No!" Reggie cried.

Suddenly Quinn dropped to his knees in front of her, holding his deformed right hand by the wrist with his left hand. He stared at it in horror and started screaming. Black splotches spidered out across his hand and along his forearm, the marks of a Vour. Quinn was under attack now, too, enslaved by some fear-induced hallucination.

But this time, Reggie could see it, too. She backed away, staring at him in horror.

"You see it, don't you, Reggie?" Aaron asked. "He's still a Vour—look at him!"

"No! It's some new power she has, because of what she is—she's putting these things in our heads!"

"Ha!" Macie laughed derisively. "That's nothing. See what else I can do."

Suddenly, the wooden floor beneath them turned to a solid sheet of ice. The walls around them fell away, revealing the winter night sky, and a dark, spiky silhouette of pine trees sprouted up all around them. The temperature plummeted, and their breath steamed. The gun in Aaron's hand stretched and morphed into a tire iron. He looked at it, terrified.

They were back on Cutter's Lake, the scene the same as it had been a year ago, down to the two bodies that lay comatose beside a hole in the ice.

Henry's limp and nearly naked form was crossed with black marks, and Reggie's lay next to him, her hand clutching his.

Aaron rushed toward Reggie, sliding across the ice and landing on his knees by her side.

"It's okay, Reg. I won't let anything hurt you," he whispered, running his hand across her ice-cold forehead.

"I'm right here, Aaron," Reggie called. "This already happened. You protected me, remember?"

But Aaron didn't look at her. Instead, he turned his eyes to something moving a little way away. Quinn rose to his feet. His missing fingers grew back like the spindly arms of a starfish. He waggled them back and forth, grinning.

"That's more like it." Black smoke spilled from Quinn's eyes and mouth as he spoke.

Aaron jumped to his feet, brandishing the tire iron.

"Take a step closer and I'll beat you senseless."

"Yeah, I'm shaking."

"Guys, this isn't real!" Reggie insisted, but Macie only laughed.

"They can't hear you anymore. They think you're unconscious. Don't you understand yet? This is a fear construct, one of my expanded powers. I can create whole worlds."

"They're false worlds." Reggie stamped her foot. "This is a wood floor, not ice."

"Perception is reality, dearie," Macie replied drily. "They'll each see the things they're most afraid of here, and that will be their reality. Aren't you dying to know what those things are?"

Quinn circled around Aaron; the latter stayed close to the prostrate bodies, always keeping himself between them and the Vour. They were oblivious to the real Reggie and Macie.

"Please, hear me, Aaron," Reggie pleaded. "You know what's real and what isn't. You can fight this." But Aaron didn't even glance her way, so focused was he on what he thought was his enemy.

"What do you want?" Reggie demanded.

Macie shrugged.

"I want to see who wins."

Every detail was so crystal clear, so perfectly re-created — even though she knew it was fake, it was hard for Reggie not to believe they weren't out on that lake again. She was even shivering from the cold.

If she couldn't make Aaron and Quinn see reality, she had to stop the vision at its source.

The cold. Perception was reality. But did the perception extend to Macie's own mind?

Reggie glanced at her watch. Twenty minutes to midnight. Maybe there was still time....

She whirled around and dove at Macie, knocking her onto the ice. The Vour was momentarily stunned and cried out as her skin touched the frozen water, but in another instant she was back on her feet and had pushed Reggie to the ground. Despite her aged body, she was very strong, and she knelt down on top of Reggie, holding her by the throat. She leaned down so close that her steamy breath brushed Reggie's cheek when she spoke.

"You think you can overpower me? Foolish girl. I can crush your windpipe with my thumb."

"You should see what I can do with my thumb," said Reggie, and she gripped Macie's cold wrists, pressing her fingers against the Vour's pulse. The last thing she saw was Macie's surprised expression before the black closed in around her.

Macie wasn't the typical Vour, and Reggie knew not to expect to fall into the typical fearscape. But nothing could have prepared her for the place she was about to enter.

When Reggie traveled between worlds, there was always a vague tug on her body before she woke up in a fearscape, as though ocean waves were pushing her about. It wasn't really her body, of course, but her consciousness that crossed deep into the mind of the person she was trying to save. The sensation had taken some getting used to, but it wasn't painful—more akin to unnerving motion sickness. Darkness would envelop her momentarily until her mind settled into the manifestation of her body in the fearscape. When she opened her eyes and first took in her surroundings, she never knew what she was going to see, but wherever she was was the starting line. For her brother, it had been a horror-filled carnival. For Quinn, a decaying elementary school. She had seen untold terrors come to life in the hundreds of fearscapes she'd now visited, nightmares that could strip the sanity from a mind, black holes of dread that sucked in and destroyed all sense and reason, leaving the innermost parts of a human naked, torn apart, and splayed out for all to see, like an autopsied corpse.

Through it all, it was up to Reggie to be the light in this darkness, to be the ember of hope in a landscape that had driven hope away. It was her gift, she knew: what she could be that others couldn't. She had struggled, she had come to the brink of insanity herself, but she had kept going, because in a fearscape, she was always herself.

The darkness closed in as it always did, but right away Reggie knew something was wrong. Her mind was ripped from her body like hair wrenched from a scalp. She felt herself flip and tumble in space, and then it was as though a thousand sharpened icicles were driven into her psyche. Warmth and hope seeped out of the gashes, leaving a ghostly cold that seemed to pierce the deepest part of her. It sprouted, and tendrils of despair grew outward, replacing the blood in her veins with ice. She couldn't breathe; she choked on the frost in her esophagus.

Concentrate! a small part of her screamed. *You don't need your breath. Whatever this place is, it isn't real.*

But the cold was more real than anything she'd ever experienced before. And somehow...horribly familiar.

A chill wind gusted all around her, through her, as though she were no more than an empty husk. Screams—from the wind or something more monstrous, she didn't know—filled her ears. And then the memory, like déjà vu, of where she had last felt this kind of coldness fell on her, and the horror blossomed fresh.

It had been in Quinn's scarscape, when she had looked through the encased wall and known that she was on the edge of not a fantastical hell, but a real one. There she had seen the portal where the monsters entered, had felt the presence of the Vours in their true form, separated from her by only a thin membrane of psychic scar tissue. The despair had been almost overpowering, and she had only just been able to get away from it. But now there was nothing between her and the abyss. The fear was like a swarm of bloodsucking spiders crawling all over her skin, injecting her with a venom that left her aware but unable to move. She knew where she was.

She was on the other side.

She had come into the realm of the Vours.

23

She was huddled down, trying to protect herself from the wind that lashed at her hair and skin, to close her ears to the shrieks that penetrated her bones. Dread had settled on her like gooey filth, gluing her eyes shut. As long as they were closed, maybe she could go back, maybe she could wish this world away. But this wasn't a fearscape. The many months spent battling through those worlds had taught her to trust her instincts, and now they were telling her that this wasn't an imagined land that could be defeated with courage. This place was real, whatever it was. The only thing she could do was face it. Step one: opening her eyes. Never had such a simple task seemed so difficult.

Just open your eyes, Reg. One step at a time, she told herself. *Get them open, then we'll think about moving around.*

With the utmost will, she forced her eyelids to flutter and open. If there was any part of her heart left thawed, it froze now.

She appeared to be in some kind of corridor that extended as far as she could see in both directions. But everything: the floor, the walls, the ceiling, the very air—if air it could be called—was a murky, wispy gray of morphing and undulating edges. The only variation in the foggy mire was rows of glowing doorways that ran the endless length of the hallway. Most of them were a faint, sickly green, but a handful shone more brightly and were tinged with red around the edges.

Gusts of frigid wind continued to whip past her. Reggie turned her head slowly to look at the doorway nearest her. It was really more like a window, with green light spilling through from the other side. It was one of the more luminescent ones, and a dark, heatless flame licked the edges and seared inward.

Suddenly a black form, like a shadow made of ink, rushed past Reggie's face and beat against the window. The thing threw itself at it again and again, as the bloody fire ate away at the barrier shielding the opening. And then Reggie felt a burst of heat as though a furnace had come on, and the film covering the window melted away completely. There was a scream unlike anything Reggie had ever heard before, like the sound of a thousand people burning to death, and she cowered, sure that her eardrums would burst.

The shadow rushed through the window, and all at once it went black. The screaming stopped, and the heat disappeared, leaving Reggie even colder than she'd been before. But then, farther down the hall, another sharp screech started and stopped as a shadow broke through the portal. Reggie noticed for the first time that all around her the lights from certain doorways were winking out as the black shades pushed through them.

Sorry Night.

Terror dawned in her anew. It wasn't wind that she was feeling; the gusts were *Vours*, in their true forms as living shadows. They were flying all around her — through her — like ghostly bats, up and down this hellish corridor. And the windows were entrances to human brains.

This was how the Vours got in. Somehow, by entering Macie's hybridized mind, Reggie had bypassed her fearscape altogether, landing instead in the place where the Vours gathered to cross over into the human realm on Sorry Night. What she was witnessing right now was Vours ripping through the boundaries that separated the two worlds; the reddish openings were the minds of frightened humans, those that were vulnerable to the Vours this one night of the year.

So the minds of all humanity are connected somehow in this place, Reggie thought. Under different circumstances it might have been a comforting idea. The heat and light she had felt when the window nearest her had opened had come from a human being — it was what the Vours craved, what was completely absent in this world.

The shadows were in a frenzy now, flying fast and furiously up and down the hallway, bashing themselves against any opening that had the smallest tinge of red. Sorry Night was almost over, Reggie realized. The Vours had only a few more minutes in which to take over a human body, and then her world would be shut to them for another year. But what about her? Could she get out of here? And where was Macie in all of this?

As if something had read her thoughts, she heard a voice whispering close to her ear.

"Beautiful, isn't it?"

Reggie could have sworn she hadn't been there before, but now Macie was standing right next to her. At least, it was a kind of version of Macie. Her form was humanoid but strangely translucent, as though she were made of smoke. She brought her face quite close to Reggie's. Her features were like the old woman's, but elongated and sharp, like a devil's. Her eyes were hollow black sockets filled with swirling, glassy ink, and her lips curled into a smile that revealed spiky teeth.

"I'm glad you get to see this," she said mockingly. "You must be the first human ever to see the Core. It's the hub between our worlds, the passage we take to get to you. All that hope you bring to fearscapes means nothing here."

Reggie felt rather than heard her, as though her own body were an empty canyon and Macie's voice was echoing around inside it. She tried to speak, but it was like something had ripped out her vocal cords, and her lips could only mouth words. Macie laughed at her.

"That would be the despair taking over," she said. "Fear, real fear, can't be destroyed. You might as well try to stop the night from coming. Now you see. Now you see how fruitless your sacrifice has been. We are endless."

Reggie tried to speak again, and managed a gutteral whisper.

"Your...fearscape..." she croaked.

"No, I don't—or rather, Macie doesn't—appear to have one of those. Probably because we're intertwined so, part of each other in a way no Vour and human have been before. I wonder what else is different about me."

Macie stretched out her arms in front of her and flexed her

clawlike fingers back and forth, examining them curiously. They moved fluidly, and smoke wafted off of them; she was something between a gas and a solid, like liquid metal that gave off steam.

"I've never had form like this before beyond your world." She gestured to the shadows that darted to and fro. "That's what we look like normally. But then, I'm not a normal Vour anymore, am I?"

Reggie was struggling to stand. Her body was so numb that every movement took the utmost effort. It wasn't just the cold—it was like when her leg fell asleep from being in one position for too long, except that all her muscles were unresponsive and she had no control over them. Macie stopped looking at her hands and glanced at Reggie.

"Such a trouper. Always trying to be your best!" Macie's arm shot out and grabbed Reggie around the throat. She lifted the girl as if she weighed no more than a feather, and drew her in close. Reggie hung like a rag doll as Macie laughed in her face. "Don't you see, you little fool, there's nothing you can do. This isn't one of your fearscapes that you like to traipse through. You have no power here. But I do. I can feel it flowing through me. I will take back the world for the Vours. I will make all of humanity's nightmares real."

The portal lights had dimmed significantly, leaving the Core shrouded in darkness. Now Reggie emitted a sound like a sharp laugh.

"But Sorry Night's over," she gasped. "Better luck next year."

Macie pursed her lips.

"Yes, that's always the most unfortunate part." She rose and looked at the thousands of Vours swarming all around them, the unlucky monsters that would have to wait another year before again attempting to take over a human life. "At least, it has been until now."

Macie's grip loosened and she dropped Reggie, who fell in a heap on the ground. She could only look on as Macie strode up to one of the portals. The other Vours seemed to feel a shift in the energy of the place, and they surged around her like anxious children.

Macie lifted one of her hands. Talons seemed to sprout from the ends of her fingers, and with a cry of fury she swiped at the door.

The sound was deafening, like the screech of metal ripping apart, as her nails slashed through the membrane protecting the human brain from the Core. And then it was as though a dam had broken: Blood spewed out into the corridor like from a popping blister, and cries of malicious delight seemed to reverberate among the shadow Vours. Reggie saw one of them dart through the gaping hole.

"Yes. YES!" Macie cackled, staring excitedly at her bloodied fingers. She cast one maleficent look back at Reggie, who lay in the pool of blood, then strode off down the hall, her arms outstretched. She tore at each portal she passed, like a tigress ripping apart its prey. More and more blood flowed into the Core, carrying with it other horrors as well—giant flies and maggots, bones picked clean, and tissue that Reggie suspected was brain matter. The devilish shrieks filled the air as Macie shredded portal after portal, and every time one was forced open, a Vour bolted into it.

Reggie couldn't tell if the blood was real or a manifestation of the terror all around her. The fear and the despair and the unnatural sounds had paralyzed her. Her body was like an empty shell. She could only watch Macie's form disappearing down the corridor. Unger's experiments had finally yielded results: He had created a being that could destroy the barrier between worlds. Sorry Night didn't matter anymore—Macie had the power to open any fearscape she wanted to, and all around her the Vours were flooding into human bodies.

"I'll make it nice and slow, Cole." Quinn took another step toward Aaron. The ice crackled beneath his feet, hinting at its thinness. "I'll let you cry and scream and piss yourself before I snap that twig of a neck and drop you into the lake." He gestured to Reggie's still body beside the hole in the ice. "I don't get why she bothered to give you the time of day. I mean, look at you."

Aaron glanced down at his body. The lean muscle he had built out over the past six months in his training with Machen dissipated like fog before his eyes. He looked skinny and awkward and weak. The tire iron in his hand trembled.

"You're no hero, Cole. You're just a nerd with a crush. She couldn't care less about you." Quinn's smile widened. "You're nothing to her. Air and noise, that's it."

"She cares more for me than she does for you." Aaron clenched the metal tighter.

"Really? Is that why she always tries to get me alone? Why she kissed me earlier?"

"You lie."

"Ha. Hardly. I'm the bad boy, Cole. The one who leaves the good girls like Reggie all aquiver. You—you're the pimply-faced mouth breather with sweaty palms and bad breath. Good for nothing but some SAT tutoring and a laugh."

Now Aaron could feel himself shrinking, losing the inches he'd grown in the past year. His arms jutted out like spindly tree limbs, and acne sprouted across his cheeks.

"This isn't me! I'm not weak anymore!" he yelled. "I changed!"

"Did you, though?"

The familiar voice spoke calmly behind him, and Aaron turned around.

Eben Bloch. He stood on the ice dressed impeccably in a pressed white oxford and black slacks, his cane steady at his side.

"People don't change, Aaron. Not really. You can fool yourself, but you can't fool me. And you certainly can't fool Reggie."

"Eben—you—you're dead—"

"Your weakness killed me. Remember?"

Blood slowly flowered out across Eben's white shirt.

"But we fought together. We saved Reggie—"

Eben pointed to Reggie's body on the ice.

"Saved? You saved no one."

"But I remember—"

"Remember what, boy? Remember this?" Eben snapped his own wrist and his flesh tore, exposing blackened bone beneath the bloody tissue. "Do you remember the pain I endured because of you? The bullets that riddled my body in the caves below Thornwood?"

"I didn't mean for any of that to happen! I just wanted to get Reggie out of there!"

"Yes, you'll sacrifice everything and everyone for her. And how does she repay you? She falls in love with a Vour."

Quinn chuckled.

"You know it."

Aaron ignored Quinn but looked desperately at Eben.

"No, she would never—I won't believe that."

Blood dripped down Eben's pant legs and spilled across the ice, coloring it red.

"She told him her secrets and left you in the dark."

"She thought she was doing the right thing—"

Eben shook his head.

"So naïve for such a smart boy. It's like I said—people don't change. There's no hope for you."

The old man turned away and began to shuffle back across the ice, leaving a small and gawky Aaron standing openmouthed by the two bodies. The tire iron was heavy in his bony arms. He looked down at Reggie. How could he possibly hope to protect her when he was such a pathetic weakling?

A strong, cold hand gripped his throat, and Quinn hissed in his ear.

"Time to die, Cole. Try not to get your self-pity on me, okay?"

Anger suddenly sprouted in Aaron. Using all of his strength, he whirled the tire iron backward, cracking Quinn in the skull.

The Vour dropped him and Aaron splayed across the ice. For just a moment, the ground looked more like wooden floorboards than frozen pond water, but before Aaron could think too much about this, Quinn was dragging him by his foot to the hole in the ice.

Aaron kicked violently and, in his attempt to wrest his leg out of Quinn's grasp, slammed the tire iron on the ice. There was a sickening crackle, and the surface beneath them broke. Both Aaron and Quinn plummeted down into the dark and frigid water.

24

You have no power here.

Above the screams, above the roaring of the Vours rushing past her, above the maniacal laughter echoing down the hallway, Macie's words filled Reggie's head.

You have no power here.

She didn't. She couldn't even stand, much less mount an attack against the super-Vour. And even if she wanted to, how would she go about doing such a thing? Macie had all of the power in this place, and Reggie had none of it.

Reggie rolled over onto her back. Her hair was wet and sticky with blood, and her muscles throbbed with pangs of cold. How long, she wondered, before Macie ripped open the portals to all the humans in the world? Days? Hours? How long before every living person was infected by a Vour, taken over, and forced into a fearscape? Would the world look different when that happened? Would it start to look like this place?

When would Macie get to the people Reggie loved? To Henry, to Dad, to Aaron? Reggie's thoughts turned to her best friend. She didn't know how long she'd been lying here, but it seemed like years since she'd seen him. He had been on the ice, trying to protect her. He and Quinn were ready to kill each other, but that was wrong. They weren't enemies anymore....

Her thoughts grew more focused. Aaron and Quinn were still stuck in Macie's fear construct, and they were going to fight each other until one of them, or both, were dead. There was always the possibility of saving someone who had been Vourized, but there was no rescuing someone from death. She might already be too late. But if not, she had to stop Macie—somehow—and destroy the fear construct before Aaron and Quinn destroyed each other.

Aaron.

Aaron.

Aaron.

She repeated the name in her head over and over and over again, as though the word were a piece of flint she was striking against steel.

Aaron.

The screams in her ears lessened.

Aaron.

The blood seemed to recede.

Aaron.

Finally, a spark seemed to flame up inside her. It was small, but it was the first bit of warmth she'd felt in this place. She might be some kind of hybrid, but she was still mostly human, and to survive here she needed that humanity. She filled her mind with images of her best friend, dredging up every memory she had of him, everything he had done for her, everything he meant to her. The flame grew, slowly spreading out through her limbs, so that she didn't feel quite so hollow anymore.

But it was so easy for that emptiness to return. The second one of those awful shrieks pierced her thoughts, the warmth would ebb away, but she persevered, focusing all her energy on remembering her human life.

Her fingers twitched, and then her toes. She moved her head back and forth, and then she sat up slowly, carefully. She pushed herself up onto one foot.

Only a handful of Vours flew past her now; most had followed Macie down the passageway. But every time one got near her, she felt an icy prick in her heart and had to redouble her concentration. Gray fog wisped around her.

She was crouched on both feet now, and with every ounce of effort left in her she straightened her legs and stood. She wavered for a moment, holding out her arms for balance, but she stayed upright.

Reggie took one step, and then another, jerkily stumbling forward. Her limbs responded like molasses, but at least they were responding. The cold still penetrated her, but she was able to fight against it now. With every step she grew a little stronger, a little bolder, a little faster.

But the farther she went, the more the dread clung to her as well. The hall was much darker now, the screams distant but replaced by a low moaning. It was as though the corridor itself were alive but badly massacred by Macie's claws. The membranes that had covered the portals hung raggedly like skin torn from a bone, and pus seemed to drip from the walls.

It was so *violent*. However much Reggie hated the Vours, there had at least been some laws that governed what they could and couldn't do. Macie was destroying this balance — forcing open a brain was an act of pure savagery and unnaturalness. The portals were now like open wounds that would never heal.

And through these wounds, in addition to the blood and pus, seeped the fear. Visions swarmed past Reggie's eyes as she passed doorway after doorway to the fearscapes. She swatted at them like flies. A snake leaped out at her and wrapped around her neck, strangling her, then disappeared. A chain saw buzzed at her ankle, and she felt its teeth rip through her skin with a searing pain, and then it was gone. She came to the edge of a cliff and, moving too quickly, stumbled over it, only to land on her knees on the floor of the hall. The walls began to close in around her, so that she was forced to crawl forward through the blood and smoke.

She was so exhausted, both physically and mentally. Her brain would not be able to take the stress much longer. And besides that, what was she going to do when — and if — she ever caught up to Macie? How could she possibly fight that demon when she could barely move in this world? The despair was like a weight around her neck, pulling her down into a swamp of horror.

And then her fingers brushed against something small and hard on the ground. Reggie stopped, surprised, and gripped the object. It was a metal disc of some kind. She drew it up out of the smoke and brought it close to her eyes, peering at it through the dimness. It gave off a tiny glow of its own, and Reggie let out a small cry when she realized what it was. She had seen it before, a year ago, locked behind a wall in Macie's basement, draped on the skeleton of Jeremiah.

It was a St. Giles medal.

Quinn propelled himself up through the icy water. The shocking cold had stunned his brain momentarily, but luckily his body's survival instincts had sprung into action. Why had Aaron done it—pulled him under like that? Where was Aaron now? Somewhere underwater still?

Quinn reached the surface and somehow managed to haul his body onto the ice. His teeth chattered so violently he thought they might crack, and he knew his skin was turning blue. A little way away, Reggie and Henry lay sprawled on the ice. At least they still seemed safe.

Aaron had just gone nuts—talking to himself and yelling crazy things. Come to think of it, Quinn couldn't remember how they'd gotten out here in the first place.

He crawled a few feet, then collapsed on his stomach. The cold was beyond numbing; it was painful, like one of his limbs was being sawed off. He coughed, and black sludge poured out of his mouth onto the gray ice. Quinn looked at it, perplexed.

"I knew it." Aaron's shoe appeared next to Quinn's cheek, and he tapped it up and down.

"Knew what?"

"What you are. You can try to hide it, but I see right through you."

"What are you talking about? You're the psychopath who dumped me in a frozen lake!"

"Only to prove a point. Get him up, boys."

Strong arms grabbed Quinn by the shoulders and hoisted him up. Glancing to either side he saw that Machen and Mitch were the ones playing the roles of Aaron's henchmen.

"What's going on? What are you doing?" Quinn demanded.

In answer, Aaron pulled out a switchblade and held it to Quinn's palm.

"Why did you come back?"

"What do you mean? You brought me back, remember?"

Aaron swiped the blade across Quinn's hand. Quinn yelped in pain, but Mitch and Machen held him firmly.

"Did you come back for her?" Aaron nodded toward Reggie.

"I came back—I don't even know what you mean! I came back because my life was here!"

Aaron picked up a lump of snow and crushed it into a ball with his hands.

"Tell your buddies—no Vour's life is here."

"Vour? Whoa, Aaron, I'm not a Vour anymore. Reggie saved me, remember?"

Aaron shook his head, smiling at Machen and Mitch.

"Such acting chops, this one. I almost believe him. Really, I do. But you've got to work on your tell."

Aaron smashed the snowball into Quinn's bloody palm, and Quinn howled in agony. But that pain was not as great as the horror he felt when he saw his hand wither into a blackened stump at the touch of the snow.

"No!" he cried. "I swear, it's a mistake—I'm not a Vour!"

"But you tried to kill me, Quinn."

Reggie had rolled up onto her feet. She walked slowly toward them.

"When I was a Vour, yes, but that wasn't really me!"

"What about last week? When I was in your room—you almost strangled me to death. Remember?"

"I don't know what that was. I'm so sorry....I never meant to hurt you."

"I guess it's just a coincidence that everyone around you seems to get hurt, then."

"I'm not evil. I'm not. I won't let it take over."

"It's not a choice thing. You are what you are," Aaron said. Reggie nodded.

"You're *infected*, Quinn. You'll never be human again. We can prove it another way, if you like."

Machen and Mitch forced Quinn onto his knees and pushed him over so his head dangled above the hole in the ice.

"You ready? Hold your breath," said Aaron, and he shoved Quinn's head under the water. He held it there for a couple seconds, then pulled it up again. Quinn coughed and sputtered, and a plume of black smoke erupted from his mouth and nostrils, along with black flecks of ice.

"Yahtzee! That's the money shot!" Aaron rocked back on his heels as Quinn continued to spit out the water from his lungs. All of his skin was turning black now, as if hypothermia were creeping across his body.

"Not human," said Reggie, shaking her head. "It's a shame, too. I always thought you were cute."

Aaron went in for another dunk, but Quinn was ready this

time. He pulled Machen down first, shoving him into the water, then scrambled out of the way as Mitch grabbed at him. Mitch landed hard and his leg poked through the ice and caught there.

Quinn bit his lip in fury and ran at Aaron. The two rolled across the barren winter landscape, kicking and biting and pummeling each other. The rest of the world seemed to disappear.

25

It was the one thing that could have inspired Reggie to keep going. This place might not be a fearscape, but the St. Giles medal was a bread crumb. It belonged to Macie—the human Macie. It had been her brother, Jeremiah's, and it was a symbol of her crusade against the Vours. Most importantly, it meant that there was still some human part to the monster that was now tearing apart the fabric of the world. Reggie just had to find her.

Macie was so far ahead, and this corridor was endless. But maybe Reggie didn't have to catch up. The Vour was proud and wanted to prove she was stronger than the human. Reggie just had to put up more of a fight.

She stood as tall as she could and breathed in the foul air around her. She didn't feel very brave, but she was going to have to fake it if she was going to get Macie back. Clutching the medal in one hand, she bellowed down the passageway.

"MACIE!" she yelled as loud as her voice could bear. "Macie, I'm not finished with you yet!"

She took a few more steps, shouting at the top of her lungs, which burned each time she drew in another breath, filling them with the frigid air. The shadows that had dissipated began to return, surging around her. They seemed to laugh at her; they flew into her mouth and down her throat, so that she coughed on her words and choked them back up. But still she called out for Macie.

The temperature continued to drop as more and more Vours filled the passage, turning the air black with their swarming. And then she heard the low cackle. It grew louder, and the black shades parted to let Macie through. She had grown taller already, and her arms looked like bloody pitchforks used for the sole purpose of ripping bodies apart. Viscous skin and muscle hung from her talons, and when she smiled a cruel, wicked smile, Reggie saw the same matter stuck in her bloodstained fangs. She had apparently taken to ripping open the fearscapes with her teeth as well as her hands. Like Reggie had done, she was now, in a way, literally devouring fear, and it had made her stronger.

"You want to go another round?" Macie spat.

"I do," Reggie replied. The medal felt hot in her clenched fist.

Macie shrugged, then sped toward Reggie, her fangs bared, her claws outstretched. Reggie could not move fast enough, and the Vour was on top of her in seconds. She gripped Reggie with her nails, piercing the skin on her back, and sank her teeth into Reggie's shoulder. Reggie cried out as smoke rose from the wounds and the thousands of Vours around them jeered at her.

Macie threw back her head and chortled, and in that moment Reggie whipped out the medal and slung the chain around the

Vour's neck. Surprised, Macie fell backward, unsure what had just happened. But when she looked down and saw the silver medallion *thump* against her chest, her face twisted with rage.

She dove again at Reggie, but the girl was already probing into Macie's mind, searching for the human part. The touch of the token had split the two sides, at least momentarily—Reggie could sense the fear that the real Macie felt. And then, her thoughts like fingers, she grabbed at it, pushed at it, like she had in Unger's and Mitch's minds. Only this time, she was going to push it further. She had to get the human part alone, away from the Vour. She had to build her own fear construct.

Reggie closed her eyes, using all of her will to concentrate. When she opened them again, she was in the basement of Macie's old farmhouse.

She looked around. It was exactly the same as she remembered it: the dark, the cold, and a glass wall at the far end, behind which a skeleton sat in a rocking chair—Jeremiah, Macie's brother.

This was the room where Macie had locked up her brother the Vour. Unable to save him, she had devised a way to trap him. She had sat with him for hours, days, years, until old age had taken his body, and his soul had finally been released. The Vour, however, had remained imprisoned behind the glass, and this was the creature that Reggie herself had devoured that cold December night almost a year ago.

But there was no sign of Macie herself now. Anxiety prickled across Reggie's skin. Had she failed to bring the human Macie here? But she couldn't have—this was what she had seen in the woman's head. She had constructed the scene based on very specific fears.

"Macie?" Reggie called out into the room.

There was no answer, but she heard a tiny squeak.

"Macie?" she asked again, peering into the dark corners.

Squeak. Squeak.

Reggie walked the perimeter of the basement. Every few seconds she would hear the faint noise, but she couldn't tell where it was coming from. And then, as she neared the glass wall, it grew louder.

It was dark behind the glass, and hard to see, but Reggie drew close, nearly pressing her face against the window. She thought she saw movement.

Squeak.

The rocking chair pitched back and forth, and Reggie saw the glint of something shiny within.

"Why am I here?" asked a low voice.

"You tell me, Macie."

The figure got out of the chair and approached the window. Reggie was surprised to see a young girl, not an old woman. Her skin was pale and almost translucent, like a ghost's. Flaxen tresses hung straight off her scalp and looked more like yarn than hair. Her eyes were small and black, like a doll's. The St. Giles medal hung around her neck.

The young Macie drew her finger down the glass.

"I locked him in here, you know. For years. He begged me to let him out. He cried. He whimpered like a sick dog. But I hardened my heart."

She spoke so softly and so low that Reggie had to press her ear to the glass to hear her. Her voice was like crickets chirping, faint and hollow.

"I don't mean for you to relive this," Reggie said. "I just needed to get you away from ... from the other. I needed you to be locked away someplace safe, where we could talk."

"You think this place is safe?" Macie asked.

As if in response, the entire room shuddered like an earthquake had hit. Reggie glanced around. The walls flickered. Macie shook her head.

"No place is safe," she said.

A noise like beating drums sounded outside the room.

"Please, Macie, I need your help," Reggie pleaded. "We're not in a traditional fearscape, but it's the best I can do. This is your Vour. You need to conquer your fear once and for all to beat it. No pressure, but I am not exaggerating when I say the world is at stake."

"But I'm in a cage," Macie replied.

"Yes, I think you've been trapped for a long time. You never got to have a life—not once you saw your brother get taken on the cross. After that, your existence was tied to the Vours. Your sanity got locked deeply away. I think you're afraid of being free. But you don't have to be!"

The basement windows exploded, showering the floor with glass. Black smoke began to pour inside the room.

"It's as simple as tearing down this glass wall, Macie," Reggie said, trying to ignore the rumbles that shook the basement. "We can go back together. It's not too late for you to have a life."

The stone walls were cracking on both sides of the glass wall, and dim light filtered through. Reggie saw human bones scattered on the floor around the rocking chair. Jeremiah's bones.

"Look—pick up that femur and break the glass!"

Macie swiveled around and saw the large leg bone. She knelt down by it but hesitated.

The walls groaned, and the ravenous forces beating against the basement tore a piece of the ceiling away.

"There's no time!" Reggie shouted. "You have to do it now!"

But instead of taking the femur, Macie picked up a tiny rib bone. She looked at Reggie and cocked her head.

"It's not about the glass."

"What do you mean?" Reggie demanded.

"We're part of each other now, it and I. One can't exist without the other. There's only one way to stop it and set myself free."

Reggie's heart fell and she beat her fists against the glass, but it held firm. On the other side, Macie took the sharp bit of bone and sliced open her throat. As black smoke gushed out of the wound, a scream echoed through the basement, ripping away the rest of the ceiling and bringing the walls down completely. In the same moment, the glass splintered and fell, and Reggie rushed to the other side. She caught the small girl in her arms.

Macie looked up at her, a mixture of blood and inky smoke seeping from the gash in her neck. Reggie held her hand to it, trying to staunch the flow, but the girl pushed her hand away. Before Reggie's eyes she aged eighty years, until she looked just like the old woman in the hospital bed. Only this woman had no fear in her eyes, and she smiled at Reggie.

A cyclone of black smoke formed around Reggie and the body of the old woman, whipping at them, screeching in their ears. Reggie felt cold fingers press down on the wound on her shoulder, and she winced in pain. She looked up to see the haggard, demonic face of the Vour in the smoke. It gnashed its teeth and howled at her, but Reggie stared it down, until it was lost amid the rest of the swirling, spinning storm.

Reggie closed her eyes and held Macie tightly. Slowly the wind ebbed, the haunting shrieks faded away, and warmth crept back into her body. When she opened her eyes, she was kneeling on the floor in Eben's apartment, Macie's body spread across her lap. They were both covered in her blood, which spurted out of the gash in her neck. Macie's breaths were coming fast and shallow.

"Hang on, Macie. You're going to be all right," Reggie insisted. It's what people always said, no matter how hopeless the situation.

Macie shook her head only slightly and gripped Reggie's hand. She said nothing, but her breath slowed and, to Reggie at least, when the last one came, it seemed like a sigh of contentment.

At long last, Macie Canfield was free.

26

The pond, the forest—all of it vanished, though the boys were still very cold. Aaron and Quinn blinked several times. They had each other in a headlock and were draped over the side of the fire escape at Eben's apartment. A mound of snow fell off the landing and smacked on the ground two stories below.

"Guys! Stop! It's over!" Reggie was shouting at them from the living room, trying to crawl through the window to get to them.

Aaron rose first and nearly slipped on the ice that covered the iron platform. He grabbed the railing just in time and stopped his fall.

"Jesus, be careful!" Reggie cried.

"I got it. I'm okay." Aaron rubbed his neck. It was sore, and he was having a little trouble swallowing. Quinn sat up and groaned.

"What happened? It was so real." He turned to Aaron. "You tried to kill me!"

"You tried to kill me!" Aaron shot back. They looked like they might attack each other again.

"You both tried to kill each other," Reggie exclaimed,

exasperated. "Macie made you see the things you were afraid of. You saw each other as enemies, even though that's stupid because we're all on the same side now. Now come inside."

Moving slowly, because of both their cold limbs and their sore bodies, Aaron and Quinn managed to make it back inside the apartment. But they each snapped to attention when they saw Reggie covered in blood.

"Reggie, oh my God!" Aaron burst out.

"It's okay, it's okay, it's not my blood."

"Well, whose blood is it?"

Reggie exhaled deeply.

"Macie's. It's Macie's blood. She's dead."

Aaron and Quinn followed Reggie back to where Macie's body was sprawled across the floor. Her head was cocked to the side, and her eyes were still open. Aaron knelt down beside her and shut them.

"Machen will know what to do," he said. "Reggie, tell me, are you okay? Are you hurt at all?"

She shook her head.

"And the Vour…is dead? You're sure?"

"Yes, I'm sure. We're going to have some other problems, but we can consider this Sorry Night officially closed for business."

Aaron nodded.

"I want to hear everything that happened, but I think we should take care of this…er…situation as soon as possible. Plus, Machen should be here for the story."

The three of them looked at one another. Besides Reggie's bloodbath and some scarring from the Vour's attacks, the boys had welts and cuts all over them, and their clothes were ripped. Aaron's neck was particularly bruised, and Quinn had a gash running the length of his hand and what looked like rug burns on his cheeks and forehead.

"Are you guys…okay?" Reggie asked doubtfully.

Quinn raised an eyebrow and glanced at Aaron, who exhaled a low chuckle.

"Yeah, we're okay."

"We just had to straighten some things out."

"And they're straight now?"

Both guys shrugged.

"Yeah."

"Sure."

"Ugh. Boys," Reggie muttered.

It wasn't until later the next day, however, that the four of them were seated around Eben's living room, sipping coffee that Machen had brought over. As Aaron had prophesied, the ex-Tracer had called upon some "friends" to take care of Macie's body. He himself had spent most of the night trying to keep the Tracers off their trail and had not realized until later how much danger the three of them had been in.

Sitting on the couch, wrapped in a blanket, Reggie told them her tale. The three men listened without interrupting until she had finished. Then Quinn wrapped an arm around her and kissed her forehead.

"You're amazing," he said. "You saved us all."

"I didn't save Macie."

"I think you did," Machen countered. "I think she was right, that she was inextricably linked to the monster. While one lived, so did the other, and vice versa, like Siamese twins."

"She went out on her own terms," Aaron added. "And she took a super-bad Vour with her."

"Well, at least now she really is free," Reggie said.

"So are you," Machen said.

Reggie looked up at him, surprised.

"I've reached an agreement with the Tracers. As long as you agree to stay out of trouble on future Sorry Nights, so that you don't go getting yourself turned into a Vour, they're not going to come after you. I think there's even potential for a partnership. With everything that's happened—Macie, and the discovery of all of Unger's research—they know there are more questions that need answering."

"They're changing their zero-tolerance policy?" asked Aaron.

"Well, I don't know about that, but they're not going to shoot any of us on sight, which is an improvement in our relationship, I think."

"What about all the damage the Macie hybrid did?" Reggie asked. "There are a lot more Vours out there after this Sorry Night."

"And their fearscapes were forcibly ripped open," said Aaron. "We don't know what those places will be like."

"We'll deal with them," Machen replied. "But not today. I think that today everyone has earned a good rest. And I think Reggie's earned a night in her own bed."

Reggie's head shot up.

"What?"

Machen smiled at her.

"The immediate danger is past. You can go home, Reggie. I think that you *should* go home."

"But my dad..."

"After what happened at Home, I don't think he'll be sending you off to any more hospitals. That man just wants his daughter back."

Reggie glanced at Aaron, and he nodded at her.

"I'll take you."

So within the hour Reggie was belted into Aaron's car, leaning back against the headrest with her eyes closed. She was so tired. They drove in silence for a few minutes, then Reggie opened her eyes and looked at her best friend.

"I didn't tell them everything," she said.

"What?"

"When I was talking about that Core place, I left out a bit. But I think you should hear it."

"Okay. You can tell me anything, Reg."

Reggie took a deep breath.

"When I was lying there, and I thought there was no way I could get up, and I thought I was just going to waste away and die, I started thinking about you. And I just repeated your name over and over, until I felt like I could move again." She paused and bit her lip. "I just wanted you to know. Even when you're not there, you're with me."

A smile played on Aaron's lips, and he seemed to sit a little taller.

"Okay," was all he said as they pulled into her own driveway.

"I'm still not sure about this—" Reggie began, but Aaron squeezed her fingers.

"It's going to be fine."

They got out of the car, and Aaron helped Reggie up the icy front walk. A Christmas tree glittered in the front window. Reggie had almost forgotten that the holiday was just a couple days away now. Warily, she pushed open the door and stepped inside.

It was so warm, and she could hear the crackling of a fire in the living room. With Aaron following behind, she walked slowly into the house.

Henry was doing a puzzle on the coffee table, and Dad sat on the couch, reading a book. They both looked up as Reggie appeared in the doorway.

"Reggie!" Henry yelled, and he jumped up, scattering the puzzle pieces everywhere. He ran to her and hugged her, and she squeezed him back so tightly he had to tell her to loosen her grip.

She looked over his head at her father, who had risen to his feet.

In two strides he was across the room and had drawn both Reggie and Henry into his arms.

"Hi, guys," Reggie said. "I'm home."

EPILOGUE

"Wake up, sleepyhead."

Reggie's eyes fluttered open. It was dark in the room, but she could feel someone sitting next to her on the bed. Fingers reached out and stroked her hair, and sweet-smelling breath brushed against her cheek as the figure bent over and whispered in her ear.

"Time to wake up."

A shiver speared through her when he touched her.

"My dad will kill you if he finds you in my bedroom in the middle of the night."

Quinn muffled a chuckle.

"Technically it's almost sunrise. But I don't think that distinction would make much difference to him, so we should probably try to be quiet."

"Too early," Reggie groaned as she rolled over to face him. Quinn leaned down and kissed her. Her eyes drooped closed again as she happily let his lips explore hers. They were soft and warm, and she liked the pressure of his body against hers. She was in a lovely state of semiconsciousness when he pulled away.

"No, no, you temptress, I'm here to get you *out* of bed."

Reaching over, Quinn snapped on the bedside lamp. Reggie squinched her eyes shut in the glare, but Quinn took both her hands and pulled her up into a sitting position. Reggie could feel the finger nubs on his right hand, but she barely noticed them anymore. They had become as familiar to her in the last several months as the faint scars that lined Quinn's cheek. She opened her eyes and ran a finger across one of these now. Quinn shied away.

"Don't," said Reggie. "I like them. They make you look—"

"Tough?"

"Real. Different. Special. All of the above."

"I think they make me look human."

"I like that, too."

Quinn smiled and kissed her again.

"Okay, now we're really running late," he murmured after a couple of minutes. "You get dressed, and I'll go get the car started."

He rounded her bed and ducked out the window, the same way he had entered. Reggie watched as he crept along the eave below her bedroom to a nearby tree and swung himself down to the ground. She'd seen him do this many times before, but she was still impressed by his athletic grace. She always felt like a discombobulated monkey when she attempted the move.

She dressed quickly and before long had joined Quinn in his car, which he had parked a safe distance down the street from her house. As he revved the engine and headed off, he handed her a slim stack of manila folders, each labeled with a name.

"Today's crop," he said.

Reggie sighed as she perused the contents of the folders. Even though this was now a regular part of her routine, it always felt a little intrusive to study a compendium of a person's fears, like she was breaking into a private part of another person's self. She was fully aware of the ironies there, since she would, in less than an hour, literally break into these brains to try to help these victims conquer their fears; still, there was something cold and clinical about reading up on them first. But she couldn't deny how helpful these dossiers were in defeating fearscapes, the best defense being a good offense, as it were.

In another bit of irony, she had the Tracers to thank for this assistance, or at least some of them. After Sorry Night, the organization had faced a crisis of conscience, and small factions had broken off from the group, split by disagreements as to how to handle the "Halloway Factor." But Machen had managed to garner support from the majority of the membership, and they had formed a tentative alliance with Reggie and her friends. Reggie had quickly discovered that fighting a war with resources such as the ones the Tracers possessed certainly had its benefits, and a team of investigators who researched victims' histories and the possible terrors she might encounter in fearscapes was one of them.

And that was hardly all. There was a special squad devoted to seeking out and capturing Vours, and a group of scientists who were studying Dr. Unger's research and monitoring Reggie's health and body chemistry. Quinn, who possessed the extrasensory Vour detector, had joined the former and had been responsible for bringing in several of the monsters. Mitch Kassner, after spending some time in the hospital following his encounter with

Macie, had also been prevailed upon to join the ranks of the new Tracers.

They drove for a little over half an hour, and the sun was up by the time Quinn parked the car behind a ramshackle brick building that looked like an abandoned factory. It had in fact at one time been a factory that produced sneakers, but it was now the headquarters for Machen's team of Tracers.

Reggie and Quinn entered through a side door. Reggie had still not quite gotten used to the disparity between the building's exterior—that of a crumbling old building—and its interior, which had been completely gutted and refurbished. Labs and equipment were housed on the first floor, and the Vours' cells were in the basement. The second floor contained training rooms and gyms, as well as the place where Reggie spent most of her time: the Icebox.

The Icebox was a room specially designed for entering the Vours' fearscapes. It was cool, of course, but after some experimenting, the Tracers had found that Reggie was able to move about more easily in the mental worlds if she herself was not subjected to the frigid temperatures that the Vours were. Tracer engineers had constructed a special couch for her that kept her body temperature high, similar to a car's seat warmer. Vours were strapped to a different couch containing cooling panels that made the creatures weak enough for Reggie to enter their fearscapes.

And so, for the last few months, one or two mornings a week before school, Reggie had sat in the Icebox and, one by one, tried to save the humans trapped inside their own minds.

The decision that she would continue going into fearscapes, especially after Machen had confirmed that the very act of defeating Vours was changing her biological makeup, was not made lightly. But a lot of damage had been done on Sorry Night. Macie's actions had resulted in a huge number of Vourings, and though she had been defeated, the Vour world still existed. Until she and her friends figured out another way to combat the monsters, Reggie would take them out one by one. It was the only way she knew how. But at least now she had some help.

Machen came out of his office and greeted them.

"Good morning. Did you have a chance to look at the files, Reggie?"

"Yep, in the car."

"Good. All pretty basic today, I think."

Reggie sometimes marveled that any of this could be considered "basic," but she chose not to mention it.

"I've got to go on a raid," Quinn said. "See you at school?"

"Sure. Be careful."

"You too."

He kissed her and headed off to one of the training rooms. Reggie was about to go into the Icebox when her cell phone buzzed in her pocket. She looked at it and hesitated; the number was blocked.

"I have to take this," she said to Machen, unconsciously gripping the phone tighter. Machen raised an eyebrow but nodded.

"Use my office."

Reggie hurried to the end of the corridor and clicked the answer button as she was shutting the door behind her.

"Hello?" she asked breathlessly.

"Hey, you." The voice was scratchy, and the connection not entirely clear, but it was unmistakably Aaron.

"Oh, it's so good to hear you," Reggie said, sinking into a chair by the window. "How've you been?"

"Getting my ass kicked, but that's not a bad thing."

"If you say so. I don't suppose you can tell me where you are, or what they've been doing to you?"

"No, I'm sorry, Reg. You know the secrecy drill with Tracer training. It's hard enough to make the occasional phone call."

"I know." Reggie tapped distractedly on the glass.

"But I want to know about you. How are you feeling? Everything still good? What are the doctors saying?"

"So far my blood work is consistent with what it was in the fall. It hasn't plateaued, like Macie's, but the rate of change has slowed. So, you know, I'm still at least part human."

"I don't like it. It's too dangerous for you to be going into all these fearscapes when we know they're affecting you in this way."

"We've been through this, Aaron. There's no other way for the moment."

"I swear to you, Reggie, we are going to find another way. I've seen some of the experiments they've been doing here—we're going to figure out a way to reverse this thing in you."

"I believe you, Aaron."

They were both quiet for a moment.

"So it's been a real bummer not having you here to help me study for finals," Reggie said, trying to keep her tone lighthearted. "You know, I'm going to have to take summer school to catch up for missing the fall. That's probably the biggest travesty to come out of this whole mess."

"Yeah, I'd take a fearscape over summer school any day. But other than that, how are things? How's your family?"

"Great, actually, if you can believe that," Reggie said. "Dad even went on a date the other night. The woman was hagsville, but I was proud of him for giving it a shot."

"So your mom…"

"Haven't heard from her, no. But, you know, I'm okay with it. Things feel *solid* at home, for the first time in, like, ever. Dad trusts me again, and Henry hasn't had any more episodes, although he's been talking about wanting to join the Tracers, which I've had to put the kibosh on."

"You might not be able to do that. Look at what you do — it's only natural that he'd want to help."

"He's *ten*, Aaron. We're at least going to wait until he starts shaving before we send him halfway around the world for super-secret Tracer training." Without meaning to, Reggie had let a note of irritation creep into her voice. Aaron caught it.

"They asked both of us to come, remember? And I know why you said no. I know that you have to be with your family right now and that this is the way you need to fight. But that's exactly why I had to say yes. I need to finish this — to see it through. It's the best way I know to help you. I don't want to be that scrawny nerd who does other kids' homework anymore. I *can't* be that guy."

"I liked that scrawny nerd."

"Not enough," Aaron said, so quietly that Reggie almost

didn't catch the words. But before she could respond, he went on. "Look, this is not why I called, and I don't want to fight. There's going to be plenty of time for us, Regina Halloway. Right now, this is where I need to be."

"I just…I just miss you."

"I miss you, too. So much." Aaron was silent again. "Okay. I should go. Give my best to everyone—except Quinn. Quinn you can give my mediocre."

Reggie laughed.

"I'm sure he'll appreciate that."

"I meant what I said. Working with the Tracers now, we're going to find a way to bring down the whole Vour world, and we're going to do it without making you less human. There are already some really promising leads."

"I believe you," Reggie said again.

"Bye, Reggie."

"Bye, Aaron."

She clicked off the call, leaving a little part of her heart on the other side of the line, wherever in the world that might be. But Aaron would be back soon enough, and he was right: There would be plenty of time for them.

She took a moment to compose herself, then left the office. Machen was waiting for her by the entrance to the Icebox.

"How's Aaron?" he asked. "His parents still believe the story about him attending a prestigious engineering school?"

"I think so. It's not a hard story to buy. He said to say hello."

Machen eyed Reggie for a minute.

"Are you okay to do this now?"

Reggie slipped the phone back into her pocket and squared her shoulders.

"Yes. I am."

Machen smiled at her and held open the door to the Icebox. The chill floated out into the hall, and she disappeared into the dark room. A technician was waiting for her inside. Next to her was the Vour, a twelve-year-old girl, strapped into the specially modified couch. She hissed at Reggie, but the sound was weak and powerless. Reggie felt a surge of confidence; this one didn't stand a chance.

She sat down in her chair, and the technician turned on the radiator, then set about linking Reggie's and the Vour's arms together.

She still did believe that Aaron would find a way to reverse whatever was happening to her physically. And she even believed that it might be possible for the Tracers to use her blood, or DNA, or whatever they could, to discover an alternate method for fighting the Vours, one that could be utilized on a grander scale. What she wasn't so sure about was Aaron's claim that they could wipe out the Vours altogether. Because, really, how could anyone eradicate fear? It was as endemic to the human species as the need for water. And Reggie thought that where there was fear, there were Vours. They were inextricably linked, and so, in some ways, humans and Vours were just as inextricably linked.

But for all the horrors that Reggie had seen, she had also witnessed the wonder of the human spirit fighting back. It wasn't about eradicating fear; it was about overcoming it. And that was something that was of so personal a nature that if she had to keep entering fearscapes one by one, seeking out the souls trapped in hell one by one, then that was what she would do. It was her gift.

The technician finished with the binding. Reggie cast one last glance at the whimpering girl.

"It's okay, Sara. I'm coming to find you."

The blackness closed in.